AE

Nort
Tel:

**Return to** ................
**or any other Aberdeen City Li**
Please return/renew this item by
by phone or online

Bu 8/2/16
No 9/2/16
5/1/17.

# TIGER COMMAND!

When Germany's leading tank ace meets the Steppe Fox it's a fight to the death. Faced with overwhelming odds Kampfgruppe von Schroif needs a better tank and fast; but the new Tiger tank is still on the drawing board and von Schroif must overcome bureaucracy, espionage and relentless Allied bombing to get the Tiger into battle in time to meet the ultimate challenge.

# TIGER COMMAND!

# TIGER COMMAND!

*by*

Bob Carruthers and
Sinclair McLay

**Magna Large Print Books**
Long Preston, North Yorkshire,
BD23 4ND, England.

British Library Cataloguing in Publication Data.

Carruthers, Bob and McLay, Sinclair
    Tiger command!

    A catalogue record of this book is
    available from the British Library

    ISBN    978-0-7505-3888-6

First published in Great Britain in 2013 by Claymore Press
an imprint of Pen & Sword Books Ltd.

Copyright © Coda Books Ltd., 2011
Published under licence by Pen & Sword Books Ltd.

Cover illustration © David Ridley by arrangement with
Arcangel Images

The right of Bob Carruthers and Sinclair McLay to be
identified as the authors of this work has been asserted by them
in accordance with the Copyright, Designs and Patents Act,
1988

Published in Large Print 2014 by arrangement with
Pen & Sword Books Ltd.

Magna Large Print is an imprint of Library Magna Books Ltd.

Printed and bound in Great Britain by
T.J. (International) Ltd., Cornwall, PL28 8RW

*For Mr McWhinnie whom we are both privileged to have as a friend.*

# CHAPTER 1

## ROSTOV

'Panzer rollen!' SS-Hauptsturmführer Hans von Schroif jerked his clenched fist downwards as if pulling on an imaginary bell chain and gave the familiar command. Responding with a smooth discipline bred from years of familiarity, driver SS-Panzerschütze Bobby Junge disengaged the clutch and the battered Panzer IV lurched violently into motion as it rolled forward towards the front.

Had the tank not been festooned with a motley selection of grenadiers precariously holding onto everything they could, the thankful landsers, sundry rear area warriors and the overworked engineers left behind in the assembly and supply area near the company workshops, would have noticed the neatly stencilled word *Magda* on the side of the vehicle.

Dutifully, the remaining tanks of his SS-Panzerkompanie fell in behind. They were followed by four SPW half-tracks, each packed to capacity with shivering grenadiers, as Kampfgruppe von Schroif began to rumble over the river of mud which constituted the main rollbahn to Rostov. The muddy morass of the Rostov road was unmistakeable, its route clearly marked on each side by the remains of thousands of stranded cars, trucks and carts which formed an almost unbroken verge of worn out and dilapidated wrecks. The few spectators, both military and civilian, watched in sullen silence as the column slithered its way past.

In addition to a prominent identifying number on the side of the turret, each of the succeeding tanks also bore the name of a wife or sweetheart left behind in the security of the Reich. Greta fell in behind Magda and one by one the small column of panzers skidded into position and began the treacherous journey towards Rostov.

Mounted in the turret of his battle-scarred Panzer IV, SS-Hauptsturmführer Hans von Schroif reflected ruefully on the fact that the twenty-two tanks which had come under his command in February had so recently constituted an impressive mass of ironclad might. He glanced backwards and counted the machines again.

'Seven? That's it? Christ, this is getting serious!'

Time and time again over the last two months he had watched in horror as comrades were blown apart or died screaming in a mass of flame. No one who had heard it could ever forget the cries of dying men trapped in a burning tank ... but the terrible sights and sounds of this godforsaken war in Russia crowded in on each other, and what had once seemed earth-shattering was now commonplace. There had been far too many funerals for death to make any further impression. Too many good men were now biting into the grass.

Russia had taken its toll. It wasn't just the fighting either. In the logical side of his over-tired brain von Schroif knew and gratefully acknowledged that SS-Hauptscharführer Klaus Rubbal and his team at the battalion workshop did an amazing job keeping the tanks rolling forward, but the mud of this muddy season, the second which they had endured out here, tested the men and machines of the Panzerwaffe to their limits. The locals called it the rasputitsa, but von Schroif couldn't give a damn what they called it. No single word could ever be sufficient to express his disgust and contempt. He was not well disposed to the locals and grumbled bitterly to himself that if the lazy bastards spent less time inventing stupid names and more time building a proper civilised road system, then none of them would be in this mess.

The desultory drizzle of misty rain which had been falling since 03:30 hours now gave way to a heavy fall of sleet, and the muddy surface was soon coated in a dispiriting blanket of grey. To von Schroif it seemed that this second Russian rasputitsa was even worse than the first season they had encountered in October '41. That first time, the unexpected phenomenon, with its endless and seemingly bottomless ocean of mud, had tested the vehicles to their limits and now, just six months later, here it was again. In his fatigued mind the two recent seasons of mud blended together to form one gruelling nightmare of muck and filth. The only redeeming feature was that the intervening horrors of the merciless Russian winter were temporarily forgotten as the grim nightmares of the white hell on earth now lay buried under a tidal wave of liquid clay.

As they rolled along, past groups of vaguely interested landsers huddled beside the miserable panje huts which passed for human habitations out here, the grenadiers and tank men alike cursed the rain, sleet and melting snow which had again turned every metre of the primitive Russian road network into one bottomless alley of mud. This awful bone-chilling and cloying mess stuck to everything and everyone.

Hauptsturmführer von Schroif considered himself relatively lucky; he at least had a vehicle to ride on. He had, of course, to dismount for track failures, engine failures and a potential host of other irritating reasons, but nothing was sufficiently annoying to make him envy the hapless wayside figures he passed by as the tank slipped and slid through the mess. The despatch riders suffered most. To a man, they were coated in a uniform skin of sludge which gave them the look of elemental creatures formed in some demented kindergarten glory hole.

Faced with this new and implacable foe, the German horse-drawn transport system had completely broken down. The horse teams floundered in their efforts to make progress and the exhausted animals died in harness, overcome by the viscous morass. The only remaining solution to a host of day-to-day mobility problems had been to use his newly issued tanks as workhorses, and they were soon being requisitioned for every task imaginable.

It was now, too late, that the further limitations of the Panzer Mark IV came to light. The tracks, which seemed adequate by European standards, were hopelessly inadequate out here, beyond the reach of civilisation. The narrowness of its tracks made life nigh on impossible, but von Schroif knew, and reluctantly accepted, that his job was to make things possible.

The few tanks which had survived the fierce battles of the winter were now, once again, being pressed into service as recovery tractors, supply lorries, glorified staff cars and ammunition schleppers. Nothing else could get through the mud and there was simply no alternative. Already worn down and in need of spares and repair, Krupp's finest were called upon for every conceivable job faced by a modern army. Engines which were already overworked were pushed to the limits as the panzers crawled through the sea of filth. Their road wheels and tracks barely visible, the few remaining panzers could usually be found dragging trucks from muddy pools or hauling staff cars to distant field conferences. Air filters and carburettors soon became clogged with mud. It seeped into every nook and cranny, obliterating vision ports and forcing the crew to drive with the hatches open, under a constant spray of mud thrown up by the tracks.

The only man who appeared immune to the misery of the muddy season was SS-Panzerschütze Otto Wohl, von Schroif's main gun loader – and full-time comedian. The 'schiessekrieg' was Wohl's catch-all description of the war in Russia. To Wohl, the whole Russian experience could be summed up very simply.

'A shit country, run by a shit, full of people covered in shit, fighting a shit war, for possession of a pile of shit about which I couldn't give a shit!'

With his free flowing Bavarian sense of fun

and irrepressible outlook, Wohl could always be relied upon to lift the spirits with a relentless stream of droll observations. It helped morale, but von Schroif had to keep a lid on Wohl's natural exuberance. In the wrong ears, Wohl's remarks could easily be interpreted as defeatist. Now that events had turned sticky, the Gestapo were always keen to hear of any potential dissenters and the last thing von Schroif needed was to find himself without the services of Otto Wohl. Nor, for that matter, could he do without SS-Panzerschütze Bobby Junge, the wizard at the steering controls, who somehow managed to keep Magda going forward when virtually nothing else could get through the rollbahn of endless mud. Or, as Otto Wohl so aptly called it, the 'scheissebahn.'

An unofficial truce appeared to have been declared for two months, with both sides seemingly immobile, stuck in the endless mire. The season of mud had exercised such a deadly grip that, until 02:30 hours this morning, even the Ivans had been forced to halt most of their activities, but now the cunning bastards had shattered the peace at the worst possible time, with an artillery bombardment of a scale and intensity which even von Schroif had not witnessed. The old military cliché was being reinforced once more, and von Schroif sensed that the months of boredom were about to be replaced by brief moments of sheer terror. Everything which had formerly seemed so unimportant now needed to be done in a tearing hurry, mud or no mud. Suddenly there was no time to get the Kompanie in order. He had been given thirty minutes notice of the mission and here he was with seven tanks ... just seven!

Russia had indeed taken its toll alright and, as they rolled past another identical stretch of panje huts, von Schroif was forced to come to grips with the reality of his situation. No matter how hard the battalion and divisional workshop engineers worked, the reality was that the latest strength report stated there were five total write-offs awaiting replacement, four more of his panzers were under short-term repair at the battalion workshop and six were at the divisional workshop, awaiting engines.

Logically, Hans von Schroif accepted that there was nothing that could be done, but the tired, cold and hungry part of his brain railed against the fates which had brought him here. Stuck in the damn turret hatch of an ailing vehicle, he could clearly hear the ominous, fitful, spluttering sounds emanating from the engine compartment and the rasping noise of the gears which told him that his own machine was about to go the same way as eleven others.

He needed more force for this mission and his tired brain was not easily satiated. Defying all logic, it screamed back at him that surely some of the other panzers could have been made ready! Mentally, he inveighed against the gods once more. Irrationally, he convinced himself that this was obviously just another excuse from the rear-area echelons to hide their rank incompetence.

Following a further wave of internal cursing, von Schroif decided that he could at least get warm inside the tank. He had performed the move a thousand times, but on this occasion, perhaps because of his extreme tiredness, as he moved to close the hatch his knuckles somehow caught on the catch side of the open turret hatch lid and a sharp pain flooded over him, bringing him back to resentful wakefulness. This new indignity triggered a fresh mental tirade as the fast receding pain was conflated with dislike for the mission, with life in a tank, and the war in Russia.

'Fuck! Fuck them all, fucking bastards. It can't be that fucking difficult. Fuck Voss and his stupid fucking death fucking mission. Fuck this fucking war!'

Hans von Schroif was right, there were clearly insufficient tanks for this mission, but then there were insufficient tanks for any mission these days.

He had attended the 04:00 hours emergency briefing and his heart sank when he learned that his Kampfgruppe would once again be thrown against Hill 15. Old man Voss had detailed the mission, which was to provide fire support and reinforcements for the few desperate grenadiers still fighting to stabilise the line, but surely Voss knew that the whole area was now the preserve of Ivan's T-34s. Their wide tracks gave them a huge advantage over the battered Panzer IVs of Kampfgruppe von Schroif. They could still move if necessary and they carried a deadly high-velocity main gun. Countering the T-34 demanded mobility, and a better weapon than the short and stubby low-velocity gun of the Panzer IV.

As every East Front tank commander knew only too well, the Panzer Mark IV had originally been designed as an infantry support tank. They weren't supposed to be tank killers. The standard tactical doctrine proclaimed that engaging enemy tanks was the job of the Panzer III. Von Schroif ruefully reflected for the thousandth time that, against the T-34, the main gun of the Panzer IV was all but useless. It was essentially a howitzer, to be used against entrenched infantry positions, and once again von Schroif cursed the lack of real tank-killing potential. What was needed was a high-velocity Kampfwagenkanone which could match the T-34.

The theorists back in Paderborn would no doubt pronounce that tank duels were intended to be the exclusive realm of the Panzer III, but that was the theory. In practice, this was impossible, as the Panzer IIIs in his Kompanie were now all out of action. In any event, the puny 50 mm weapon on the Panzer III was demonstrably no match for the strong, well-sloped cast armour of the T-34. And when it came to facing up to the monstrous KV-1? Well, it was time to pack up and go home.

It was a badly kept secret that the design boffins were already working on a long-barrelled, high-velocity 75 mm gun for the Panzer IV, a new and much more effective Kampfwagenkanone, which could still fit inside the smallish turret of the Panzer IV. The F2 was rumoured to be on its way, but it would take time to roll out the new machines and, out here, there was no time left any more.

His war now boiled down to a case of needs must, and von Schroif and his crew had become experts in the deadly game of cat and mouse which ensued every time he attempted to get as close as he dared to a T-34 in order to get in a side or rear shot from his unsuited main gun. The gunnery team of Wohl and Knispel did a great job and worked miracles time after time, but every time felt like it could be the last.

Mobility and manoeuvrability were the deciding issues and in deep mud, as Junge never tired of complaining, the narrow tracks of the Mark IV were as much use as a pair of ice skates. Various bodged attempts to add width had been conjured up by the battalion and divisional workshops. Even in their augmented incarnation, the tracks were no more than forty centimetres wide. Sure, they were better than the previous thirty centimetre tracks which did so little to spread the weight and made the vehicle cut into the mud, but, even with the improvised enhancements, the tracks were obviously still too narrow.

'They're slightly narrower than the tyres on my dad's Volkswagen and about as much fucking use!' was driver Bobby Junge's, only slightly exaggerated, description of the track design.

From his cramped position in the bowels of the fighting compartment, Bobby Junge certainly had his work cut out keeping Magda's forward momentum going at all, but Junge's problems were of little concern to the grenadiers in their grubby off-white snow camouflage overalls perched on the engine deck. They knew they would have to do the dirty work soon, but for now there was still time, and they fell into the rhythm of the familiar journey and rearranged themselves so that they were bunched together on the engine deck of each of the tanks, where they gladly absorbed the heat emitted by the engines.

Huddled on the back of Magda, the small group of grenadiers swayed precariously and grumbled ferociously as they clung on to any handhold they could find. Among them was SS-Schütze Fritz Müller, a slightly built youth from Hamburg. Müller had reason to curse the sleet which drove into his face, but, as always in these situations, most of his personal anger was reserved for Herr Bauer, the local Nazi Blockleiter who, unfortunately for Müller, had also been his Hitler Youth leader. It was Blockleiter Bauer who had cajoled Müller into joining the Waffen SS. SS-Schütze Müller was now a very bitter young man and had good reason to be. As he repeatedly wiped the freezing sleet from his eyes, Müller regretfully recalled the words of their last conversation in the Hamburg sunshine during May 1941.

'I still don't understand why you haven't signed up for the Waffen SS, young man. A tall, fit racial comrade like you shouldn't be hanging around, waiting to be called up. You should join now! You'll see the Mediterranean, maybe Afrika! Who knows? I have it on best authority that the Führer has decreed that the party should be represented by its own fighters in every theatre ... there's bound to be a Waffen SS division ordered to Afrika soon. You'd best enlist now... Rommel will have the British in the bag soon and you'll be too late. Trust me, you won't regret it. After all, you're a miller and I'm a farmer – we depend on each other.'

So he had trusted him, the bastard, and he had signed up – and all he had achieved was the order of the frozen meat, then the miseries of the season of mud, and now winter seemed to have come back!

Müller consoled himself by making yet another resolution to kill Herr Blockleiter Bauer as soon as he got his first leave. He wasn't sure how he would do the deed, but he intended it to be every bit as slow and painful as this shitty journey.

Müller glumly noted that, even in April, the melting snow still held sway, but the welcome sight of patches of green stony ground speckled the landscape as the fearsome Russian winter of 1941/42 slowly gave way to an unsettled spring.

The treacherous Russian weather was obviously the ally of the Russians and, in its own way, was every bit as dangerous as the Red Army which, as they had been briefed in the assembly area, was now pouring through the gaps in the line only five kilometres distant from the battalion workshops which serviced Hauptsturmführer von Schroif and his SS Panzerkompanie.

Up ahead, the columns of black oily smoke pointed the way to the front as surely as the best Zeiss compass. As they crawled slowly down the muddy rollbahn towards

Rostov, the rumble and crash of explosions grew louder and formed a continuous wall of noise which soon drowned out even the noise of the tank. Ivan was obviously throwing everything he could at the thinly-held line of main resistance.

Reluctantly, von Schroif opened the commander's hatch. A blast of freezing air hit him and, on the muddy roadside, he observed the first fleeing fugitives hurrying in the opposite direction, slipping and sliding through the mud and sleet of the rasputitsa. Many were wounded. Others appeared to be unharmed ... physically at least. Von Schroif had some sympathy for them. Two hours ago, a deadly barrage had fallen with pinpoint accuracy on the main resistance line and, just when it seemed that things could get no worse, there had come the sound of the infamous Katyusha – Stalin's Organ.

Screaming down like banshees from hell, they produced a nightmarish enclosed box of exploding fire. The avalanche of high-explosive iron rained down on a designated target area, destroying virtually everything inside the hellish cauldron marked by the barrage. Inside the barrage area, the continuous concussion of multiple detonations was enough to transform the strongest and most dedicated warrior into a shivering nervous wreck.

He noticed that many of the retreating

fugitives had thrown away their weapons, which incensed him. His sympathy evaporated and he thought briefly about stopping to round up these haunted men, but immediately thought better of it. For now, these disoriented refugees were beyond salvation as a fighting force, but a few kilometres back, he had no doubt, lay old man Voss and a welcoming committee of military police. They would catch up the residue and turn them into a fighting force once more.

Slipping down inside the tank and carefully closing the hatch behind him, von Schroif began to take an ever closer interest in the terrain outside the tank. They were approaching a bend in the track – exactly the place where Ivan might lie in wait.

Driver Bobby Junge had become an expert in handling the involuntary mudslide which accompanied every attempt to turn a corner in this godforsaken country, but it was still a difficult task. As the narrow tracks of the Mark IV slipped and slid, attempting to gain some kind of purchase, up ahead came the unmistakable and most welcome sound of the 88 mm Flugabwehrkanone, known to the troops as the Acht-acht Flak gun. Somewhere up ahead the familiar bark of the Acht-acht told him there was still some resistance and, as long as a few strong points continued to hold, there was still a chance.

'Where's the flak gun position, Junge?' barked von Schroif to his driver.

'No movement, same place as last week,' replied Bobby Junge, straining to make himself understood over the intercom as he wrestled with the controls of the sliding tank.

'OK, leave it to the others... Turn off here... Take up a position 400 metres at 3 o'clock to direction of fire,' ordered von Schroif.

Junge responded immediately and Magda began to jump and jolt as the tracks sought some form of purchase and the tank somehow ploughed its way through the mud. Now and again the odd wounded fugitive made his way back to where he hoped safety lay. Somewhere up ahead, inside that wall of smoke, there was still resistance and, as long as a few strong points continued to hold, there remained the possibility that the line could be held ... but why a fire support mission?

'Voss... Damn Voss! Has he learned nothing?' von Schroif thought to himself.

Old man Voss was his long-standing, and highly trusted, superior officer. Von Schroif grudgingly admitted to himself that Voss was a wise old fox. He would not endanger his men or their precious machines recklessly. Even in his tired and angry state, von Schroif acknowledged this, but the man was just so obdurate! It was absolutely infuriating!

They had first met at the KAMA facility in 1927 and both had been there watching the first Great Exercise near Munster in 1936, attended by the Führer himself. It was plain for all to see from way back then; the key was mobility, mobility, mobility! Why in God's name would anyone still ask for the few remaining Panzer IVs to provide fire support? That was now the job of the divisional artillery or the Sturmgeschütz abteilung! The lazy bastards ... but no sooner had the thought entered his brain than von Schroif knew to let the anger pass.

In his mind, he surmised what Voss knew for certain. He pictured the tangled remains of the divisional artillery and the Sturmgeschütz battalion after the bombardment by a brigade of Stalin's Organs. He let his feelings subside as the reality of the situation dawned. This was no place for too much anger, as too much anger got you killed. The intractable mud had forced the big guns to stay locked in the same place for too long and Ivan had done his homework. The early morning whirlwind bombardment had come with pinpoint accuracy. Obviously, Voss knew that there was no divisional artillery left and, as a result, his seven tanks had to do the job they were originally designed for.

Now completely resigned to his mission, Hans von Schroif fell into the familiar survival pattern of observe, notice and remember. Panje huts 200 metres to the east, forest 300 metres beyond that, open ground to the west, a river, a lone beech tree, a single track coming out of the trees and a small hillock beside it with heavy foliage, these were all mental markers that had to be remembered if they had to veer from the mission. And when did they not have to veer from the mission? Yes, maps had their place, comfortably behind the lines or spread out in old man Voss' Gefechtsstandfahrzeug. He pictured Voss in his converted SPW at a safe distance and swore again! But now von Schroif was getting angry... 'Concentrate! Concentrate!'

He decided to use the man he had come to trust as his other eyes and ears – SS-Panzeroberschütze Karl Wendorff. Von Schroif considered him without a doubt the finest radio man in Army Group South. Wendorff functioned like a second brain for von Schroif, a brain which could identify the most important, and filter out the irrelevant, pieces of information from the storm of traffic that swirled around any operation.

'Any radio traffic, Wendorff?' demanded von Schroif.

'...Nothing, Hauptsturmführer.' Wendorff was hesitant. He was always hesitant. His modus operandi was silence, an almost interminable silence, punctuated only very occasionally with words, fine-tuned words, which concisely conveyed carefully selected information which he had decided his commander absolutely must be aware of.

Although they both occupied the seats on the right hand side of the tank, Wendorff was the exact opposite of the garrulous Wohl. Perhaps that was why they got on so well, but this time Wendorff was even more reserved than usual. He had heard something, something he had never heard before in any language or code, and he was still trying to compute what it meant. It had emanated from the German side. Amidst the babble of voice communication was this one keyed and apparently meaningless signal repeated over and over: PNKTI.EH.SFTVOCE... PNKTI .EH.SFTVOCE... PNKTI.EH.SFTVOCE.

Wendorff reflected on the strange message. There were the possible traces of words, like punkt, so could it be a friendly attack and a time? But voce? Italian for voice ... there were Italians in this sector... Or was it possibly partisans operating behind the German lines and disguising their communications by using German? There was so much traffic that it was hard to provide an immediate answer, but he would try. For now though, there was no point in reporting to the commander, no point in passing confusion on. He would only do that when he had a definitive answer, or a working hypothesis. Karl Wendorff dealt in answers, not questions.

Instead, he filtered out the signal for the time being and relayed the most important information.

Von Schroif sensed the slight hesitation in Wendorff's voice. 'You sure?' he barked over the intercom.

'Nothing to report, Hauptsturmführer,' the radio operator replied.

'Excellent,' said Otto Wohl, 'now we can pack up and go home!'

This brought a smile to driver Bobby Junge's face. From his position next to the main gun, Michael Knispel could not suppress a short laugh. What would they do without mad Otto!

'Silence, Wohl!' Hans von Schroif did not smile with them. He redoubled his gaze and picked up his binoculars. That old sixth sense had returned... nothing much up front though. Beyond the Acht-acht, there was no sign of life. There was not even the flup flup of friendly mortars firing in support of the hard-pressed grenadiers up ahead, just the smoke and thunder of Ivan's massive artillery barrage. Suddenly, something caught his eye, movement in the forest. He hurried to focus ... but it was just a frightened deer, rushing through the trees.

But what had flushed it from its hide? With a trained hunter's eye, at the limits of his peripheral vision, he registered a slight movement off to the left of where the deer had sprung from, in the trees ... but his train of thought was halted by an almighty bang and flash and he was thrown backwards and felt a searing pain across his temple and right arm.

Without even thinking, von Schroif knew what had happened. Despite the pain, he gave the hand signal to halt the column and yelled over the intercom. 'Halt! Minen!'

Karl Wendorff immediately relayed the information by radio to the following panzers and the column skidded to a halt. Despite the pain, von Schroif immediately returned to scanning the landscape for movement. Scuttling out of the forest and scrambling over the brow of the hillock, he registered the shapes of two men taking up position. One staggered under the weight of what appeared to be a radio transmitter.

'Artillery spotters. Shit!' he muttered to himself.

No sooner had he recognised this new threat than, even with the ringing in his ears, he heard the unmistakable sound of tank engines starting up. They were obviously T-34s, but still some way off. He needed to make a decision, and quick. Load with armour-piercing and await the tanks? Or attempt to dislodge the spotters with some well-placed rounds of high-explosive? But first he needed to assess his own position.

'The right track, sir!' shouted the young

grenadier who had been thrown from the front of the tank by the blast. Von Schroif noticed that the young man's forearm was missing. Instinctively, von Schroif looked around for a source of first aid. His gaze fell upon a medical orderly too nervous to step into the mine field.

'Sani, over here!' shouted von Schroif above the noise of the engine.

Responding to the direct order, the medic at last crept towards the wounded man, but he did so very slowly, each step calculated and agonisingly deliberate.

'Hurry up, man, or he'll bleed to death.' Then, using his left arm to support his own weight, von Schroif managed to clamber out of the tank and, scanning for the tell-tale signs of anti-personnel mines, he gingerly stepped down to inspect the damage.

'Damn!' he cursed on seeing the right-hand track hanging limply from the Magda's front drive sprocket.

Fortunately, the cloying mud had absorbed much of the blast and the sprocket itself appeared undamaged, so they could still hope to continue. However, even with the ox-like strength of Michael Knispel to draw upon, fixing the track would probably take a few minutes which he was sure they didn't have. Von Schroif surmised that the spotters controlled the Katyusha batteries which had destroyed the divisional artillery park. He knew that they would soon be under concentrated artillery fire from the fearsome power of Stalin's Organs.

The obvious alternative was to evacuate the stricken panzer and clamber onto one of the other tanks in the unit and retreat, but this notion clashed resoundingly with every bone and fibre in von Schroif's body. No, that was not an option; they would be driving into the zone which the Ivans had obviously earmarked for the target area. He desperately needed to buy time. While von Schroif continued to ponder his options, he was rudely interrupted by a rush of air and a loud zing as a bullet snapped past his head and ricocheted off the steel hull of the tank.

Despite his wound, the young grenadier was alive to the situation. He raised himself to his feet and, with his good arm, pointed towards the nearby hillock. 'Over there, sir!'

They were the last words young Fritz Müller ever spoke. This time, there was no mistake. No sooner had he uttered the words when a second Russian bullet smashed into his temple and he sank lifeless to the muddy ground. For young Fritz Müller, there would be no reckoning with an over-enthusiastic Blockleiter back in Hamburg.

The Sani stopped in his tracks and gaped in shock at the stricken body. He realised a fraction too late that his immobile form made a perfect target. There was a distant crack and the medic sagged to the ground beside his erstwhile patient.

Seizing the opportunity, Hans von Schroif dived behind the tank and picked up his binoculars. Once more he felt an acute pain and he was forced to operate with his left hand as he homed in on the crest of the hillock. At first he could see nothing, but with his hunter's eye he soon distinguished the long antennae of a radio set attempting to find the direction of the strongest signal.

'So, there must be an operator...' And, moving down ... there they were ... two men... 'Looks like one has a sniper rifle...'

There was another danger too. He couldn't see any trace of them, and he still couldn't hear properly above the shrill whine from the explosion that reverberated in his eardrums, but the sound of T-34 engines revving up was unmistakable.

'Grenadier!' he shouted to one of the infantrymen who had taken up positions around the stricken tank. 'The engine noise, where is it coming from?'

'Over there, sir!' replied the Grenadier, pointing to the forest, up and beyond the opening where the single track emerged.

Despite the overwhelming numbers that the Ivans had been able to bring into the field, the Panzerwaffe still held the initiative in Russia. Superior organisation and communications saw to that. The Red Army was improving, but it was still something of a blunt instrument. Soviet battle plans were set and, of necessity, they had to be followed to the letter. On the Soviet side there was none of the flexibility built into the concept of the Aufstragstaktik, which allowed even junior German commanders to take decisions on the spot. The situation was changing rapidly, but many of the Russian tanks could not take advantage of their tactical superiority as they had no radio and communicated by means of flags.

'So what would Ivan plan to do? What would Ivan do?' von Schroif thought to himself frantically.

'Quick, the artillery spotters will soon be ready to report back! So, if I'm the Russian commander, what would I do?'

'Load with high-explosive, sir?' asked Otto Wohl.

'Not yet, Wohl, await my order.' Von Schroif continued to ponder the situation, lost in his own thoughts.

'I'd probably be trying to work out what the panzer commander would do... What would the panzer commander do? In this situation, the panzer commander, if he were to do it by the manual, would order all his tanks to slowly reverse back along their tracks to avoid any more mines... So, knowing that, what would Ivan do?'

It was this ability to think himself into the

mind of his enemy that distinguished von Schroif from so many other panzer commanders on the Eastern Front, certainly in the Panzerwaffe. There were persistent rumours of an equally adept white-haired adversary on the Russian side, a KV-1 commander christened Der Weisse Teufel (the White Devil), but von Schroif dismissed such defeatist nonsense as mere campfire stories, forged in fevered imaginations after the heat of battle.

Von Schroif knew for certain that the Russians would be slavishly following a rigidly predestined battle plan... so now all he had to do was deduce what the Russian Commander would have ordered. Quickly resurveying the immediate environment, he observed, noticed, paused, thought and, with a sharp intake of cold Russian air flaring in his nostrils, arrived at his best guess.

'If I were the Russian commander, I would assume that the column is going to retrace its steps ... and so I would lay down a barrage about 700 metres behind where the last tank is now... I would hold my T-34s out of sight in the forest and send them down the track, around the hamlet, and drive them into our left flank. Now, what is the best way to counter that?'

Von Schroif's gaze returned to the fallen medic who had died on his way to attend the wounded grenadier. What a soldier! The young man had kept to his duty even after the loss of a limb. Sadly, there was no time to provide him with a soldier's grave. Germany needed men like him, but their ranks were becoming thinner every day.

Oblivious to the dangers, Wendorff opened his hatch and shouted to his commander. 'Shall I order them to back up, sir?'

'No!' replied von Schroif, a trifle too quickly. 'Tell them to stay put and keep their main guns trained on the forest. We are expecting a few guests and maybe a present from the Popovs... Everybody else, get down here. Let's get this fixed.'

As von Schroif considered his options, he was unaware that all the time he was being closely observed from the nearby hillock by Andrey Basilevsky of the reconnaissance unit of the Guards tank battalion. Andrey too loved to hunt, and in better times the two men would have enjoyed each other's company, but today Andrey was hunting fascists and von Schroif was the prey. Having already claimed two victims, Basilevsky knew all he had to do was wait.

Within a few seconds he smiled as he saw the crippled tank's crew emerge with tools and spare track links. One figure quickly scuttled under the tank, leaving the other three to start work on the track. Basilevsky did not fire immediately though, as Koniev was still struggling with the dials in a vain attempt to connect the radio to HQ. That momentary hesitation was to cost him his life.

At any minute Basilevsky expected to hear the roar of engines as a column of panzers revved up their engines from idle as they retraced their steps from whence they came, back along their tracks towards the muddy rollbahn. He began to plot the distance at which the barrage would fall. '700 metres should do it...'

Basilevsky calculated that there was no need for a tell-tale spotting round; Stalin's Organ would obliterate the whole area. Arranged behind him was an entire brigade of lorry-borne Katyushas which had been brought to just behind the front by a super-human effort, and those efforts were about to be rewarded by the death of the best German tank commander in the southern sector. The intelligence had been perfect. This was a cakewalk, all he had to do was wait for Koniev to connect the radio to HQ and Kampfgruppe von Schroif would be history.

In the meantime, there was sport to be had. As Sergei Koniev continued to struggle with the bulky radio set, Andrey Basilevsky once more took up his rifle, readjusted his position, and muttered quietly to himself. 'Keep going, you fascist bastards. You offend Mother Russia with your presence, and she is about to make you pay!'

Those were the last words he would ever utter. Suddenly, as if from nowhere, the bullet from a Sauer hunting rifle sliced clean through his face and, speeding through the recesses of his brain, blew away the back of his skull.

His compatriot looked on in horror before instinctively going to the aid of his comrade. He should have taken cover, for he was the next target. A German bullet crashed into his skull through his left ear and exited through the right, taking most of the side of his head with it.

Noticing the tell-tale puff of smoke, Hauptsturmführer von Schroif peered under the tank. As he suspected, lying prone under the crippled panzer was gunner Michael Knispel, who patted the telescopic sights of the Sauer and looked back at von Schroif and smiled.

'I thought we said no poaching?' said von Schroif.

'That wasn't poaching, Hauptsturmführer ... that was culling a few rats.'

'OK, but no non-standard weapons aboard my bus, understood?'

'Jawohl, Hauptsturmführer.'

There was no need for any more words. Von Schroif was damned if he could find the hiding place where Knispel managed to conceal his beloved hunting rifle in the cramped interior of Magda. It was against all regulations to carry a personal weapon, and von Schroif obeyed regulations scrupulously. He had deliberately searched the bus at night while the crew were in their billet and had come to the conclusion that Knispel probably slept with it.

He knew what that smile meant; once a poacher, always a poacher. Somehow, the Sauer would be smuggled aboard and, although he conscientiously did his duty to prevent it, secretly von Schroif was glad to know it would be there in future ... just in case.

'Ok, we've bought ourselves some time. Now let's get this track back on!' ordered von Schroif.

Working feverishly, the five men set to their tasks. Von Schroif was fully aware that, in the absence of contact from their spotters, the Russian gunners would do a quick calculation of how much ground the column should cover before letting loose. For now at least, the small formation of panzers was safe from that particular danger.

In the meantime the cold had not abated. if anything, it seemed to have intensified. Just one more reason to hate Russia, hate the shitty war, and curse everything that went with it. With stiff, blue and bloodied hands, the crew worked with a discipline born of familiarity to repair the damaged track, each man knowing that failure would mean death or, even worse, capture by the Red Army.

For a relatively small man, Michael Knispel displayed a remarkable strength. His large hands worked quickly and, when an extra burst of muscle was required, the former boxer was able to deliver the necessary power. The job was progressing well, but von Schroif knew it was only a matter of moments before the barrage would fall.

Flecks of snow now came in on the cold Easterly wind, freezing not just their faces but spreading throughout their bodies and hurting hands and feet, but there was absolutely no time to rub their hands or stamp their feet in an effort to get warm, nor was there any point in thinking of the massed T-34s in the forest or the units of Siberian Devils that would surely follow them.

Just then von Schroif heard the clanking of T-34 tracks. 'Hurry boys, the Popovs will be opening up any second now!'

Then it started, the familiar moan and then the earsplitting roar as the first Katyusha barrage landed behind them, the ground shaking, the trees splitting, mud and rock shooting across the pale, white landscape.

'Keep going, boys, keep going!' von Schroif shouted. 'Stay on the job!'

And then came wave after wave, each one sounding louder than the previous, a roar

40

from the very depths of Hell itself, the ground rippling and rolling under them as the shock waves spread out across the land.

Every neuron of the brain sent the message, 'Take cover! Take cover!' But each man knew that they had to stick to the job at hand, every natural impulse towards self-preservation had to be resisted. Then suddenly the barrage halted, to be replaced by an eerie silence which was soon broken by the screeching of disturbed birds.

'Had the other panzers survived?' thought von Schroif. No time to look. Nearly there!

'Come on boys, one last heave!' ordered von Schroif, but the crew involuntarily halted as they heard the roar of thousands of human voices. 'Hurrah!' It was the deep-throated war cry of what sounded like a whole army of Russians, charging through the trees.

'No point in looking, no point in thinking, just get that track back on and get back into the tank.'

Then came another roar, a deeper roar, the sound of a force of twenty T-34s revving up and rumbling through the trees. Von Schroif dared not glance up. Even if he did, he would have seen nothing. The smokescreen from the smoke shells blew down from the opening of the forest and engulfed him and his men. There was no time to cough, no time to rub smarting eyes. All that mattered was, 'Track! Track! Track!'

'Grenadiers!' shouted Von Schroif, without taking his eyes away from his main preoccupation.

The smoke would clear soon and they would be stranded and out in the open. Hopefully, God willing, the Russian tanks would engage with the main group of panzers and they would only be of interest to the Russian infantry. The grenadiers took up positions around the Panzer IV and still the crew worked on.

Then came the sound of main guns opening up and he could hear both enemy and friendly fire. Suddenly an explosion followed, a huge explosion, the unmistakable sound of a tank being hit then blown apart by its own ammunition exploding. The question for von Schroif was now 'Ours or theirs?'

'No time to look... Sounded distant, so likely to be theirs... Bet it was Bolter in Greta... Good man, Bolter. Not long now...'

At that moment there was suddenly something else to occupy the mind. With a further blood-chilling cry of 'Hurrah!' which echoed around the valley, the first wave of Russians came running out of the forest and down the hill towards them.

As he worked with his crew von Schroif could hear the Unterscharführer in charge of the grenadiers intoning quietly: 'Hold... Hold... Hold... Fire!'

There was the familiar ripping sound as the MG 34 barked into life. The other grenadiers opened up with rifles and automatic weapons. A deadly hail of steel cut the Russians down, screaming and falling like rag dolls as the grenadiers let loose. The fusillade lasted for about thirty seconds, then silence, but for the howling and plaintive cries of the wounded.

Suddenly it was done! The track was back on! No time for congratulations, no relief, just the simple order, 'Get back in the bus!'

Even as the crew began to scramble into their tank, there came another great cheer and a second wave of Russian infantry came charging out of the forest. Again, the order was given: 'Hold... Hold... Hold... Fire!' The grenadiers opened up, and again scores of men were wiped from the face of the earth.

'Now!' ordered Von Schroif.

Otto Wohl kissed the hatch as he jumped back in, shouting, 'No home could be finer!'

At last the crew were able to settle back into the welcoming interior of Magda.

Gazing from the turret, the smoke clearing, von Schroif could make out the rest of his panzers just south of the hamlet, perfectly positioned for the emergence of the T-34s as they came forward from the forest. But where were they?

Just then he saw a flash from out of one of the panje huts and a split second later his heart sank as he saw SS-Panzerstandarten-junker von Mausberg's Helga explode into flames, the turret careering up into the air like a giant flaming frying pan. A second later came the noise of the explosion. There was no time for reflection. Another experienced and capable crew gone.

Karl Wendorff, with one eye alert for targets for his bow machine gun, listened intently as the FU7 radio receiver burst into life with directions, ranges and locations. The panzers swivelled their turrets in the direction of the hamlet, but not before another flash from the same building and another tank, Greta, was hit. A fire took hold immediately, thick black smoke billowing out of the crippled vehicle. Despite the distance, they could hear the unmistakable sound of men trapped, screaming and burning to death.

'Anti-tank gun in the panje hut far right!' barked Knispel over the intercom.

Wendorff swiftly conveyed the target information and the four surviving panzers instantly opened up on the target building with high-explosive rounds, blowing the flimsy wooden panje hut apart and revealing the source of the danger. Knispel had been mistaken. It was not an anti-tank gun as he had predicted, but the hulking shape of a concealed Soviet KV-1, lying in the perfect ambush position.

They were now faced with 45 tonnes of

nigh on impenetrable steel. There was only one sure way of destroying this mobile fortress of iron and that was with a point-blank hit to the rear. That would be impossible for the other panzers; they were out in the open and fully in sight and range. They were returning fire with well-aimed AP rounds, von Schroif could see the bits, but the shells were ricocheting harmlessly off the monster's 70 mm thick hide.

'Junge,' barked von Schroif to his driver. 'Take us in by the forest and come in at him from behind.'

Bobby Junge immediately shifted the gears, turning Magda on the spot before spinning off the track and heading up to the edge of the forest, and in the process turning to mincemeat the fallen Soviet infantry who lay in their way. This was a highly risky strategy and von Schroif knew it. There were T-34s in the forest that could come roaring out at any minute and attack from the rear, and an adversary up ahead with a combination of armour and armament which made it the undisputed master of the battlefield. What if he saw them coming up from behind?

The KV-1 was picking off his panzers at will. He was expertly positioned and he still hadn't called in for support. Who was this Russian commander?

The battle-scarred Panzer IV raced up on

the firmer ground leading to the edge of the forest. As Bobby Junge spun her around, almost as if she were a figure skater, von Schroif turned and looked back up the track, and there they were! A score of T-34s on the muddy rollbahn, pressing slowly up the hill towards the German rear.

'Faster, Junge!' ordered von Schroif, and Magda picked up speed as she came down off the incline of the hill and sped up across the open ground. The KV-1 would have to wait. This once in a lifetime target was just too good to miss. The mud was making progress difficult, even for the enemy. In their arrogance, the T-34s slowly making their way up the hill each presented him with the coveted rear shot.

At that moment the ever alert von Schroif noticed a new danger; a Soviet tractor pulling an anti-tank gun raced from the forest and took up position in the open. The Russian crew spilled out and began working frantically to get the gun into action. At this short range there was no chance that Magda would survive a hit. There was no time to load with high-explosive, but, instinctively, driver Bobby Junge knew what to do.

'Anti-tank gun, 200 metres, 12 o'clock. Overrun attack!' ordered von Schroif.

Magda's engine screamed as the panzer streaked towards the gun in a desperate race against time. It was a near run thing. Just as the Soviet gunner threw his first shell into the breach, Magda crashed into the gun, which buckled as it was forced backwards. There was insufficient mass to destroy the tractor, which now flew into reverse and careered towards the forest.

Bobby Junge tried reversing, but the tangled wreck of the gun was now intertwined with the panzer.

'Halt,' ordered von Schroif.

Everyone knew the KV-1 could wait. The perfect target had appeared. It was a tank man's dream and was too good to miss. Stretched before them, rolling slowly up a steep hill, was the entire column of T-34s.

Wohl needed no second invitation and loaded with armour-piercing. Knispel knew instinctively what his commander required. The Kampfwagenkanone barked out and a shell smashed through the rear deck of the lead T-34, which was now approaching the crest of the hill on the rollbahn. With no room to pass the stricken T-34, the Russian column immediately ground to a halt, and some vehicles began to slide backwards. With ruthless efficiency, Wohl and Knispel picked off the rearmost tank, which was still on flat ground. The Russian column was now boxed in, halted and immobile.

Von Schroif watched in satisfaction as many of the halted machines slithered backwards and crashed into each other. Normally, he would have ordered the T-34s taken prisoner and put into action against their former masters. Beutepanzer had been pressed into service since 1941, and an influx of fresh machines would be welcomed by Hauptscharführer Rubbal and his team, but his blood was surging from the death of the comrades in two of the tanks under his command.

'Now, you bastards, now it's your time!' He watched in grim satisfaction as, one by one, the Soviet tanks were targeted and blown apart by the experienced team of Wohl and Knispel.

As Magda, still entangled with the wreck of the anti-tank gun, edged forward between shots, the lurking KV-1 gradually came into view. In the excitement of finding the new target von Schroif had momentarily forgotten the KV-1, and he was horror-struck by what he saw. The monster was hull-down in a superb defensive position, backed up against a wall. A mound of earth protected her flank and the whole area was further obscured by the debris from the flattened panje hut. He wouldn't be able to get in behind her! Worse, the turret was swivelled in the opposite direction, which spelled death for the remaining four tanks of his Kompanie. He couldn't have chosen a better spot himself. There was only one option left, hardly an option at all, and there was little or no time left...

'Wendorff! Tell the others to concentrate on the T-34s. Knispel, let's give him a little notice that we are here.'

Otto Wohl knew there was little point in wasting a hollow-charge round on the turret of a KV-1, so he selected the Kanone Granate rot Panzer, the standard armour-piercing shell, identified by its red band, and in an instant Knispel had aimed and fired the round. The projectile flew from the short barrel of Magda's main gun, streaking towards the turret of the KV-1 at 385 metres per second. The short delay felt like a lifetime, but Knispel's aim was perfect, and two and a half seconds later there was an almighty metallic flash as the speeding projectile hit the turret of the KV-1 and gouged a small piece of metal from the massive structure before ricocheting harmlessly skywards amid a huge cloud of white smoke and sparks. The sound of the violent clash reached them a few moments later.

'Well, we certainly rang the doorbell,' whispered Knispel, as slowly the turret of the KV-1 began to turn. There was no possibility of a penetration, but the round had done its job. The deadly 76 mm gun would soon be brought to bear against them.

'He knows we're here now,' intoned von Schroif. 'Knispel ... we only have one choice left, can you do it again?'

49

'Jawohl, Hauptsturmführer!'

'Load with hollow-charge.' The command was really a question, but it was superfluous. In moments like these, von Schroif inevitably deferred to the superior hunting instincts of SS-Hauptscharführer Knispel. Michael Knispel mistrusted the accuracy of the hollow-charged Granate Holladung. From his cramped position, Wohl knew what Knispel would require for this one vital shot and had already rammed another red-ringed Kanone Granate rot Panzer into the breach.

'Junge! Bring her to a halt by that tree to the left, facing 45 degrees to target.'

It was a scant hope, but von Schroif knew that the oblique position had the effect of presenting more armour to a projectile striking Magda's frontal armour. He had already calculated that, at their current distance, if the panzer was positioned at 45 degrees relative to the KV-1, they should, in theory, have enough protection to survive a frontal hit.

'I'll do what I can, sir,' replied Bobby Junge, '...but I'm not sure that the repair is holding!'

The massive turret of the KV-1 continued its turn. There was now no doubt about it. They had been spotted.

'Now, Junge! Schnell! Vorwarts!'

But, instead of a surge of speed, Magda crunched to a grinding halt. The already weakened track had given way under the pressure from the entangled anti-tank gun. There was nothing left but to try the impossible.

'Range 1100,' announced von Schroif.

'962, sir,' countered Michael Knispel.

'Take the average,' commanded von Schroif, as the KV-1's gun started to turn ever closer towards them.

'By my calculation, that's also 962, Hauptsturmführer,' replied Knispel.

It was now all or nothing. This was their only chance. Von Schroif either went by the rule book average, or he trusted his gunner.

'Alright ... 962!' barked von Schroif. 'Fire!'

This was it! At a range of less than 1000 metres, if Knispel missed, the next shot from the KV-1 would blow Magda to smithereens. Knowing that this could be his last moment on earth, even the godless Hans von Schroif said a brief prayer to himself as the 75 mm Kanone Granate rocketed from the short barrel and sped towards the KV-1. The impossibly small target was not the tank itself, but the gun barrel of the 76 mm main gun, which was now revealed in almost perfect profile as the turret of the KV-1 swung slowly towards them. Exactly two and a half seconds later there was a flash and a shower of white hot sparks, then the welcome sound of a hit.

The wait seemed like an eternity as the smoke cleared, but then came the heaven-sent sight of a shattered, smoking barrel on the KV-1, neatly penetrated by the armour-piercing shell deliberately aimed and fired by Knispel the poacher ... from exactly 962 metres distance.

The small cheer from Magda's crew was drowned out by the screaming whistle of armour-piercing, hollow-charge and high-explosive shells as the four remaining panzers opened up on the confused jumble of T-34s. As fire began to spread through the column, the Soviet crews sought desperately to escape. All the while, the survivors of Kampfgruppe von Schroif cold-bloodedly stuck to the task of destroying the remaining Russian tanks, without a hint of mercy.

The column of T-34s was soon turned into a confused mass of fiercely burning scrap metal. A few desperate flaming figures emerged from the smoke as they tried to escape the flames, but the jubilant grenadiers now joined in the fray, machine-gunning the escaping crews and taking no prisoners.

Magda's exhausted crew climbed out of their crippled tank and sat on the front of the vehicle, where they could better enjoy the spectacle. They lit well-earned cigarettes and watched in amusement as one miraculously unharmed Russian appeared and, raising his hands in surrender, jogged towards the German lines. The solid figure of SS-Sturmscharführer Braun, the senior

NCO in the battalion, appeared from his muddy hide with fixed bayonet and gestured the frightened Russian towards him.

As the unsuspecting Russian tank man approached, Braun suddenly took a mighty backswing and, in textbook fashion, thrust his bayonet through the startled victim, twisting once and withdrawing with absolute precision. As the Russian fell to the ground, Braun finished his man off with a second thrust which could have come straight from the training ground.

With their bloodlust at its height, the grenadiers gave a heartfelt and spontaneous cheer. In recognition, SS-Sturmscharführer Braun smiled and bowed deeply, as if he was a performer in a Berlin night club.

Hans von Schroif wasn't the type of man to celebrate during combat, his concept of soldiering was too professional to permit that, but he couldn't resist a passing smile when he heard his crew cheer their colleagues on.

The primeval bloodlust would take some time to recede and von Schroif was impressed by the calculating manner in which Braun had driven a lesson home to his boys. SS-Sturmscharführer Braun was no parade-ground martinet, he was hard as steel, unmoved by emotion, and he knew that if his boys learned to act in the same way they may all just get out of this mess.

At the sound of a labouring half-track engine, all eyes turned to the crest of the hill. Another cheer, this time stronger, went up from the survivors of the German battle group as the familiar sight of old man Voss's half-track crested the hill and began to slither and slide down the steep incline, past the wrecked column of T-34s.

Von Schroif suspected that something special must have occurred to bring old man Voss and his Gefechtsstandfahrzeug this far into the combat zone. He marshalled his frazzled nerves in readiness for orders to be given for the next task.

As the commander's half-track skidded its way past, the grenadiers, ignoring the accompanying shower of mud, cheered and raised their right arms in salute of their veteran commander. Eventually, the command SPW squelched to a halt by the stricken form of Magda.

Von Schroif dismounted in order to greet his commanding officer.

'By God, you've had some sport today!' beamed Voss, his craggy features giving way to a fleeting grin.

'That's one way to put it, sir ... a bit of a rougher sport than I'd have liked. I have to report the loss of two Panzerkampfwagen Mark IVs and ten fine comrades,' replied von Schroif.

'That is unfortunate, but that's war,' came

the stern reply from SS-Sturmbannführer Helmut Voss.

'As you say, sir. I'll get this track repaired and report as soon as I can.'

'You'll do no such thing. Leave it to the recovery crew. You and your crew must climb aboard. You have been summoned to Rastenburg, immediately. There are to be no delays. My orders are to have you there within forty-eight hours.'

'Rastenburg...? May I be permitted to ask why, Sturmbannführer?'

'No time to wonder why. You must not delay. These orders come right from the top. They must be scrupulously observed. Time is now of the essence. You are wanted in Rastenburg, and I am to see that you get there. Climb aboard, gentlemen.'

'Jawohl!' barked his crew enthusiastically.

Wohl, Wendorff and Junge needed no second invitation and were aboard the half-track in a flash, happy to leave someone else to wrestle with the job of replacing a muddy track in the stinking smoke which arose from burning oil and charred flesh.

Knispel took slightly longer. He ducked back inside the tank for a few moments before emerging with a cloth-covered article which seemed to magically vanish as soon as he was aboard the half-track.

As von Schroif was driven off past the scene of carnage in the crowded SPW, three things struck him as he gazed in bemusement over the smoking, tank-strewn vista. His first thought was more of an observation, his attention drawn to the distant sight of the Russian commander climbing out of the momentarily forgotten KV-1 and standing on the turret, one foot propped on the barrel. The commander took his time and stood briefly surveying the scene of carnage. He removed his cap and mopped his brow.

Through his Zeiss binoculars, von Schroif noted that he was unusually tall, and white-haired, with heavy black eyebrows above clear blue, cold-blooded eyes which seemed to be looking right back at him in particular. There was something disconcertingly familiar, but von Schroif could not force his tired brain to make the final connection. He was left with the distinct feeling that he had seen this man somewhere before.

Ignoring the bullets now falling around him, the white-haired Russian commander slowly raised his right arm and made as if to fire an imaginary pistol, which seemed to be aimed straight at von Schroif. As he did so, the KV-1 began to slowly back into the forest, as if it were on a Sunday drive. In the instant that the machine was enveloped by the trees, von Schroif caught a final glimpse of the commander, settling back into the turret, which he also noticed bore the stencilled outline of a cloven-hoofed figure grasping a pitchfork.

The distant encounter was unsettling in the extreme for von Schroif. 'Maybe this is him after all... Could it be that there actually is a white devil? He certainly knows his tank tactics,' thought von Schroif, who was painfully aware that, had Knispel not saved their bacon, it would have been this man leading the victors in a frenzy of cold-blooded bayoneting worthy of SS-Sturmscharführer Braun.

The second thought to cross von Schroif's mind crystallised into a firm conclusion as they passed the smoking wrecks of Greta and Helga. Von Schroif had final proof that too many good men were dying in inferior tanks, and he resolved to do everything in his power to get better equipment.

The third question was one which, in his exhausted condition, he was not yet able to address, let alone answer... Why was the whole crew being summoned to Rastenburg?

# CHAPTER 2

## RASTENBURG

'Shall I take us back to the battalion work-shops, Comrade Korsak?' asked Dimitri Levinski, driver of the wounded KV-1. To Dimitri, it seemed like a rhetorical question. Devoid of its main armament, there was little prospect of a successful action for the damaged tank.

'No, that's what they'll expect us to do,' replied Korsak.

'But what else can we do, Comrade?' asked Dimitri Levinski in genuine confusion.

'We've still got the machine guns,' intoned Korsak.

'No good against armour though, Comrade Korsak,' mused Levinski.

'Fuck the armour, we're soon going to find a rich target. Stop the engine.'

The harsh tone said it all. Dimitri Levinski obeyed the command immediately.

Korsak lit a cigarette and soon busied himself with a series of radio conversations.

From the fringe of the forest, Dimitri and his fellow crew members smoked and watched in frustration as the bulk of the

Waffen SS grenadiers loaded up into three of the half-tracks and followed the surviving German tanks as they slowly withdrew from the battlefield and climbed the steep hill to a well-earned rest. Other than the smoking hulks of the T-34s and the two Panzer IVs, the only feature of interest was the remaining half-track with its small screen of grenadiers and the forlorn feature of the disabled Panzer IV marked Magda. The grenadiers seemed satisfied that there was no imminent danger and busied themselves making a fire, smoking, and brewing ersatz coffee.

Levinski reported the latest development. Korsak was immediately live to the situation and made a further radio call. Levinski was fascinated to witness a lieutenant appear, as if from nowhere, leading a squad of forty sub-machine gunners. They were followed by the unmistakeable sound of T-34 engines.

'God, this man must have some pull,' thought Dimitri, as half the infantrymen disappeared to positions undercover on the fringe of the forest, while the rest climbed onto the reinforcement tanks that now took up supporting positions under Korsak's careful guidance.

All was soon quiet and the sound of bird song returned to the forest. The peace seemed to stretch into an eternity as first minutes and then hours passed.

Eventually there came the sound Korsak had been waiting for. Two recovery vehicles slithered over the crest of the hill and, following gingerly in the tracks of the disabled panzer, drew to a halt behind Magda.

This was the moment Korsak had anticipated. On his signal, Dimitri Levinski revved his engine into life and engaged gear. The KV-1 sprang forward and, followed by a wave of cheering infantrymen, charged down the slope. The fresh T-34 tanks sprang from their ambush positions, each wreathed in yelling sub-machine gunners, firing wildly in all directions.

As this overwhelming force hurtled towards them, the unwary grenadiers forming the thin security screen around Magda had little opportunity to resist. The machine gun section did manage to open fire, and a few desyanti were swept from the leading T-34, but the return fire was like a steel whirlwind and the machine gunners fell wounded. The disabled gunners had no prospect of salvation and were mercilessly crushed under the onrushing tracks of the KV-1.

From his position inside the buttoned up KV-1, Dimitri Levinski was surprised, and more than a little disturbed, to hear a yelp of delight from the commander's position, the sound of a man with a feral bloodlust upon him.

Engaged in the painstaking business of

preparing the stricken tank to be towed back to the workshop, the men of the tank recovery section had been taken completely by surprise. There was no chance to grab their small arms and they could do little but raise their arms in surrender. A small group of grenadiers attempted to withdraw to the rollbahn, but a flurry of machine gun bullets and high-explosive shells cut them down within a few yards.

The KV-1 swept up to the stunned survivors of the recovery section detachment, which consisted of the ageing SS-Scharführer Brommann and four youths, the oldest around nineteen. Surrounded by Soviet submachine gunners, the terrified youngsters raised their hands in terror as the gaunt white-haired Russian tank commander dismounted. He carried a razor sharp Cossack battle axe in one hand and unsheathed a long, sharp dagger. To the surprise of the Soviet troops, he spoke in perfect German.

'So, you see the destruction you have caused. Look at the crimes which arise from German hands. No one makes a run for it. Drop your pants.'

The men began to lower their trousers. One young man was slightly slower than the others, which seemed to send Korsak into a fury. Without, warning he lashed out at a German soldier with his battle axe, severing his hand from his arm as if it were paper.

The young man screamed and instinctively grabbed with his other hand in an attempt to stem the fountain of blood. Korsak merely laughed and slashed at the other wrist, leaving the handless and bleeding man to gaze in stunned horror at the stumps.

The tank recovery man then fell to his knees. This seemed to suit Korsak, who grabbed his head and slowly inserted his dagger into the terrified man's left eye. Korsak did not allow the dagger to pierce the brain. He wanted his victim to live to suffer the agonies of helpless blindness. Without pity, he surgically inserted his dagger into the man's right eye. The youth began to scream. In a flash, Korsak swept his dagger across the exposed genitals of the stricken young man and, grabbing the severed organs, stuffed them into the prisoner's mouth.

'Now you really can talk bollocks.'

This provoked some laughter from the Soviets. Korsak handed the axe to the nearest of them.

'See if you can do better. Send a message home to the fascists.'

This almost proved his undoing as, in this brief moment of distraction, SS-Scharführer Brommann seized his chance and sprang at Korsak, throwing him to the ground and locking his hands around his throat.

'You fucking traitorous bastard!' he

screamed at Korsak.

The Scharführer spoke no more as six simultaneous bursts of machine gun fire from six different angles hit him like a lead-dispensing fire hose and ripped him to pieces. The bloodied pulp fell onto the prone body of the White Devil, turning his hair pink and covering his chest in bile and ordure.

Clearly discomfited by his experience, Korsak sprang to his feet.

'Now you've seen what to do! Make sure you leave them as a warning of what every bastard can expect!'

With that, he leapt back into the tank, and the KV-1 headed back in the direction of the forest as the submachine gunners began to set about their prisoners with medieval ferocity.

SS-Hauptsturmführer Hans von Schroif came suddenly to a state of full awakening. His brain sprang into gear. The nightmarish images of white demons which had filled his sleeping hours instantly departed, but the familiar morning terror instantaneously gripped him in its place.

Had he nodded off? Was Ivan creeping up on the bus? Were he and his unguarded comrades about to be on the receiving end of a Soviet hand grenade?

No. He was in a real bed, with real sheets. 'Great, that's a good sign,' he thought to himself. There was no White Devil. Just a dream? 'Yes, just a dream.'

So, here he was in a proper bed...

'Am I wounded? No! Good.'

It would appear that there was no pain, and Hans von Schroif had been injured often enough to know what it felt like, so that was another good sign. At last his inner consciousness broke into the reverie and resolved the uncertainty.

'Ach! It's Rastenburg, you idiot!'

As the reality hit him, von Schroif was able to relax, and he began to feel anxiety being replaced by the flush of excitement.

So, after a week of frantic activity, the day had finally arrived. It was much too early, but this was the day, the day when he finally got to meet with him. Not just to meet him; he had done that so many times over the last twenty years that the familiarity had taken away any sense of awe long ago. The meetings so far only consisted of a perfunctory shake of the hand and a new decoration gratefully received, which brought the added cachet of being able to swagger into the beer hall and the occasional unspoken leverage during a difficult field conference.

Hauptsturmführer von Schroif was only human after all. More often than he really should, he managed to turn a conversation to the point where he would be forced to reluctantly admit that ... 'er, yes, he had met him actually.' Hans knew the mere fact that he had met, shaken hands and exchanged a formal German greeting with the great man was enough. The girls certainly loved it, they always wanted to know everything about him.

'Were his eyes really so blue? Was he tall? Did he have large hands and feet? Do you think he has a sweetheart of his own?'

This time would be different. This would not be a conversation that could be idly repeated in a beer hall to impress a willing fräulein or out-boast a beer-filled comrade. Even so, a momentary flicker of doubt crossed von Schroif's mind.

His inner voice spoke to him once more, 'The geburtstag?' In an instant an inner debate was raging. 'Sure it's the geburtstag, so what? So what if it's his birthday, he won't care. All that matters to him is beating the Ivans.'

He gathered his thoughts and quickly came to the rational conclusion that birthdays were for peacetime. Hauptsturmführer von Schroif was sure that he only paid lip service to the idea anyway. Events had taken over. The very idea of celebrating a geburtstag was history, at least for now. Now, the only thing that mattered was to win the war, to annihilate the Popovs, and then there would be time for birthday celebrations once more. Birthday or no birthday, everything was now too important to let domesticity interfere.

He soon overcame his fears and, for the first time, von Schroif was sure that they would talk. At last, Hans had a chance to get his own points over to him in person. The Möbelpackwagen, the furniture van, it just had to live, it just had to have a future.

With the methodical approach of a trained military mind, Hans von Schroif ran through the requirements for the big day and ticked them off. Was his dress uniform clean, pressed, and shiny? Tick! Was his Iron Cross polished to the point where it would reflect the late East Prussian spring sunshine? Tick! Was the van fully fuelled and armed? Tick! He knew everything was in order, but he ran through the list mentally one more time, then turned his thoughts to his long-serving crew.

As one would expect of the driver and sometime engineer, Bobby Junge had spent the whole of the previous day going over every nook and cranny of the Möbelpackwagen. Hans knew that, if Bobby gave things the seal of approval, everything was indeed in order.

It certainly had its share of teething troubles and, if anyone was hardy enough to engage him on his new favourite subject, a morning could easily be lost as Bobby Junge expanded upon the tinkering which was now required to put things right.

Bobby Junge was by no means a bore. In fact, he had a great way of lucidly explaining mechanical concepts in layman's terms, and Junge was all too aware how often his accumulated knowledge could be lifesaving on the battlefield. For that reason, he was always anxious to pass his precious lessons on to other crews, especially newcomers.

It was in everyone's interest that they survived to help in the struggle ahead and SS-Panzeroberschütze Junge would therefore happily use his own precious free time to describe the essential maintenance tricks and techniques to new comrades in detail. If they happened to have the spare hour or two, his advice came free, along with some excellent technical drawings made on the spot in order to help new comrades understand the complexities of the Panzer VI which were not apparent from the stuffy manuals produced by Messrs Krupp.

Despite the obvious teething problems, the Panzer VI, better known to its crew as the furniture van, had its good points too, and over the past week or so Junge waxed increasingly lyrical about these features. Nice wide tracks almost one metre wide helped spread the weight and, amazingly, generated less ground pressure than the Panzer IV. Although the Panzer VI was more than twice as heavy as the Panzer IV, it would obviously be able to cope better with Russian mud, much better than old Magda ever could.

Despite the massive extra weight, the thing could turn on a sixpence and on-board it was smooth, unbelievably smooth. The suspension was amazing and the Maybach engine seemed just about man enough for the task. In a very short space of time, Bobby Junge had grown to adore the lumbering furniture van and his obvious love of the Panzer VI was infectious.

Gunner SS-Scharführer Michael Knispel, too, was already enthusiastic to the point of devotion. For an experienced gunner, the optics were what really mattered, and they were first class. The furniture van was equipped with the extremely accurate Leitz Turmzielfernrohr TZF 9b, but then von Schroif had expected that in a new tank. The additional thrill for Knispel was to have the mighty Acht-acht at his fingertips.

The 88 mm Flugzeugabwehr-Kanone was the flak gun which had saved the skin of the Wehrmacht in Russia and in Libya. Knispel knew only too well that it was the only weapon which could defeat the T-34 or the KV-1 at anything less than suicidally close range. It was widely known and recognised as one of the most effective weapons on the battlefield, but it was nonetheless an anti-aircraft gun. To Knispel's delight, here it was transformed by the boffins into a tank gun, an amazing adaption by which the former anti-aircraft weapon had been turned into a Kampfwagenkanone par excellence.

The new tank gun had been issued with a new official designation, the KwK 36 L/56, but Wohl reckoned it should be known as the KWK (PE). Although smaller, it retained all the essential characteristics of the Acht-acht. Knispel noted, with obvious delight, that the new gun had a very flat trajectory and a massive high-velocity impact, which would certainly turn the scales on Ivan.

Hauptsturmführer von Schroif noted to himself that, if only they could get the powers that be to approve production of the furniture van, next time there would be no race against death with Bobby Junge desperately manoeuvring to get a rear shot on the KV-1. Next time, all that Knispel had to do was to line him up on the middle triangle. SS-Panzerschütze Otto Wohl, with his lightning fast reactions, could be relied upon to ram a shell home and boom, whoosh, Ivan would-be no more.

From Wohl's point of view, the furniture van certainly had plenty of capacity. To have a hundred shells for the wonderful Acht-acht on board was heaven for Wohl, and this was despite the fact that each of the new 88 mm rounds was so much bigger and bulkier than the 75 mm carried on board the old bus.

Wohl in particular seemed to have adapted

seamlessly to the less claustrophobic con-
fines of the Möbelpackwagen. In the training
runs, it was as if nothing had changed. No
sooner had Knispel pressed the electric
firing button than Wohl, as if by magic, had
the breach cleared and a new shell in the
chute, almost before the last shell had hit the
target. The quick reactions of Otto Wohl had
saved their skins so many times in Russia.
Von Schroif respected the views of his talk-
ative subordinate. He knew that, if the
furniture van was right for Wohl, it was right
for the rest of the Waffen SS and the Heer,
and, on their behalf, von Schroif was ready
to fight for the Möbelpackwagen all the way.

The last member of the team appeared to
be fine too. Radio operator SS-Panzeroberschütze Karl Wendorff, as far as von Schroif
could discern, approved of the communications set up in the Möbelpackwagen. The
funkmeister declared himself happy that the
receiver worked like a dream and, as the
wandering philosopher of the team, Wendorff
reported in his cautious and pedantic manner that, as he wasn't on the receiving end of
the transmission, he had no accurate way of
knowing how well the transmitter worked.
However, it certainly appeared to work fine.
That was enough for von Schroif.

It crossed Wendorff's mind at that time to
mention the unusual radio signal he had
picked up again yesterday. There was a fami-

liar ring to it. He was sure it used the same code he had intercepted during the engagement outside Rostov, but two things prevented him from discussing it with von Schroif: firstly, his commander obviously had enough on his plate today, and secondly, he was still puzzled himself and needed to give it further thought. He planned to leave the subject fallow as the crew were due to meet with Henschel's chief engineer, Kurt Arnholdt, straight after breakfast.

As the crippled KV-1 pulled into the workshop, Dimitri Korsak thanked his lucky stars. By claiming the half-track and the recovery vehicles, he'd done just enough to claim a result. After all, the Russians held the field, and the engineers would be burrowing like demented badgers and wouldn't be disgorged from their positions without a new assault. Sure, there had been losses, but they were replaceable (by Soviet standards). What mattered was that the fascists were being ground down. One day Russia would be free of them, and perhaps one day Germany, too, would be free.

As he prepared to make his report, Korsak reflected on how close he had come to a reckoning with von Schroif. The intelligence had been good and accurate, but it hadn't been enough. Next time, there could be no mistakes. Radios were becoming standard, but the Germans still held the advantage over the Soviets. There was too much opportunity for his foe to manoeuvre.

Korsak calculated that what he really needed was to be able to draw von Schroif onto marshy, wooded terrain, where the German's ability to manoeuvre would be curtailed, and perhaps a screen of anti-tank guns could do their work. Woods were what he thought were needed. He thought of the trackless forests outside his native Leningrad; difficult going with plenty of tree cover. Surely there had to be a way to level the playing field and draw von Schroif northwards.

'Heil ... and good morning, Herr Arnholdt,' Von Schroif said to a rather dishevelled looking Kurt Arnholdt.

The engineer returned the German greeting, shooting out his right arm with the enthusiasm of one who has fully subscribed to the National Socialist vision.

'Heil Hitler ... Heil von Schroif! It's really you!'

'Astonishing ... haven't seen you since KAMA,' said von Schroif. 'You've obviously been eating well!'

'You haven't changed a bit ... thank God you are here!' replied Arnholdt.

'That's the question I've been asking ... why me?'

'That's down to me, I'm afraid. I've been

agitating for you to have this assignment. It's been the devil's own job. In the end I had to get old Sepp to pull a few strings and have a word in the ear of the Führer. Things don't look good, Hans. I've heard he's going to cancel the whole Mark VI contract and project, and stick with Krupp for everything.'

'We can't allow that to happen,' said von Schroif anxiously. 'I can't blame him though. Seven kilometres from the railhead to here and the damn thing broke down 15 times. Junge had to drive pins into the final drive mechanism just to keep her going. Mind you, Dr Porsche's effort was even worse... I did offer to give it a tow, on the most polite of terms, you understand.'

Arnholdt gave a wry smile. 'It's a good design, but its engine is too over-engineered. A hybrid petrol/electric he calls it. Great on paper, but it eats copper and you just can't get components like that these days. Ours is much better... Maybach will never let you down.'

'You would say that,' replied von Schroif with a friendly grin. 'You've put enough in their pockets.'

'It's not just that, its professional pride ... and a genuine concern for my racial comrades at the front. She's still a prototype Hans, it's a work in progress. If we can have two years, the Mark VI will be the finest fighting vehicle in the world.'

'Two years! You want us to hold out there for another two years while you tinker around back here? How about we swap jobs? You fight the Ivans in Krupp's tin can, and I'll hang around in Kassel with the fräuleins!'

'No thanks, Hans... You wouldn't want me at the front ... unless you want the Russians to win the war! Seriously though, I am glad you are here.'

'And I am glad to be here, Herr Arnholdt. It is vital that we bring something a little more robust to the front line. We are losing too many fine crews. If I can do my bit to rectify that, then you can count on me.'

Given von Schroif's description of the shambolic nature of the journey from the railhead, a panzermann could be forgiven for having some anger at the raw state of the machine, but Hans von Schroif had known Kurt Arnholdt for many a year, and Arnholdt was quick to make him aware of the short time frame involved.

The order for the Mark VI heavy tank had only been received on the 26th of May the previous year, and the engineers and designers had worked every hour God sent to meet their obligations, but von Schroif knew and trusted the fact that Arnholdt was a tanker's designer and that he had their best interests at heart.

'You're right, we've got to have it. The Acht-acht is essential,' said von Schroif.

'Exactly! I think it is vital to the interests of the Reich that we win this trial today. I say that not through professional pride or, God forbid, for … er … commercial reasons, but for the sake of our men at the front. I believe in my heart of hearts that you will be driving Germany's best option today, but it is important that you know the machine and its capabilities. It has many strengths, but unfortunately some weaknesses too, although nothing that a good crew will find too daunting.

'You, young man,' Arnholdt continued, gesturing at Bobby, 'your role cannot be overestimated today. This exercise will not be about gunnery, or bravery, or steadfastness on the field of battle – this will be about engines, about speed, reliability and manoeuvrability. It's about you, SS-Panzerschütze Bobby Junge.'

'Don't worry, Herr Arnholdt,' interrupted the incorrigible Otto Wohl. 'Bobby ate all the technical manuals for dinner last night, and he's been regurgitating this stuff all day.'

This seemed to put Kurt Arnholdt in a better mood, and he said in an almost conspiratorial tone to Junge, 'So, you'll remember, it's all about the regenerative steering final drive gearbox…' at which he tapped his nose and smiled. From the blank looks on four faces it was obvious that this meant nothing to anyone, except Bobby Junge, who nodded and smiled appreciatively.

Korsak was not a man to be thwarted by a tank in need of repair. As the workshop platoon sucked in air through their teeth, like mechanics everywhere, and calculated the time needed to find and fit a replacement of the barrel, he bluntly refused the offer of a replacement T-34.

Captain Androv, the officer in, charge of the repair platoon, was visibly nervous when suddenly confronted by Comrade Kommissar Korsak. He stood by, ready to take a roasting over his failure to immediately get the tank back in fighting shape. To his huge relief, the request from Korsak was an innocuous one.

'Can you please arrange for three cavalry horses and a Protivo-Tankovoye Ruzhyo Degtyarev anti-tank rifle with two hundred and forty rounds to be at my disposal tonight?'

'Why certainly, kommissar. I am on good terms with Major Demjinski over at the cavalry HQ, and I am sure he will oblige.'

'I know, that's why I asked you, and please make sure that two are equipped for riding, and a third pack horse is equipped as shown. I require them at 10 o'clock tonight.'

Korsak handed the bemused officer a scrap of paper containing a diagram of some simple but unusual horse furniture.

'I think the workshop can deliver such an article. May I be permitted to ask the purpose?' queried Androv.

'I plan to use the spare time for a little hunting trip,' came the curt reply.

'Won't the shells be too large? They will surely blow a deer apart!' asked Androv.

'This is war, Comrade Androv. My quarry is not deer. The White Devil hunts only fascist tanks.'

'I understand, Comrade Korsak,' said Androv nervously, '...but if it is tanks that you are hunting, would it not be better to use one of the T-34s which can be placed at your disposal?'

'Not for what I have in mind. You see, the horse has the definite advantage of silence, and the ability to negotiate wooded country, where tank travel would be extremely difficult. My comrades in the mounted formations have successfully equipped cavalry with antitank weapons, and have used mounted men in an innovative and highly distinctive type of action.

'This simple piece of equipment which your men will produce allows for packing and, in action, provides a firing platform for the Protivo-Tankovoye Ruzhyo Degtyarev anti-tank rifle. I like this weapon. In my opinion, it is very much underrated. Unfortunately, it is only a single-shot, bolt-action shoulder weapon, but it does have a powerful punch with which I have destroyed many fascist tanks. However, its efficiency comes from the remarkably long barrel. It is therefore difficult to transport on horseback and can only be carried on a pack saddle, or an ordinary cavalry saddle with these modifications.'

'But who will load for you?' asked Androv.

'You will, comrade.'

'As you command, Comrade Korsak,' said Androv with mock enthusiasm. However, the fact that his shoulders sagged in dismay gave away his extreme nervousness. '...but I do not know how to ride a horse.'

'You will by tomorrow. It will be a good learning opportunity which will allow you to better understand the fascist war machine, and to learn a valuable new skill. We must learn to think that everything is possible.'

Korsak returned to the technical diagram. 'Now ... for transportation on a cavalry-type riding saddle, we require the production of this metal pack device shown here, which consists of a beam with five holes to receive the U-clamps and the brackets, one fixed and one movable.'

'Why movable?' asked Androv, who was now resigned to his fate and less inclined to deference.

'I'll come to that,' barked Korsak.

'Please accept my humble apologies, Comrade Korsak,' muttered Androv, impressed by Korsak's grasp of engineering detail.

'Good, then no more interruptions. The fixed bracket is welded to the beam, and the movable bracket is fastened to the beam with a bolt. The fixed bracket has a top strap and a lock, both of which are hinged. The movable bracket has a revolving yoke with a hinged fastening strap and a lock. In action mode, it provides a firing swivel and aids accuracy. The two U-clamps with nuts and washers hold the metal device to the saddle bows.

'The saddle bags carry the boxes with 120 rounds of ammunition. The breast band and the breeching with the tail strap keep the saddle, with its packed load, from slipping forward and backward with a change of pace, or in going over rough country. The saddle-girth, an additional belly-band, strengthens the whole pack arrangement, including the feed bag and spare parts and appurtenances.

'The feed bag holds the things necessary for the horse's care, the spare parts, and the equipment belonging to the PATR rifle. The wooden boxes carry the ammunition. The shape and dimensions of the boxes must correspond to the inside dimensions of the saddle bags.'

'I understand, Comrade Korsak,' said Androv. 'May I be permitted to ask how the horse equipment is to be assembled?'

'You may, Comrade Androv. Take careful note, as I shall say this only once.'

As Androv grasped for a pencil, Korsak began to list his requirements.

'The assembly of the riding saddle is carried out according to the following directions. It is recommended that a second saddle cloth be put underneath, for greater softness. The breast band and breeching are fastened on by means of connecting straps to the breeching and breast band rings of the saddle cloth cover on the right side. The breast band and breeching are next fastened onto the left side at the time of saddling and adjusting. The breast band is then connected to the front saddle bow by the neck pad straps. The breeching is finally connected to the rear saddle bow and the tail strap by two straps, fastened onto the bow and tail strap.

'The saddle bags are put on the saddle bows in the usual manner. The metal pack device is fastened to the saddle bows by two U-clamps. For this, the U-clamps are passed underneath the saddle bows so that they encircle them and project across the clamps. The beam is placed fixed-bracket forward, with its holes over the U-clamp bolts, and is fastened down with washers and nuts, tightened as far as possible.'

Barely pausing for breath, Korsak continued to spout forth a detailed stream of instructions.

'The saddle as it is assembled is to be packed as follows; the wooden boxes with the shells are put into the saddle bags and fastened with pack straps. Saddle pockets with oats are packed on top of the front saddle bags and fastened with pack straps. The feed bag with the articles necessary for the horse's care, and the spare parts and equipment for the PATR rifle, are placed in the middle, across the saddle, and fastened down with the saddle by the saddle girth.

'The PATR rifle is then put into the bracket yokes, breech forward, muzzle to the rear. The gun is placed so that the sight is up and the back plate is in a horizontal position; the mounting collar of the rifle must be even with the edges of the yoke of the rear bracket. The rifle is fastened to the device by means of the top straps and locks of the yokes. If the horse's neck permits, the gun may be fastened from four to six inches forward of the normal position. Unpacking is done in an order reverse to that of packing.'

Driven on by fear, Captain Androv had, by 22:00 hours, somehow managed to assemble everything Korsak had ordered. With Korsak leading the pack horse, the two men slipped out of the Russian lines and into German-held territory. They travelled across country for 15 kilometres, then made a wide turn for the rollbahn. It was a perfect moonlit night and Korsak seemed to know what he was looking for. With a hunter's instinct, he was tracking down his familiar prey. Androv sensed that he had done this many times.

As they rode along, Korsak delivered a stream of precise instructions. Androv grew in confidence. He sensed that he was with a master tank killer and his nerves began to ease. Korsak was a supreme motivator, and even the art of horse riding began to feel within the art of the possible. Korsak did not have to explain what both men already knew. The German tanks would go into laager for the night and he intended to find them. He knew they would be in the vicinity of the Rostov rollbahn, but where?

As the night wore on, they continued their search. Korsak used the time to explain the tactics they would adopt.

'In the event that I am killed or wounded, Comrade Androv, you will have to take over the gun, and it will be your duty to fight to the last round. It is important to remember that for a distance of as much as 400 metres, the effect of the wind on the PATR need not be considered. Also remember the deflection correction for the movement of the tank. At a speed of twenty kilometres per hour, a lead of one metre is required for every 100 metres of range.

'We are looking for the Mark IV machines. If we find them, I will destroy them, but if they destroy me, you must stay calm and remember to aim for the rear of the turret, as you know the gunner and ammunition are there. If you hit the ammunition, you can blow up the tank. This is a wonderful sight, comrade, when a fascist machine explodes and the turret is hurled into the air. It makes one's heart beat with joy.'

'I should very much like to see that, Comrade Korsak,' replied Androv.

'I hope you will get your wish tonight, but in the event that you find yourself in command of the gun, and if a shot at the rear of the turret is not possible, which it will not be if the gun is swung towards you, then fire at the centre of the rear half of the tank. As you know well, the motor and the fuel containers are there. If you hit either one, you will put the tank out of action.'

'I had no idea the anti-tank rifle was such a potent weapon,' said Androv.

'Indeed it is, Comrade Androv, but it takes courage. It's no use at long range. When firing a PATR at a moving target, it is essential to let the fascist tanks come within 200 metres or closer. The best gunners will allow the tank to approach to within 100 metres. A well camouflaged anti-tank rifle crew can put any fascist tank out of action with a few well-aimed shots, and don't forget that the fascists stick to the rollbahn like glue, so one burning machine can easily be used to block the road for a whole column of tanks.'

Initially, the hunt for the German tanks proved fruitless, and even Korsak seemed to grow weary and eventually fell into silence. It looked as if their mission would end in failure, until just before dawn, when they emerged from a small wood bordered by a wide lake.

Responding to Korsak's gesture, Androv was able to make out the shape of six German tanks parked up on the side of the rollbahn. Among the panje huts on the other side of the road were the shapes of half-tracks and supply trucks, but Korsak only had eyes for the tanks. The side of each parked vehicle was parallel to their position and perfectly exposed to their fire. Korsak was inwardly elated. Androv was terrified, and he felt the adrenaline pumping in his veins, his mouth dry, and the pounding in his ears.

This far behind the lines, the German crews considered themselves relatively safe, safe enough to sleep in the rough huts of the small village which bordered the road to the right. Nonetheless, the German commander had selected his site with care. To the left of the tanks was the wide lake, some 100 metres broad, which gave the tanks protection against any Soviet tanks approaching from that direction. Unfortunately, it also formed a barrier, making pursuit of any attacker impossible.

Unobserved, the two men dismounted and tied their horses to a tree. Together they stealthily unpacked the anti-tank rifle and mounted it on the swivel of the device manufactured by Androv's men, and now attached to the saddle of the pack horse. Assembly and loading was soon complete and the anxious Captain Androv expected them to open fire. To his intense frustration, the panicky Androv had to wait in an agony of fearful torture as Korsak, cool as ice, delayed opening fire and whispered his final instructions.

'Now is the time to show daring, Comrade Androv. As I told you, the best range is 100 metres. When the firing starts, don't let the enemy fire lead you to forget your duty. Fix this in your mind: as long as I am not in-capacitated, you must keep loading the rifle, whatever else happens.'

Androv was just about able to speak. 'Understood, Comrade Korsak.'

'Good. Now, this anti-tank rifle can fire eight to ten rounds per minute, if the gunner and his loader use teamwork. At this range, it's just as effective as a 76 mm gun at 1,500 metres. We have the perfect target. I shall aim for the first tank then switch fire to the rear-most tank. I shall then proceed from the rear to the head of the column. Is that clear?'

'Yes, Comrade Korsak,' came the whispered reply from Captain Androv, his mouth parched and his heart pounding in his chest.

'Once we open fire I shall open and close the breech, aiming and firing. You must be careful to clean and oil each of the shells before you place it in the chamber. In the event that I am wounded or killed and the turrets are turned towards you, you must fire at the centre of the rear half of the tank. Remember, the motor and the fuel containers are there. Good luck, Comrade Androv.'

With that, Korsak finally took aim and fired at the lead tank. The first four shots all produced hits on the lead tank, but there was no explosion. All hell now broke loose as figures came running from all directions and sprinted towards the tanks. Hatches were flung open as black clad figures disappeared inside the tanks and turrets began to traverse towards them.

Cursing his luck, Korsak switched to the fuel tanks. With his ninth shot he finally got his reward as the foremost tank burst into flames. The crew, who had only just got into the vehicle, immediately leapt out and began to fire wildly in their direction with their small arms.

Dragged from his brief sleep by the sound of firing, SS-Sturmbannführer Helmut Voss rushed from his hut and began to take stock of the situation. From the muzzle flash it was clear that they were under attack from what appeared to be an anti-tank rifle, firing from a position just behind the tree line. The lack of supporting machine gun fire suggested a very small group.

'Partisans? Potentially a diversion...' thought Voss, and immediately sent a platoon to cover the other approach to the village before he turned his attention to the tanks.

Korsak and Androv were only too aware that the fire of the remaining five tanks would soon be trained upon them, so they had to work fast, but Androv's trembling hands would not permit the smooth flow of new rounds which would make for the rapid stream of fire that Korsak now needed. Eventually, a new round was rammed home by the cursing Androv and, despite the hail of bullets now whistling uncomfortably close by, Korsak calmly lined up the rear tank.

This time he got his reward. The turret of the last tank had not yet been turned towards them and the shell from the anti-tank rifle found its mark in the ammunition locker. The Panzer simply disintegrated with the force of the resulting explosions. The turret performed a perfect parabola as it flew through the air and crashed into the lake. Voss and the grenadiers were thrown to the ground by the blast and he felt the heat wave surge over him.

The other tanks, however, were undeterred and coaxial machine guns soon began to sweep the forest edge. Korsak and Androv had to act fast, and his flustered loader struggled to keep up as Korsak switched tactics and ran along the column, putting a disabling shot into each engine compartment.

Time was now running against the Soviet pair. A high-explosive round barked out of a number two tank and exploded in the edge of the lake, with co-axial machine gun fire from the other tanks ripping through the trees and creeping closer. Korsak signalled to Androv that the time had come to withdraw.

Voss got to his feet to scan the tree line with his binoculars. He was just in time to witness a Soviet army officer step out from the tree line and take off his cap, revealing a shock of white hair, before bowing deeply and retiring back into the trees.

As a stream of high-explosive shells crashed into the forest around them, Korsak calmly led the pack horse into the shelter of the trees and, accompanied by the shaking figure of Androv, equally calmly repacked the gun and remaining ammunition, loading everything onto the pack horse. He then untied the two riding horses and handed the reins of one of the horses to a stunned Captain Androv.

'Two destroyed and four out of action. Not a bad night's action. Shall we return to the workshop, Comrade Androv?'

Androv needed no second invitation. His fear had transformed him into a natural horseman and, jumping into the saddle, he cantered off in pursuit of Korsak.

# CHAPTER 3

## DER GEBURSTAG

All week they had been preparing for the moment of truth. Today was Hitler's birthday and he had decreed that, on this day, he would choose between the two rival designs for a heavy tank; the long awaited Mark VI.

The Waffen SS crew led by von Schroif had been allocated to the Henschel prototype machine. Despite an infuriating series of breakdowns, they had successfully put the Henschel through its paces and had easily outscored the army team on the gunnery trials. For convenience, their machine was designated the Mark VI (H), while the rival design was the Mark VI (P). The Porsche prototype was crewed by an army outfit which had been fighting in the Northern sector, up by Leningrad, where, judging by their boasts, they were single-handedly fending off the entire Red Army.

'So we come to the trial at last, eh?' said von Schroif. 'Two machines, but only one contract! The Waffen SS versus the Heer, no holds barred?'

'I'm afraid not,' replied Arnholdt. 'I wish it were that simple, but there will actually be three panzers in the final trial.'

'Really...? Why three?' Hans had expected something out of the ordinary, but he was taken aback when the identity of the third competitor was revealed to him.

Just at that moment came the sound of a familiar engine being revved up and Arnholdt pointed towards a small garage-type structure, out of which trundled the familiar shape of the Krupp Panzer Mark IV, but now sporting the long-barrelled 75 mm high-velocity gun.

'Ah, this must be the much rumoured F2, but it's a medium tank!' said von Schroif, with a tone of clear disappointment in his voice.

Knispel and Wohl immediately wandered over and admired the new version of the familiar machine, which now seemed like a stranger with its long-barrelled 75 mm gun. They, were soon engaged in conversation with the army crew of the F2, all of whom were highly enthusiastic concerning the new machine.

'I don't understand it, Kurt ... what's happening? I thought this was to be a straight trial – the Henschel versus the Porsche ... best man wins.'

'It's partly your fault, I'm afraid. Due to the number of breakdowns, the Führer is of a mind to cancel the Mark VI project. He feels both designs are still too unreliable.'

'My fault! Why my fault! You're the damn engineer, not me!' exploded von Schroif in frustration.

'Apparently it's got something to do with an action outside Rostov... On the strength of which, I am given to understand that a certain Hauptsturmführer von Schroif is to be awarded the Knight's Cross today. He and his crew destroyed twenty Russian tanks in a Panzer IV. Naturally, the Führer is being guided towards the obvious conclusion that there is merit in up-gunning and continuing with the Krupp design. Even I have to admit that it's probably a match for the T-34.'

'That's madness! We don't want to settle for parity! It's a fight to the death out there ... you want to outgun your opponent! Not match them!' As he spoke, von Schroif glanced around and noticed Knispel returning from his inspection. 'Look ... it's like old Knispel here ... as a boxer, you want to outreach your opponent. Why have a 75 mm gun when you can have the Acht-acht fitted in a panzer?'

'I agree with you.' Arnholdt turned and gestured towards the massive bulk of the Mark VI. 'But this thing doesn't come cheap. They're going to cost 250,000 Reichmarks each! You can have two Mark IVs for the same price, and they require less labour, less raw materials ... less time. There are a lot of factors weighing in against us, Hans ... but let's enjoy a moment of joy first, eh? Knights Crosses are not awarded every day. Your crew certainly deserves the recognition.'

'I don't care if they awarded me a papal medal. We need this bus at the front! Just who are we fighting here?'

RSHA Kriminalassistent Walter Lehmann was another man weighing up the factors ranged against him. His situation was different to von Schroif. Walter Lehmann's enemies actually thought they were his friends. Looking out from his office in Prinz-Albert Strasse, over the rooftops of Berlin on a wet but muggy summer's day, he could not help but reflect on how he had got here, and how long he would last.

His stock had surely risen with the accuracy of the information he had provided in the past. He had given them absolute accuracy concerning Kampfgruppe von Schroif. As a source, he must have been vindicated. Surely he couldn't be blamed by the failure to eliminate von Schroif. Surely that was someone else's department. Stenner was the man on the ground, he would have to take the blame.

At first, duplicity had come easy to Lehmann, but now the different faces and fronts were becoming more difficult, as were the demands. The uncertainty of it all was beginning to wear down his resolve. Now there was the demand for information about this new heavy tank, and Beria had begun pressing him hard. This wasn't the kind of information that came easily. He knew he could twist Borgmann round his finger, the poor deluded idiot thought he was doing his bit for the Reich, but collecting the information was one thing, fooling Borgmann into transmitting it from Rastenburg was an altogether more delicate undertaking.

Despite his increasing unease, he couldn't help but allow himself a smile. Whatever happened, he, Walter Lehmann, son of the murdered Uwe Lehmann, the former communist street fighter, was now working for the Reich Main Security Office, with executive responsibility for preventing the Soviets spying on the German Armaments industry... The gamekeeper had certainly turned poacher! His late father would have loved the fact that he was now the prime source for the NKVD!

Yes, it could be funny, and it had its benefits, pecuniary as well as carnal, and he was a man of big appetites! But sometimes the tightrope was strung up so high between his different facades that walking between them gave him vertigo.

Carrying out the odd interrogation brought its own cathartic rewards. Torturing Nazis gave him a measure of revenge over the death of his father. One day soon he'd get even with the flash aristocratic bastard who had throttled him to death... but for now he was trapped, his daily wish that the Soviets would win this war and, as promised, make him mayor of Berlin. Then the bastards would definitely pay.

The brown folder bearing the name of von Schroif was so well thumbed that it stood out from the small pile on Lehmann's desk, but he resisted the urge to flick through it once more. Lehmann hoped that his quarry would live to see the day of reckoning. There was still a chance that he might meet a soldier's death, trapped in a burning tank, which would be just, but disappointing... Lehmann wanted him to survive, so that he could suffer an agony of medieval tortures.

The tide was certainly turning. Now that the stupid little corporal had declared war on the Americans, it was just a matter of time. What a dangerous little idiot! Dragging the biggest industrial nation into the

war in order to pander to the yellow men –
who then refused to attack Stalin! Priceless!
Absolutely priceless! What a clown! Lehmann allowed himself a smile but wrenched
himself back to the matter in hand. 'This
damned heavy tank? So, what does Moscow
expect this time?'

Drawn up in parade order, von Schroif
listened to the over-familiar strains of the
marches and waltzes played by the Waffen SS
military band. He waited impatiently for a
sign of the Führer. As first thirty minutes
then an hour passed, the bandsmen appeared
to be nearing exhaustion when suddenly
there was a flurry of activity and a cloud of
staff officers emerged from the unprepossess-
ing collection of huts which comprised the
'Wolf's Lair'. In their midst was the familiar
figure of Adolf Hitler.

Hitler wasted no time in approaching the
spot where the three machines were drawn
up, with their crews proudly standing to
attention. The band played on as Hitler was
introduced to the army crew of the Panzer
IV. Like von Schroif and his team, the men
from Army Group North had obviously performed valiantly and each was awarded an
Iron Cross. The Führer exchanged some
words with the crew then moved on to the
team tasked with putting the Porsche
machine through its paces.

It had been the week from hell for the crew from the Gross Deutschland Division. The Porsche machine had exhibited all of the signs of a seriously flawed design, not least because of the obvious problems arising from the turret being set forward, at the front of the superstructure. Turning corners was a real problem, as the combined length of the barrel and the tank made it impossible to navigate in tight spaces.

Bobby Junge had spotted that flaw straight away. Von Schroif wondered why one tank driver was instantly able to spot what hundreds of Germany's finest engineers apparently couldn't. As von Schroif continued his musings, once again there was a brief presentation of medals, and then Hitler moved on to von Schroif's crew.

Hitler smiled when he was introduced to von Schroif and turned to Reichminister Albert Speer, standing at the forefront of the dignitaries and top brass.

'This is SS-Hauptsturmführer von Schroif. He's the one I've been telling you about... the hero of Rostov.' Turning to von Schroif, Hitler continued speaking. 'A Berchtesgadener, if my memory serves me right? My neighbour across the valley from the Berghof ... Maximilianstrasse, isn't it?'

Completely taken aback by the ability of Hitler to recall tiny details, von Schroif found himself at a loss for words.

'That is correct, mein Führer... May I offer you my fondest Birthday greetings.'

Hitler's piercing blue eyes were now fixed earnestly upon him.

'Thank you, Hauptsturmführer, but the significance of today means nothing to me. There are far more important matters to deal with. I dedicate this day to you and this fine crew. The news of your exploits outside Rostov was the finest birthday greeting any-one could offer me. I am honoured to find myself in the company of true German heroes. Siegfried himself could not have achieved what you achieved that day – that was a mighty red dragon which you slew! The Empire needs men like you, the true shield of the German people. You represent authentic German virtues, valour and courage. You have the honour of Parsifal and the goodness of Lohengrin. With men like you, Germany has no equal in the world.'

As Hitler spoke, the crew each felt them-selves grow in importance. The man was mesmeric. His honeyed words seemed to produce in the listener the conviction that, despite all her enemies, Germany would prevail. The familiar conviction of belief in the final victory flooded back. How could they ever have doubted it, even for a mo-ment?

Barely pausing for breath, the Führer con-tinued.

'There are three types of people who inspire me to keep up my work: German farmers, German workers and German warriors, and you are the finest of the three. On behalf of the grateful German nation, it is my privilege today to bestow upon you a token of our grateful and humble thanks for your sacrifices and your courage.'

Hitler was like a hypnotist and healer combined. As he spoke, the cares of the world were lifted from the shoulders of the listener, to be replaced by the unshakeable belief that everything would get better. Every member of the crew felt the same devotion. They would do anything for this great man and this great people.

As promised by Arnholdt, Hitler stepped forward and presented the Knights Cross to von Schroif. Then, to his delight, he presented Knispel with the Iron Cross First Class. Wendorff and Junge each received the same coveted decoration.

Finally, he came to Wohl and presented him with the Iron Cross Second Class. Wohl seemed to grow in stature. His chest swelled as, with tears in his eyes, he finally achieved some recognition from the world which had been so unkind to him. In that moment, Wohl at last felt as if he belonged somewhere. His days as a Munich street urchin melted away into history.

The day had been memorable, but the

most important purpose now resurfaced as von Schroif grappled with the significance of the moment. Here in the balance lay the fate of the machine which could be the key to victory in the East and the fate of not just Germany, but also of the German people and the Führer himself.

The retreat from Rostov to the Mius had been a setback, and it was now in the interest of the whole country that the Wehrmacht regain the initiative. In modern warfare, this was a matter of material just as much as it was manpower. So von Schroif rationalised this new attitude inwardly by deciding that yes, he would take great pride and enjoyment from his meeting the Führer, but only after the trial had been won!

'It's true,' thought Von Schroif to himself, 'the man has an almost encyclopaedic memory.'

'On behalf of my crew, I thank you, mein Führer,' replied von Schroif, temporarily blown from the course he had intended to take.

'I'm sure you will drive well today,' said Hitler, 'but I have a feeling that perhaps this time an inferior design might let you down.'

Von Schroif could feel the moment slipping, but he plucked up the courage to reply.

'Mein Führer, in my personal opinion, the Panzer VI we are privileged to drive today has admirable qualities and, if the tests were designed on parameters other than speed over a rally course, which, as commander in chief, you know is but a small part of the operational requirements of a panzer in the field, then I am convinced that the result will be different. I respectfully request that the trial be conducted not just on the basis of manoeuvrability, but also upon the ability of each machine to overrun its opponents. My experience at the front tells me how important this factor is; we almost lost our battle with the enemy outside Rostov as a result of our inability to overrun a small tractor and an antitank gun.'

'I am sorry,' interjected a staff officer. 'Allow me to introduce myself. I am Oberstleutnant i.G. Borgmann. In case you have forgotten, today is the Führer's birthday. We just don't have the time to conduct another trial.'

But the Führer, with a gentle wave of his hand, brushed this consideration aside. 'I think, gentlemen, that the welfare of our men on the Eastern Front is of more import than whether my birthday cake remains undisturbed for another hour or two!'

The assembled group burst into sycophantic laughter, all except Oberstleutnant i.G. Borgmann. Von Schroif made a mental note to find out more about this gentleman.

'Regrettably, Hauptsturmführer, time is

against us,' said Borgmann, 'and there are also the immutable laws of economics. It has been my painful duty to inform the Führer that the designs of Dr Porsche, and also Henschel and Sohn, suffer from engine failures, and I'm sure you don't need that outside Rostov.'

'We need a better overrun capability,' said von Schroif, stubbornly sticking to his point.

'I have no doubts about that, Hauptsturm-führer, but we would require dynamic and conclusive proof that this expensive and un-trustworthy vehicle has that ability. If it doesn't run, it can't overrun,' said Borg-mann smugly.

There was more laughter, but von Schroif noted that Hitler did not join in. There was the faintest glimmer in his eyes, which von Schroif interpreted as a communication from soldier to soldier.

'But the overrun is an important part of the armoury,' ventured von Schroif.

Borgmann was quick to counter von Schroif's argument. 'No buts ... we have very limited time, and the parameters have been set and cannot be changed.'

Not surprisingly, with Knispel on the team, the gunnery tests had given the Henschel design the clear lead, but today was to be a speed trial, and mechanical reliability was what was required. They had been taken through the four kilometre course, with a number of nasty twists and bends.

As they climbed back inside the Möbel-packwagen for what could be the last time, the first thing, as always, that struck all of them was the space compared to the cramped interior of the Mark IV; it was a veritable cathedral, it was wonderful! It was amazing even with 100 Acht-acht rounds aboard!

Bobby Junge sat down in his seat and ran his hand along the various controls, levers and switches. It was heart-breaking to have come so close, but even Bobby Junge with his rally driving skills could not perform mir-acles. They could possibly beat the Porsche, but they could never hope to beat the Krupp. The Mark IV had been given a slight handi-cap and would not start until both Mark VI prototypes had covered 500 metres, but it was certain to finish the course first.

Junge was now back in rally mode. As soon as the signal was given they started off. The two heavy tank prototypes seemed to have the measure of each other, but then the Porsche model began to pull away.

'What's wrong, Junge?' asked von Schroif.

'I can only get her up to twenty-five, sir, and she's starting to heat up.'

Von Schroif and Michael grimaced as they watched the Porsche prototype edge ahead.

'She's doing nearly thirty,' added Bobby.

The test was only a short four kilometre speed test, two kilometres out and two kilometres back, and it looked like it was soon to be all over. The Henschel machine was destined to be still-born, and with it, the whole of the Mark VI project.

However, as they started to reach the turn, von Schroif could see the deficiency in the other tank; it lumbered and slowed when it had to make the turn. The Henschel on the other hand completed the turn in what seemed like half the time and space and actually came out ahead! So this is what Arnholdt meant! The regenerative steering final drive gearbox, that's what gave it its manoeuvrability!

'Well done, Bobby Junge!' cheered Michael Knispel, who for once was really along for the ride, but he seemed to have spoken too soon as the Porsche came out of its turn and started to catch them and finally overtook them. The one thing the Porsche did have was an amazing turn of speed.

'Junge, give her everything, we're on the final straight!'

The Mark IV had not yet made up enough ground and it suddenly looked as if they might do it.

'Right, Junge,' said von Schroif, 'let's show the world what she can do!'

'There's nothing left and she's getting hotter. If I don't slow her down, the engine is going to melt!'

Junge's words came like a dagger to the heart, but from his experience at the front, von Schroif knew to trust Junge's judgement. There was no point in countermanding him, so he came to the only decision he could.

They came towards the brow of the final hill, watching the Mark IV as it gradually pulled level. They reached the brow neck and neck with the Porsche and were about to charge down the final slope together when there came an almighty bang and the Porsche stopped dead in its tracks, a cloud of smoke issuing from the engine deck.

'Slow her down, Junge,' ordered von Schroif.

'It's worse than that, sir. We're going to have to stop now, or no one will be able to drive this bus again.'

With a heavy heart, von Schroif gave the order. With only 350 metres downhill to the finishing line, the Henschel came to a halt, perched on the brow of the steep hill.

Von Schroif could see the Mark IV pull past the finish line, then turn broadside on before the victorious crew members piled out and went to meet the dignitaries. The nodding of heads and smiles told their own story; they signalled general agreement among the chiefs of staff and dignitaries. The consensus was that they would move ahead with the Mark IV. He hung his head when he saw the disappointment on Kurt Arnold's face. He felt that he had let him down.

As the Mark IV crew reached the dignitaries, a ripple of applause reached the dispirited men sitting despondently inside the Henschel. Behind them there was even greater disappointment for the Porsche crew, who were now fighting a small fire in the engine compartment. The crew sat dejectedly in their places, listening to the sound of the rapidly cooling engine.

Eventually Bobby Junge broke the long silence. 'That wasn't a fair fight. There's much more to this machine than running around a damn rally track.'

'Damn right!' said Michael Knispel. 'With this bus we could have overrun every anti-tank gun in Russia... Now what?'

'I assume its back to tin cans again. At least we'll have the new Kampfwagenkanone,' said Wohl, glumly accepting the result.

'Yes, indeed, but that's no consolation,' thought Von Schroif. 'The Acht-acht is what is really needed.' It just wasn't a fair fight, and that irked him.

Knispel was now warming to his theme. 'If only we could have had an overrun test ... the very mass of this beast is a real weapon. Junge could crush T-34s and save Reichminister Speer the ammunition,' said Knispel in obvious frustration.

Suddenly, a very dark thought dawned on

von Schroif. 'Knispel, you're right.'

'Thank you, Hauptsturmführer, but, right or not, we have to give up now.'

'We're not giving up that easily,' said von Schroif. 'There is still one part of the test to go...'

'What do you mean, sir?' asked Junge.

'Prepare for overrun attack!'

As the Mark IV crew lined up for photographs with the Führer and his entourage, and the flash bulbs popped, a Propaganda Kompanie crew appeared and a film camera turned over as they began to interview the successful crew.

Von Schroif could hear a fresh round of applause for the victors and it felt like a knife cutting into him once more. He took a deep breath. Hitler was not only the chancellor, but head of the German armed forces. What he was about to do was the biggest risk of his career and the supreme commander may well have a different opinion. This was going to be an unspoken dialogue between two military men about what was best for the German soldier.

'Is the engine cool enough, Junge?' asked von Schroif.

'Just about,' replied Bobby. 'It's downhill. We are not going to be running now, we are going skiing!'

'Can we do it, Wendorff?' barked von Schroif.

'What can you get her up to, Junge?' asked Wendorff.

'On this slope, probably forty kilometres per hour...'

'So what do you think, Wendorff?' asked von Schroif impatiently.

'Well, the math is simple. Forty multiplied by sixty tonnes ... yes, that should do it.'

'Alright, I order we do it... If we fail, it's a punishment battalion. This could go spectacularly wrong. Anyone who is not needed for the demonstration must now dismount and leave with his honour intact.'

There was no movement.

'Knispel, Wendorff, Wohl... I order you to dismount.'

Nobody moved.

'That's an order,' said von Schroif solemnly.

Still nobody moved.

Finally, Wendorff spoke. 'There seems to be a problem with the intercom, sir. We can't hear you.'

'As you wish, gentlemen... Start her up, Junge.'

The noise of the Maybach engine being revved up halted the conversation in the Führer's entourage. All eyes turned towards the heavy panzer perched at the top of the hill. Suddenly it lurched forward and began to pick up more and more speed as Bobby Junge expertly ran through the gears. The group watched in puzzled silence as the heavy panzer sped towards the Mark IV. Gasps of consternation were emitted as the realisation dawned that there was about to be a collision. The Henschel was now speeding down the slope. Inside the speeding tank, all eyes were on the Mark IV, which they were fast approaching.

'What are we doing?'

'Fifty-five,' said Wohl. 'Hold tight, here we go!'

As sixty tons of steel crashed into the lighter machine, the box structure of the main hull immediately gave way and collapsed inwards. The turret was forced from its mounting ring and the far side hull was forced outwards, leaving the Mark IV a flattened heap of junk.

Alerted by the sound of the crash, the assembled staff officers turned as one, but no one spoke. They simply could not believe what they were witnessing. They watched open-mouthed in stunned silence as the Henschel machine reversed over the wreckage, crushing the turret, then turned towards them before rolling swiftly forward and finally drawing up in front of the Führer. As the heavy tank drew to a halt, von Schroif jumped down from his hatch and saluted the Führer.

'Birthday greetings, mein Führer ... overrun test completed.'

Suddenly the cameras and the Propaganda Kompanie movie crew were focused on von Schroif and his crew.

'It was certainly conclusive! Germany needs men of action,' replied the Führer. 'With this combination – you, your men, and this fine new tank – I think we may have something for the untermensch to think about. But husband this new weapon carefully. It may have many opponents, but it will have a few brothers.'

'We will, mein Führer,' replied von Schroif.

'We will have to find a soldier's name for this beast ... do you have one in mind?'

'Yes, my Führer.'

'Well, go ahead, commander.'

'We call it the Möbelpackwagen.'

There was a long pause. Hitler was obviously unimpressed. Eventually, he spoke. 'The furniture van? Oh no, that won't do at all.'

Hitler paused briefly for thought, and then began again.

'You and your crew have demonstrated this wonderful new German weapon. You fought like tigers at Rostov. You showed tigerish courage when all seemed lost to you. The Mark VI should have a name that befits its predatory nature.' Turning towards a smiling Arnholdt, he announced his decision. 'Dr Arnholdt, the Henschel VK 45.01 shall be informally known as the Tiger.' But Hitler wasn't finished. He turned once more to von Schroif and his crew. '...and you shall be the first of the Tiger men!'

With that, Hitler swept off towards his headquarters, trailing staff officers in his wake.

A stunned von Schroif was faced by the microphone of a Propaganda Kompanie. As the camera whirled away, he began trying to compose rational answers to the questions.

Dimitri Korsak was not in a patient mood. The workshop was going as fast as they could, but he had a score to settle and there was no time to lose. Captain Androv had pulled out all the stops to have a new barrel delivered. The final adjustments to the main gun of the KV-1 were nearing completion. Soon it would be fine-tuned to his satisfaction. The reinforcements had brought his company up to strength, and he still had his line to the divisional artillery. If necessary, he could call upon any amount of firepower, so there was plenty of muscle at his disposal, but caution urged that he use his resources sparingly. The events at Hill 15 outside Rostov had been embarrassingly close to a defeat. This time, there must be no mistake.

It was infuriating that he still did not have a full complement of radio-equipped tanks. He was suspicious that he was not being given the resources that Moscow had promised. If he was being sold short, the reckoning with those responsible would be sudden and vicious, but that was a score to be settled on another day. The facts that took up all of his thoughts were that only two of the tanks at his disposal had the means of both sending and receiving radio communications, twenty-three could receive but not send, and the remaining thirty still used signal flags.

As usual, all the machines provided were T-34 types, whereas Korsak swore by the KV-1. He could have spent time and effort arranging a complex method of intercommunication and response to suit the changing battlefield situation, but he knew he was not working with the finest material; the crews only understood how to advance with dogged courage, and tactical finesse was out of the question in any event. It was obvious that the only real option was to use his superior numbers to bludgeon the enemy into submission. The obvious route was to agree a simple but strict battle plan, and stick to it.

Korsak's intelligence told him that von Schroif had been transferred back to Germany, which left his old battalion vulnerable to counterattack, but, even with the less than gentle prodding from Moscow, it had taken a week to assemble a strike force. As the ground dried out it was clear that the fascists were going to throw themselves against Rostov once more. Korsak had prevailed in the rough and tumble game of politics, and against the local Russian commander, who had reluctantly weakened his front. He had received the messages from Viper. There was to be another German attempt at Hill 15 with tanks and assault guns. Korsak knew that the German attack would be preceded by a major bombardment lasting two hours, and that the tanks would then advance under a heavy smoke screen.

The attack had twice been postponed due to wind conditions, but as dawn broke the new day promised to be a beautiful still spring morning, and when the first German range-finding shells began to scream into the Soviet position, Korsak sensed that his time had come.

The German bombardment grew in intensity. First it was mortars and infantry guns of increasing calibre, then the 150 mm guns began to add their weight to the barrage. A wall of explosions marked the edge of a ferocious barrage, and the concussion caused by the heaviest shells reached far beyond the front lines to pound the chests of Dimitri Korsak and his waiting attack force. The shocking force of the initial bombardment was unimaginable, but astonishingly it built over the next hour and grew in intensity as more and more batteries joined in. Soon Korsak was able to discern the unmistakable punch of the massive shells from the 210 mm heavy howitzers as they added their fire to the appalling maelstrom of steel and high-explosive. The dirty grey-brown plumes of smoke climbed into the sky and, on this windless morning, towered over the front line like an immense wall of a castle built for giants.

Korsak was disconcerted, but not sur-prised, when his radio communication with the front line abruptly ceased. Nothing could be expected to survive under a bombardment of such intensity. Still he watched and waited. Finally, as the intense shelling began to overwhelm the senses, there came the gentle plopping sound of smoke shells hitting the soft earth, and a cloud of pure white smoke began to spread from the foot of the brown wall. The time had come. Korsak gave the signal and fifty Soviet tanks began to roll forward into position, just below the crest of the hill which stood between the Russians and the German front lines.

Korsak crept his KV-1 to the crest of the hill; he was now just 2000 metres from the front line. At first the field seemed empty, save for a few Soviet refugees who could be seen crawling back from the bombardment, but as the fire slackened there came the sound of German tank engines. Finally, the shape of a Mark IV emerged from the stillness of the cloud of smoke. It stopped while its machine guns took the fleeing Russians under fire, sending the distant figures of men spinning to the ground. Its stubby main gun spat its message of death towards a further group of fugitives.

Korsak knew that he could potentially destroy the German tank. At this distance, the German had no chance of hitting him. He, on the other hand, with his long-barrelled 76 mm main gun, could destroy the Mark IV, but he chose to wait. The trap had been baited and was now about to be sprung. He smiled grimly to himself as he noted that, on each side of the lead tank, other German tanks were beginning to emerge from the smoke.

'Come on, you fascist bastards, show yourselves. You'll get what's coming...' thought Korsak as he watched the events unfold.

He was happy to see that the tanks were soon joined by two squat turretless vehicles, which Korsak recognised as Sturmgeschütz – army assault guns, alert for field defences which might hold up the waves of infantry which Korsak calculated were still hidden by the cloud of smoke. His suspicions were confirmed as the lead Sturmgeschütz was followed by clumps of infantry in camouflage pattern. As yet, there was no sign of the half-tracks carrying more infantry, which Korsak felt sure would follow.

Korsak watched with detached interest as the lead Sturmgeschütz identified the lone Soviet anti-tank gun which remained in action between the front line and Hill 15. It was quickly engaged with high-explosive rounds fired by both assault guns, and the gunners were all too soon thrown to the ground, the distant shapes remaining motionless, killed by deadly shards of shrapnel which flew in all directions. Through his powerful binoculars Korsak could discern the faint pools of dark red blood which widened as the prone bodies were crushed under the wheels of the advancing Sturmgeschütz. He could easily have destroyed the Sturmgeschütz through its weak roof armour, but still Korsak did nothing and the German tanks began to advance warily across the open ground. He counted them: five, seven, eleven. This was it, the fascist attack had begun.

Unable to resist any longer, Korsak ordered his gunner to take careful aim on the lead German tank, which was now little more than 1200 metres away. The gun was already loaded and the armour-piercing round barked out, but frustratingly flew over the German tank.

Korsak cursed the gunner. 'Aim lower, you cretin! Or you'll end up in a punishment battalion!'

His tank was expertly concealed behind

the crest of the hill, but Korsak knew only too well that his position had now been given away by the tell-tale puff of smoke and his gunner's carelessness. There was no time for a second round as, according to plan, on seeing his tank fire, the first wave of Russian tanks began to charge up the slope and over the crest of the hill. Although his own tank was still motionless, he had ordered all of his tanks to load with armour-piercing and, on his signal, the first wave of ten tanks had broken cover and charged towards the German forces.

As expected, the German tanks came to a halt as soon as the T-34s emerged from over the brow of the hill. With the advantage of their static position, the German tanks were able to fire accurately, but Korsak was confident that his tanks would not suffer at these ranges, and he had other things to occupy his mind. He gave the order to pull out while continuing to observe the battle-field.

Korsak was stunned to see four T-34s explode into flames as the massive impact of the armour-piercing rounds stopped the lead tanks dead and further rounds found a home in the ammunition lockers of the stricken T-34s. The first victims were shortly followed into oblivion by a further two tanks.

Korsak was mystified. There was only one tank commander who was capable of such a feat. 'Was von Schroif still here?'

Despite the loss of six tanks, Korsak remained confident that his superior numbers assured him of victory. The trap had been sprung, and he watched over his shoulder as his next wave and a further ten tanks advanced over the hill and into combat.

The plan was clearly working. Korsak expected his opponents to stay pinned in position while they engaged the Soviet armour frontally. His well-constructed plan was to lead the remaining thirty tanks around the hill in order to engage the Germans on their flank. Korsak urged his driver to turn right and stay below the crest of the hill. The battle plan was now underway, and there was no way to change it. Korsak knew that, by closing to such a short range, his two leading waves of tanks would become vulnerable to the German tank guns, which would become more and more effective as the range closed. He expected losses, but six in short order gave him grounds for concern.

Korsak could hear the declining sounds of firing and the sound of tanks being hit by armour-piercing rounds, but the die was now cast as he and the other thirty tanks raced around the contour of the hill, preparing to burst triumphantly into the flank of their enemy. He calculated that his tanks would be around 800 metres from the German machines, and firing into the weak side armour guaranteed a kill.

As he rounded the corner of the hill the slower KV-1 was joined by the faster moving T-34s, arrayed below him and to his right. Gathering speed, they rolled onto the plain and slowly came to a halt in firing positions on the German flank. It was then that Korsak realised that he had a problem.

The T-34 nearest to the smoke cloud suddenly burst into flame. The sound of the gun which had fired at the T-34 was drowned out by the noise of the continuing bombardment which had now been lifted to the slopes of Hill 15, otherwise Korsak would instantly have realised the magnitude of his predicament. The destruction of the first T-34 was quickly followed by five more machines which were all blown apart in a matter of seconds.

Korsak was stunned. To his left he could see the carcasses of all twenty T-34s, but there were no German tanks on the field, nothing, not even a wreck. He could see from the track marks that the German tanks had all withdrawn into the bank of smoke.

Something was wrong... the German tanks had the field, but they had withdrawn. The attack must have been a feint. Quickly, Korsak gave the order to withdraw. Those tanks with radio receivers immediately began to leave the field. Flags were being waved frantically to the others, which one by one began to withdraw. As the smoke began to clear the source of the danger became all too apparent. Korsak's worst fears were vindicated.

Under cover of the smoke, a battery of 88 mm anti-aircraft guns had been expertly pulled into position. The destructive power had come from the mighty Acht-acht. His situation was now desperate. The fleeing Soviet machines offered an easy rear shot, and the greedy Acht-achts were quick to find their targets.

Voss watched in grim satisfaction as his boys destroyed the fleeing Russian armour. He was distracted as a group of grenadiers passed and SS-Sturmscharführer Braun stepped out of the ranks and gave the stiff-armed salute.

'May I offer my congratulations on your victory? This White Devil is more of a puppy dog, I'd say.'

Voss smiled. 'It's not my victory, its revenge for our recovery boys that bastard mutilated. Make sure everyone knows that the planning was by Hauptsturmführer von Schroif. His legacy lives on in his absence.'

'I'll make sure the inhuman pigs continue to pay. The untermensch will learn. We look forward to the return of the Hauptsturmführer.'

'So do I, Braun. We'll need him soon.' Voss

made a mental note to commend von Schroif on the effectiveness of the battle plan that he had drawn up.

The mutilated recovery team had been avenged, and the scores were now even, but this vicious war was becoming more and more barbaric by the day.

# CHAPTER 4

## PADERBORN

'Paderborn?' asked Bobby Junge.

'After the birthplace of the River Pader,' replied Karl Wendorff. 'The river originates in nearly 200 springs near Paderborn Cathedral, last resting place of St Liborius, the Patron Saint of a good death.'

'Obviously not on the side of Brommann and his recovery team,' said Michael Knispel in a sad tone. 'Nothing could ever make up for that.'

'The word is that old man Voss, with the help of the boss here, gave them a heavy punishment in return,' said Wohl, trying to lighten the atmosphere.

'SS-Scharführer Brommann would have thanked you both for it. He was a great friend of mine. Boy, could he drink beer,' said Knispel, warming to his subject.

'Yes, I know. He was at KAMA with me. He was a good man, but he was suddenly sent home ... some incident I never quite got to the bottom of. He didn't speak much. He certainly didn't deserve to die like that. It's not over, it's unfinished business.'

'I bet he didn't go quietly,' said Knispel, 'not old Brommann.'

'So this Laborious, how did he die?' asked Bobby Junge, turning the subject away from the horror of what had happened to the tank recovery team outside Rostov.

'In the arms of his best friend,' replied Karl Wendorff, his voice trailing off as the powerful image evoked by his answer struck him.

All went quiet. Von Schroif gazed out of the train window at the beautifully tended countryside of North Rhine-Westphalia, a view that gave no hint of the carnage that was enveloping the entire world, but a view that reinforced his deeply held conviction that this Germany, this land, these people, were worth upholding. Yes, even to the death, but, for now at least, he had no intention of dying, nor did any of his crew, and that was why they were headed to Paderborn. It was there at the Panzer training grounds that they would get to know their new machine, its likes and dislikes, its temper and its power. Once known, they could then ride into battle with a confidence probably never even dreamed of by any warrior in any age, but it wasn't going to be an easy introduction.

After arriving at Paderborn, the crew headed straight to their quarters and snatched at what little sleep they could.

Dimitri Korsak was in a dilemma. He sat poised over the typewriter, but no words came. All around him were the intrusive sounds of frantic repairs as the few survivors of the second battle for Hill 15 were made ready for a return to the field. The clash of metal and shouts of the battalion workshop intruded on his thoughts and made it impossible to concentrate. Even with this handful of survivors, the unpalatable fact remained that he had lost forty tanks in the second debacle around Hill 15, and his reputation as the best tank commander on the Eastern Front was now sure to come under scrutiny.

Captain Androv, however, was now an evangelist, telling everyone who would listen about their adventures with the anti-tank rifle, but this wasn't a game of cowboys and Indians, that was small-scale stuff. Korsak now needed a big and unambiguous victory. His special standing in Moscow was now under threat.

He desperately cast around for a positive angle to add to his story. Eventually, the mixture of half-truth and lies emerged. He had thwarted a major German attack and he could just about spin the story around that, but why had his own attack failed? The 88 mm, of course. It was a deadly tank killer. 'Thank God the fascists can't mount that in their tanks!'

Korsak began to type:

*The fascist forces, reputed to be a force of over 150 tanks, supported by a preparatory artillery barrage of army-level intensity, attempted to break through in the Mendov Hill Sector. I managed to bring together a force of 50 T-34 tanks and threw the machines into battle in order to thwart the attack, which led to heavy losses. I personally led the flanking attack which halted the fascist tanks and caused them to withdraw into their smoke barrage.*

*The fascist advance was completely halted by the courage and sacrifice of the tanks under my command. Further losses were incurred before the fascists were forced to withdraw, leaving us the victors. I was able to gather my machines. All losses were caused not by fire from the fascist tanks, but from 88 mm anti-aircraft guns, whose deployment had been concealed by the smoke barrage.*

*Initially, it was thought that our losses were caused by a new type of armour-piercing projectile. However, there is now a real danger that the 88 mm will be mounted in a new generation of tank, the possession of which would pose enormous difficulties on the battlefield. The dis-*

*appearance from the battlefield of von Schroif and his crew needs to be investigated and reported upon by Viper.'*

'Good morning, gentlemen,' boomed the voice, snapping awake the recently-risen crew. 'Your steed has arrived! Now, let's get started! I am Major Jurgen Rondorf.'

'Pleased to make your acquaintance, Herr Major,' offered von Schroif.

'And yours, but there is no time for pleasantries here. There is a war to be won, and they tell me that you are just the men to do it... Well, we shall see about that.'

With that, he turned and led them out to the courtyard, and there she stood, almost blocking out the early morning April sun.

'Gentlemen, soon to be at your fingertips... Sixty tons of steel, which can deliver 700 horsepower, giving a speed of twenty-five kilometres per hour on tarmac, and fifteen on rough terrain. All above ground, of course, because, as you will soon find out, she can also swim... Now, I know you would love to jump in the saddle and head east, but first, I'm afraid, the boring routine... You have to read this first, then read it again and again and again, as if your lives depended on it, which I assure you my good fellows, they certainly will.'

At that, he lifted up a bundle of the newly printed paper, three centimetres thick, and handed each crewman a copy in turn.

'Much to digest, gentlemen. Here are the details of how to maintain, and fight with, the Panzer Mark VI ... or, as I believe we soldiers must now call it, the Tiger. The preliminary written examination will be in four hours' time. If you are all as good as you are reputed to be, you should all pass with 80%... Physical conditioning for four hours after that. Same again tomorrow, and the day after.'

'Permission to speak, Herr Major?' asked Wohl.

'Granted ... if it's quick.'

'When do we do some driving?'

'Unfortunately, you are not going to get your hands on 250,000 worth of hard earned Reichmarks until your brain knows every nut and bolt of this beauty ... and then the hard work begins... Heil Hitler!'

'What are we going to call her though, boys?' muttered Otto as they turned and made their way back to the barracks. 'I was fond of Magda, but I think I may have found someone else... Maria? No, maybe something a little more kittenish...' Looking up, he realised that no one was responding. They had all set off at a clip back to the barracks, each clutching the pile of papers close, like a newborn child.

'Ach, I suppose they all have difficult new routines to learn,' thought Otto to himself.

'My section will be about a page long. I'm just going down to the river – not much you can teach me about lifting and loading!'

How wrong he was to be...

Settling himself with his back to a tree, Wohl placed his papers by his side. With less than three hours to the first paper, Wohl would have been well advised to start studying, but his hand was drawn once more towards the breast pocket of his overalls, where nestled the well-thumbed copy of Die Wundertüte, which Wohl had picked up from the news stand for 50 Reichspfennigs. The small illustrated magazine described itself on its garishly illustrated cover as '100 pages of humour and puzzles in words and pictures for the Front and Homeland.' The little magazine was purpose-designed for military personnel and was made to fit in the pocket of a soldier's battle dress.

Wohl was particularly interested in the illustrations; he decided to save the articles by Hermann Krauze for another day. The racy illustrated pictures of beautiful damsels in a state of undress brought to his mind the work of Peter Jensen, his old art teacher from Munich. They hadn't seen each other for years, but his encouragement still worked its hold and Wohl dreamed of being a graphic artist. His inspiration was the female form.

Die Wundertüte was generously provided

with plenty of illustrations of young ladies, most of them in a state of undress. Wohl was soon lost in contemplation as he leafed through the magazine. His favourite strip was 'The Little King', and there came the odd small laugh as he lost himself in the comic antics. He paused at page thirty-three to study a cartoon which depicted four ghosts peering through a window at the seductive form of a naked young woman, and laughed sympathetically at the ghost turning to his colleague with the sentiment that it was not so bad being dead after all. 'You could be right,' thought Wohl to himself as he settled down to study the little magazine once again.

As the morning wore on, Wohl was soon lost in Die Wundertüte. Unfortunately, other eyes were concentrated upon him and, shortly afterwards, the telephone on the desk of Major Jurgen Rondorf started to ring.

'Rondorf speaking.'

'Good morning, Major Rondorf,' came a strange voice. 'Oberstleutnant i.G. Borgmann calling from Führer headquarters, Rastenburg.'

Rondorf was immediately alert to the range of possibilities. 'How may I help you, Oberstleutnant?'

'You can help me by turning to your left and looking out of your window.'

From his office window, Rondorf had a clear view of the ground down to the river.

He could see nothing remarkable.

'You have me at a disadvantage... What am I supposed to be looking at?'

'Do you not see the figure by the tree? Maybe the binoculars would help.'

With the aid of his trusted Zeiss binoculars Rondorf was soon able to identify Wohl, and was able to make out the name of Wohl's reading matter... Die Wundertüte.

'I see the problem now, Oberstleutnant.'

'I'm glad to hear it. We need only the best men in the Tiger crews. I trust you will deal with the matter accordingly.'

'You can count on me, Oberstleutnant.'

Rondorf replaced the receiver and sat in stunned silence. 'Rastenburg was calling him? How? How could they know what a single lowly Panzerschütze was up to?'

One thought immediately sprang to mind and Rondorf's mind was a blur of acronyms. RSHA? SD? Or GESTAPO? He quickly ruled out the SD, he got the feeling an arrest would follow. This had to be Gestapo work. As commanding officer they'd need his authority though, so he would soon know.

Four hours later, seated at their classroom-style desks, four men scribbled quickly, occasionally staring into space to collect their thoughts and find the right phrasing for their answers. Not so the fifth man, Otto Wohl, whose deeply furrowed brow dripped sweat onto a half-finished and much-amended paper with most of its answers crossed out, re-crossed out, and then crossed out again ... and the rest left blank. He had started out well, and initially the answers flowed as he scratched out each response in his untutored hand, consisting of block capitals.

*Q1. What do you do with shells with fractures or dents?*
*THROW THEM OUT.*
*Q2. What do you do with shells with a marred rotating band?*
*THROW THEM OUT.*
*Q3. What do you do with shells with leaking explosive?*
*THROW THEM OUT.*
*Q4. What do you do with shells without base plates or crimping?*
*THROW THEM OUT.*

Shell identification was straightforward too:

*Q5. Anti-tank grenade no 39 is what colour?*
*BLACK WITH WHITE TIP.*
*Q6. Anti-tank grenade no 40 is what colour?*
*BLACK.*
*Q7. HL Grenade is what colour?*
*GREY.*
*Q8. High-explosive shell is what colour?*
*YELLOW.*

So far so good, but then came questions on the cannon. He knew the answers – he just couldn't remember them! Damn! He should have been more prepared! Was this supposed to be kindergarten? His head was spinning, and he declared to himself that facing a half-dozen T-34s was easier than this. So great were his tribulations that he didn't even reach the questions on turret trouble, let alone answer them.

All too soon Major Rondorf rang the bell and then collected the papers.

Otto Wohl let out a huge sigh of relief. 'Thank God that is over! Just put me in the tank and get all these schoolboy exams away from me!'

Korsak sat in the murky gloom of the forward command dugout and reflected quietly on his situation. Outside, behind the clouds, the moon waxed towards the full. The stars were screened by the ominously dark clouds which seemed to conspire to suck the life out of the few flares that climbed into the night sky. Other than the distant chatter of a lone machine gun, it seemed as if the whole front had succumbed to darkness and lethargy.

Korsak knew that he needed to do something to regain his reputation, and quickly, but his companion in the dugout offered no immediate sign of hope. Slumped over his table and feeling extremely sorry for himself, Major Leonid Naminsky stirred and poured himself another tumbler of vodka. Korsak was all too aware that two major setbacks in a few days meant that he was dicing with death, He was viewed with extreme suspicion by Major Naminsky, the local commander, who knew that he had to tread carefully. Korsak could almost feel the legend of the invincible White Devil deflating day by day.

As each day passed, Naminsky grew just slightly less deferential. He was clearly no longer intimidated by Korsak, or he would not have had the temerity to pour a fifth glass of vodka. But Naminsky had his own troubles and, although he hardly glanced at it himself, he was very willing to share his intelligence with the legendary Comrade Korsak.

With time running against him, Korsak devoured the intelligence reports which Major Naminsky had brought with him. They conveyed very little of value, other than the fact that the same SS unit which had caused him so much embarrassment now defended two important hills immediately in front of the Russian lines. From these hills, the fascists obviously had good observation of the Russian forward positions. As a result, the Soviet positions were continually kept under highly effective harassing fire which was causing an alarmingly high rate of casualties. Korsak was painfully aware that the bold attempts of the Soviet infantry to capture the hills by advancing in a human wave had been completely in vain. As a result of these failures, Naminsky was now terrified of what might happen to his own neck. They needed each other. The commander needed a success to save his skin, and Dimitri Korsak needed a result to save his reputation.

In the stuttering light of a candle, while Naminsky fretted and helped himself to another calming measure of vodka, Korsak wracked his brain once more and agonised for a solution which would win the heights and restore his reputation.

Tired of waiting for an answer, Naminsky took out his pistol and put it to his temple. 'Come, Comrade Korsak, give me some help, or there's only one way out for me...'

'Stop drinking that shit and you might be able to think straight,' came the blunt reply. 'Wars aren't won by idiots who feel sorry for themselves,' added Korsak with mounting venom. 'You don't deserve help, but I have decided that the best solution is to attack at night, with my tanks and what's left of your infantry. We attack under cover of darkness, it's the only hope we've got.'

'It's no use, because...' began Naminsky. He got no further with his opening statement as he was suddenly seized and pinned against the wall by the snarling Korsak. Naminsky felt the unmistakable caress of cold steel against his throat. The razor-sharp blade drew a few drops as Korsak pressed close, the fug of alcohol-tainted breath now issuing in short blasts from the terrified Naminsky.

'You really are a cowardly snivelling louse,' hissed Korsak. 'I could have you shot or cut your throat now... You don't even take the time to understand the intelligence reports. If you did, you'd know they reveal that the fascist system of defence is based on the establishment of a series of separate firing points which mutually support each other. The defences are well planned. The distinguishing characteristic is the irregularity of the pattern of layout. They were designed by a wily old fox named SS-Sturmbannführer Helmut Voss. They are effective, but his resources are being stretched thin. A wide front has been covered very economically by establishing these firing points, but it is not invulnerable. They are placed along two general lines; some have embrasures and overhead cover while others are open. At distances from 50 to 200 metres to the rear are dugouts used for rest purposes, or for protection from artillery and machine-gun fire.'

Korsak pressed the dagger a little closer to the Major's throat. The drops of blood became a definite trickle.

'In the forward firing points are the fascist light and heavy machine guns. Some of these are protected by a single row of barbed wire. In the rear firing points are mortars and light artillery. All firing points are assigned regular and supplementary sectors of fire. The sectors are overlapping and, in the case of machine guns, final protective lines are also interlocking. The fascists have burned all villages on the east bank of the river, thus materially improving their observation and field of fire.

'As a commander, you must understand that it is necessary to utilise every means of reconnaissance to discover, as nearly as possible, the exact positions of the enemy's forward firing points and his main line of resistance. You were too drunk and too lazy to do this. As a result, I have had to do things myself, and I don't like to be put to unnecessary trouble. However, after careful study of the terrain and the enemy defences, which has taken four nights of reconnaissance and cost the lives of eight brave comrades, I have decided to strike by night at the enemy centre of resistance. You will support me to the end ... understand?'

'Yes, Comrade Korsak!' came the rapid reply.

'Good. On the night of the attack, your infantry is to be deployed along the east bank of the river. A plan for coordinated infantry-artillery action must then be drawn up and, by God, I want some punch in that bombardment!'

Major Jurgen Rondorf strode into the early morning light of the lecture room. His demeanour suggested that he was a less than happy man.

'A mixed bag, I'm afraid. SS-Panzeroberschütze Wendorff. Excellent! 95%. Not only do you seem like an expert in your field, but it also seems that you continue to apply yourself in that field, something many experts would do well to remember. Well done!

'Hauptsturmführer von Schroif, 91%. At what distance does a T-34 7.62 cm long barrel penetrate my armour? The answer at three o'clock is under 1,500 metres, not 1,200 metres, with a T-34 at 800 metres the answer is 300 not 250, and the answer to the question you didn't answer: if an enemy turns from 'side' to his own '45 degrees' then his target will be increased by ... 10%. Highly commendable though. I'm sure that you will be up to speed soon enough.

'SS-Hauptscharführer Knispel, 85%. I understand where you are going wrong. The magnification of 2.5 and the 26 degree first field of view on the TZF 9b are not what you are used to. I have attached some notes to help you with the new optics. Apart from that, well done.

'SS-Panzerschütze Junge. Again, it is going to take some time to get used to this particular Maybach version, but, like Herr Knispel, this should not be something which is beyond your capabilities. 81%.

'Now, Herr Wohl. It seems that you enjoy your free time. There is nothing intrinsically wrong with that, there is a place for relaxation, especially in hard times such as these, but not if it interferes with your duty as a soldier of the Reich. If you have mastered your subject, then yes, by all means, while away the odd hour...'

'I tried my best, Herr Major.'

The Major's cordial attitude changed instantly.

'Do not insult me or the uniform you wear! Idling your time down at the river reading Die Wundertüte, when you should have been studying hard, does not constitute trying your best. Believe me, SS-Panzerschütze Otto Wohl, in light of your results you are marked in my eyes, a man who has not mastered his subject and is now in need of revision. It appears that you are either stupid or vain, and there is no place for either of these inflictions on this course.'

'How the hell does he know what I was reading?' thought Wohl.

'I am not going to embarrass you in front of your fellows by revealing how poorly you did on this test, but I will say this: any man who thinks that he can step inside this new Panzer VI without having prepared himself to the highest of standards is not only a danger to himself and the machine, but to the other members of his crew. If you do not want the blood of these men on your hands, I suggest you shed this false faith you have in your own abilities and start preparing for your second paper tomorrow ... otherwise, you can say your farewells to your former crewmates.'

The words landed on Otto Wohl like hammer blows and he hung his head in shame, knowing he had only himself to blame. Soon, however, he lifted his head as a sign of his stern determination to master his task and redeem himself in front of his fellows the following morning. However, his newly emboldened heart again sank to his boots when he heard of the next day's task.

'The central ethos of what we are trying to instil in you here,' continued Major Jurgen Rondorf, 'is teamwork. A tank crew is not a collection of individuals, but a unit. Each expert in his own sphere must also be an expert in the sphere of not just one other, but of all others. You are a totality and this is total War. Hence, I want SS-Hauptsturm-führer Hans von Schroif to sit an exam on gunnery tomorrow. You, SS-Panzerschütze Junge, to study the role of the loader. SS-Scharführer Knispel to know, inside out, the duties of a commander, and SS-Panzer-oberschütze Wendorff to immerse himself in the vital task of driving and mechanics. Wohl, you are to come in here tomorrow an expert in radio operations and the operation of the bow machine gun.'

Otto Wohl appeared so utterly broken by the announcement that even the hard-bitten Major Rondorf, who now felt himself under observation by the RSHA, was moved by a small measure of pity.

'I am a fair man, and there are clearly forces out there who do not want you to be part of this crew. You are obviously unused to the world of examinations, so I will accept a 51% mark in the Funkmeister's exam. However, you are also to re-sit and achieve an 80% pass in the exam on the gun loader's duties or, for you, the course ends here! Dismissed.'

Walter Lehmann poured a glass of schnapps and thought angrily to himself, 'So why the hell has it all gone so wrong?'

He had sent that damn von Schroif and Knispel into the perfect ambush at Rostov, but even the White Devil had been foiled. What was he supposed to do now?

Thanks to Borgmann's influence, he had been present at Rastenburg on Hitler's birthday. Lehmann recalled bitterly the shock as von Schroif had appeared. Moscow had demanded that he sabotage the Mark VI project, and his discrete interference had almost killed off the whole project – until that damn von Schroif took things into his own hands.

Not unusual for a man who led a double life, Lehmann now had a number of courses of action open to him. If he could deliver a Tiger into Soviet hands, he might be allowed to interrogate the crew ... and if one of those men just happened to be Hans von Schroif, life would be complete. It was all too obvious from the Wochenschau film report now playing in cinemas across Germany that one of the reasons for von Schroif's success was his tight-knit and exceptionally talented crew. So, before the new tank was shipped to the front, one obvious option was to weaken the crew...

His first thought was of Knispel, but he was too much of a public hero, known for his boxing prowess, and his record was too clean...

But this Bavarian oaf, Otto Wohl ... he seemed to be the easiest target. Nothing in particular, but there were certain anomalies in his records and a bit of hearsay about defeatist talk. Lehmann decided to send Bremer out in the field – Bremer, his shiny little Nazi – to pull him in for questioning. Hardly an end to the Tiger project, but it might disrupt the cohesion of von Schroif's crew, and a weakened crew might just make a vital mistake at the front...

Then there was the Dane. An art teacher with a grudge, making tanks... There was something there, but that's enough for one day... For now it was time for a drink, and some female company.

'Time to let off some steam,' said Lehmann to himself. Picking up his favourite riding crop, Lehmann set off on the familiar trail to the female cell block.

In the other ranks' mess hall that evening sat four shattered men, but none more so than Otto Wohl. The morning had been mentally gruelling, and the training that afternoon equally so in terms of physical effort, but it was the humiliation in front of his fellows and the dread of mental toil that was to come which had so deflated Otto Wohl.

Hans von Schroif unexpectedly entered the room and the men sprang to attention. As he gestured for the assembled troops to sit down and pulled up a chair, he noticed the genuine turmoil written on Otto Wohl's face and immediately felt sympathy for him. How many times had Wohl saved their lives, and how could you measure such indebtedness?

'Well, where do we go from here, Wohl?' asked von Schroif, more in sympathy than anything.

No one spoke. Everyone knew that the unschooled Wohl, for all his natural wit, was unlikely to suddenly shine in written exams. As the gloomy realisation that the team could be split apart dawned, the crew settled into a glum silence.

'If only the Tiger manuals were illustrated like Die Wundertüte, he might have a chance of getting through,' said Junge with obvious frustration.

'What is this damn Wundertüte anyway?' asked von Schroif.

'Here it is, Hauptsturmführer,' said Wohl, producing the small magazine which now looked set to be his downfall. 'When all this is over, I hope to work for them as a cartoonist.'

'Joke books are for kids... I'll stick to Der Stürmer,' grumbled Knispel disdainfully.

'There are more jokes in that rag than in Die Wundertüte,' retorted Wohl.

'I won't have that! It's the Führer's favourite,' retorted Knispel.

'Only when he has to wipe his arse!'

'Wohl! Enough,' snapped von Schroif, suddenly alert to the danger. 'Walls have ears ... unless you'd like to spend some time in Dachau.'

'My father died in Dachau...' said Wohl quietly.

The mood instantly grew even more sombre as each of the crew searched for the appropriate words. Since 1933, Dachau had been synonymous with the suppression of political enemies of the Nazi state. This was the place where social democrats, trade

141

unionists, communists, anti-socials and in-tellectuals disappeared into nacht und nebel, or 'night and fog'. The mere mention of Dachau spread terror throughout Ger-man society, but the epicentre was in Wohl's native Bavaria. The place was only twenty kilometres from the rough streets of Munich, where Wohl had grown up.

For von Schroif there was a slightly differ-ent resonance; this was the place where he had suffered the ignominy of losing a battle between his much vaunted Freikorps and a rabble of communists – a painful and bitter memory.

There was a respectful silence while the crew digested the awful possibility of the fate that might have befallen Wohl's father.

The silence was eventually broken only by the impeccable comic timing of Otto Wohl. '...he got drunk and fell out of his watch tower ... broke his fucking neck!'

Even von Schroif could not contain a slight smile. The others gave a hearty belly laugh.

As he returned to leafing through the jokes, von Schroif stopped at page 33 and even gave a small chuckle. 'That's a good one with the ghosts ... not so bad being dead,' he said, handing the joke book to Junge.

The welcome spirit of levity was short-lived. Junge appreciatively glanced at a few more risque illustrations, then handed the small publication back to Wohl, as a despondent silence descended once more.

Surprisingly, it was the taciturn Karl Wendorff who spoke next.

'If I may, sir?'

Hauptsturmführer von Schroif nodded his assent.

'Well, it's just that, judging by today's events, it looks like one can just about get away with presenting one less than perfect paper at the Paderborn Panzer examinations. Major Rondorf sounds like a fair man.'

'A total bastard, you mean,' thought Wohl, who for once had the good sense to keep his thoughts to himself.

'So, tonight I propose that I will forgo some of my planned preparation for the mechanical paper and instead help SS-Panzerschütze Otto Wohl with the mysterious and hitherto inexplicable behaviour of the radio wave and its relevance to Germany's Panzerkampfwagen Mark VI. Furthermore, my fee for such a task shall be negligible...'

'I can't give up my rations ... I'm fading away already, Wendorff.'

'No, you can continue to pig out, Wohl. If you pass, and I'm sure that with my help you can, I would like you to finally give up your former life as a complete Philistine and agree to accompany me to the new production of Das Rheingold, which is being performed in Paderborn. There you shall hear the music of the master of Bayreuth, conducted by the great Fürtwangler, and learn the real possibility of what the human brain can achieve if one looks upwards and outwards, beyond the world of Die Wundertüte.'

Wendorff was a Wagner addict who could generally find something on the dial every time even a note of Wagner was broadcast from anywhere in Europe. Like his Führer, he loved Wagner to the exclusion of everything else, but he had been so far unsuccessful in his attempts to lure Wohl and his fellow crew members into the world of high culture.

'Look, I'm desperate, Wendorff... Wagner sounds more like a prison sentence to me, but, if you can keep me on the crew, I'll do it...'

'Good man, Wendorff!' exclaimed von Schroif. 'This is what a team is. Someone, and, as fate would have it, usually the right one, will step forward and offer himself when the team finds itself in trouble... And if Wohl has to suffer grand opera for his punishment, then so shall we all... I will take the extra pain and pay for the tickets.'

This was in reality no great concession from von Schroif. He had grown up on opera and loved nothing better than to attend, with its parade of attractive young women. The lure of the opening part of the Nibelungen saga was less apparent to the remaining members of the team.

'But, sir...!' began SS-Hauptscharführer Michael Knispel.

'You too, Knispel ... and you, Junge,' added von Schroif, his voice full of mock sincerity.

Wendorff did not see anything to laugh about and seized his opportunity with both hands. 'Thank you, Herr Hauptsturm-führer. I shall reserve the tickets.'

Wohl was still despondent. 'I can't see the point. I couldn't ever pass an exam at school ... all I could do was draw. How can I pass an exam? I'll never understand this stuff. These manuals are as dry as dust ... they mean nothing to me, just lists of numbers.' Turning to von Schroif, tears began to form in his eyes. 'I just can't do it, sir...'

Again Wendorff spoke. 'But this time it's different, Wohl ... we'll do the learning in Die Wundertüte style!'

Two days ago, under cover of darkness, Korsak's tank unit had been surreptitiously ferried across the river and concealed in a grove. He had spent the following day in reconnaissance, coordination with Naminsky, and establishment of communications. From long experience he knew that the attack had to be made on a moonlit night, so that the infantry could orient itself and give his tanks the signals necessary for them to maintain direction. The tanks had to be used in echelons, keeping the movement to a comparatively narrow front, and creating an exaggerated idea as to the number of tanks in the battle. During the attack, Korsak knew that the tanks must under no circumstances be separated from the desyanti, the tank-riding infantry, as at night the tanks needed the help of the infantry even more than in the daytime.

Korsak had decided to send the tanks on a flanking movement from the south and the southwest, in order to give the enemy the impression that they were surrounded by a large force. The tanks were echeloned in depth. The heavy tanks were in the first echelon, the lighter tanks with desyanti tank riders were in the second echelon, and in the third echelon were tanks hauling guns. The shells for the gun were carried on the tanks.

Standing motionless in the commander's position of his KV-1, lit by the faint glow of the moon, Korsak held his breath and looked at his watch. Naminsky had better not let him down.

For once, he was not disappointed. Twenty minutes before the attack, exactly as ordered, every available piece of artillery on the Soviet side began to rain down shells on the German front lines.

'Good, give those bastards hell,' thought Korsak to himself.

The artillery bombardment was fierce and brutal in its intensity, and for twenty nerve-rending minutes every gun was fired in a pitiless preparation on the front lines of the fascists. Exactly on cue, half of the barrels then shifted to the rear, concentrating on the possible avenues of retreat.

Zero hour was thirty minutes before dark. In these thirty minutes, Korsak's tanks moved from the jump-off positions, reached the Soviet infantry positions, collected the designated desyanti, and moved out.

On the German side of the lines the ferocity of the artillery preparation came as a disconcerting surprise. Nonetheless, SS-Untersturmführer Brand and his men followed their customary practice and scuttled into cover in their dugouts on the rear slopes. As soon as the artillery fire was lifted to the rear firing points and the reserve positions, Brand realized that the attack was about to commence. He roused his unwilling men and began to move back towards the firing positions, but so heavy was the concentration of mortar and now machine gun fire on the forward firing points that the Germans were pinned down and unable to get back to their firing positions.

According to Korsak's plan, the Soviet small-arms weapons were brought forward and proceeded to destroy the effectiveness of the few active forward firing points by direct fire at the embrasures. Meanwhile, the artillery and mortars kept up the neutralising fire on the rear firing points.

Attacking in formation, Naminsky was able to capture the enemy positions with mostly just the supporting artillery and machine-gun fire. The full moon aided observation and, soon after crossing the line of their own infantry, the Soviet tanks rolled to a halt and opened fire on the remaining points of resistance. The flashes of the few German guns firing in return and the constant stream of flares discharged by Soviet infantry aided fire direction.

From his position to the south, Korsak noted with grim satisfaction that the German artillery seemed to have been taken completely by surprise and was conducting un-aimed, disorderly fire, and often seemed to be shelling their own infantry positions. Pressed from both the flanks and the front, the will to fight suddenly evaporated, and SS-Untersturmführer Brand and his surviving men began a disorderly retreat.

Korsak realised that his tanks and infantry had taken full possession of the enemy strongpoint. He now charged after the fleeing survivors, grinding them under the tracks of the KV-1. He sensed that there was no time to rest. The tanks manoeuvred along the south and southwestern slopes of the hills, enabling Naminsky's infantry to consolidate their positions. It soon became evident that the hills were securely occupied by Naminsky's infantry, and Korsak gratefully ordered the tanks returned to the grove to refuel, take on more ammunition, and be inspected.

Only Korsak and his KV-1 remained on the field. The German dead, the equipment left on the field of battle, and the few dazed prisoners captured that night gave proof that the night attack was a complete surprise to the Germans. It felt good. The impression of complete encirclement was created, and enemy officers and men scattered in all directions.

During the night the enemy attempted a few desultory counterattacks, but they were effortlessly beaten back and, most importantly, resulted in no loss of Soviet tanks.

The mission was a complete success. The White Devil had restored his reputation. Now it was time to strike back.

# CHAPTER 5

## DIE WOCHENSCHAU

Far away from the thunder of the Eastern Front, von Schroif and his crew were experiencing a different kind of night. They worked together to get Wohl through the paper he needed to pass.

SS-Panzeroberschütze Karl Wendorff had assembled a crude kindergarten facsimile of a radio transmitter and receiver using boxes, tins, buttons and laces. Patiently, and in the most graphic style possible, he taught Otto Wohl about the right wavelengths and volumes. He encouraged Wohl to draw the positions so that he became familiar with the need to check that all the switches were in the 'off' position when not in use, and also to check the connections from the battery over box 23 in the base plate. He made a checklist of the adjustments for locking the frequency and switching to keyed mode. Then he turned to instruction on the intercom and illustrated the use of buttons for speaking and listening ... and then they went back to the radio... and then returned to the intercom.

When he was satisfied that Wohl had a firm grasp of the procedures and the thinking behind them, he at last moved onto the bow machine gun. This was easier, as SS-Panzerschütze Wohl had enacted this role in real life and in the heat of battle too. The job in hand, however, was now to turn that instinctive knowledge into something that might pass muster on an exam paper. 'Jamming?'

'Remove foot from trigger. On right, move cocking slide back. Check position of lock, check what is being ejected, anything in the way of the lock?'

'Lock is in almost forward position. What is ejected?'

'Cartridge...'

'Intact. What jams?'

'Locking catch.'

'Remedy?'

'Exchange barrel.'

'Lock is in the centre position. Barrel free. What jams?'

'Ejector rod.'

'Remedy?'

'Exchange lock. Lock does not stay in place, if it is to stop hold belt, wear on trigger, use other machine gun.'

Still he went on, memorising the chart, saying it out loud until Wohl could answer each of Wendorff's questions.

With the other three men independently

151

studying their own allocated tasks, the little hut was a hive of mental activity, the bright light of dedicated application shining all night and into the small hours as the Tiger-men prepared for the day that lay ahead.

At three o'clock, Schroif decided that they should all rest, except for Otto Wohl, who had to go back and restudy the role of the loader, a subject in which he would ordinarily be an instructor.

The next set of exercises involved the complicated physics that governed the survivability of a hit and the angle at which the tank should be set in front of a target. To help Wohl, it was explained that it was basically like a clock, with 12 o'clock facing straight ahead. Given that the enemy's shells had more metal to penetrate if they hit the tank at an angle rather than straight on, it was a golden rule to maintain the tank at an angle to its opponent.

For shorthand reasons, Wendorff developed a quick explanation. The safest angles could be equated to certain 'meal times'. For example, given that the best angles to position the tank at had clock designations of 10.30, 1.30, 4.30 and 7.30, these angles and the corresponding times were labelled for the ever hungry Wohl as 'Breakfast', 'Lunch', 'Coffee' and 'Supper'.

The Cloverleaf was a simple way of representing the areas and distances in which the

152

Tiger was safe from enemy anti-tank fire. For example, knowing the distance at which a shell from a T-34 could penetrate the Tiger's armour, and also knowing the advantage that the angle of the tank could confer, Wendorff prepared a simple diagram which resembled the leaves of a clover. This simple aide-mémoire would ensure that even the slower members of the crew could quickly calculate whether they were in danger or not.

Wendorff explained that to be inside the cloverleaf was to be safe. If any enemy tank managed to get himself within the imaginary outline, then you most certainly were not safe, and it was time to turn the vehicle quickly to one of the meal times!

The 'Goetz theory' was another expression developed by Wendorff for Wohl's benefit. It was a straightforward bit of arithmetic for Wendorff, but a difficult concept for Wohl, which was made clear by a comparison involving the popular fictional knight, Goetz, and his mighty reach.

'Look,' said Wendorff, patiently poring over the diagram, 'the Goetz reach lies between your cloverleaf and your maximum range. So, for example, if you are facing a T-34 at 12 o'clock, you know that your cloverleaf extends to 500 metres – you are safe within this distance. But you also know that, like Goetz, you can kill him at 800 metres. Therefore, the

Anti-Goetz is between 500 metres and 800 metres. This is the key, the decisive factor, you see?'

'Ah, I get it! That's simple. So, if he comes at you from 12 o'clock, turn the tank towards lunch so that he stays within the cloverleaf, then hit him before he reaches 500 metres! Easy! Why didn't you say so earlier, instead of all that angle stuff?'

'They both say the same, Wohl. One is in the language of mathematics and the other is pure Wundertüte,' said Wendorff, without a trace of sarcasm.

'Well, on behalf of the great unwashed and untutored, let's say it in Die Wundertüte style, highly effective and absolutely deadly!'

'Well,' von Schroif said, 'perhaps there should be an exception. I shall also stay up and tutor Knispel on the relatively unimportant role of the commander, perhaps the easiest of all the functions!'

So, while Bobby Junge and Karl Wendorff tried to get as much sleep as they could, Hans von Schroif and Michael Knispel went over diagrams, tactics, and the order to shoot.

'Motor cover closed, engage lock, Funker's hatch closed, Fahrer's hatch closed, lamps removed, track clear for shot,' Wohl read and then, exclaiming out loud, 'Of course, why didn't you just ask that!' However, as he read further, despite his tiredness, he now felt emboldened, his confidence growing. Despite all his enemies, he may just pass this exam after all!

The disconcerting news of the successful night attack outside Rostov had not yet reached von Schroif and his crew. They were still immersed in the anxiety-provoking business of passing examination papers and gave little thought to events on the now-distant front.

As the crew waited nervously for the results, there was a small crumb of comfort to be taken from the fact that Major Jurgen Rondorf appeared less stern than usual. Fortunately, he didn't keep them waiting long before letting the anxious crew know the results.

The marks that day were not as high as the day before, with the exception of von Schroif, who had excelled in the gunnery paper, but which now appeared irrelevant against the welcome news that Otto Wohl had passed both papers. It had been a close run thing and, even with Wendorff's help, the 51% pass mark seemed to stretch generosity to the limit.

Major Rondorf's new-found praise and encouragement masked a little inner smile which indicated that he knew exactly what had been going on, especially in light of Wendorff's lower than expected results, which were passable, but, in Rondorf's opinion, not as high as one of his obvious intellectual abilities should have attained. The men were clearly dog-tired and Rondorf appreciated the effort. He had seen the lights burning long into the night. He could have called lights out, but he had been lenient. There were no points for camaraderie, but it was noticed and approved of.

Walter Lehmann did not take kindly to the new request. 'Ensure Tigers diverted from Rostov to Leningrad? Did the Soviets have any idea how complicated and dangerous that would be?'

Hitler was taking a close personal interest in the subject. Every fool knew that the deployment of the Tiger would be his decision. How on earth was he supposed to influence Hitler's thinking? The man was renowned for his tendency to meddle in the minutiae of operational affairs. Even his generals and the chiefs of staff found it impossible to bring him around to their way of thinking – and let's give the monster some credit, his grasp, his research, his photographic memory and his ability to be ruthlessly decisive set him well apart from ordinary mortals – once his mind had been made up, God himself would have had difficulty persuading him to decide upon an alternative path.

The only possible way to get Hitler to

change tack would be to introduce credible new information, but it would have to be compelling and significant. Hitler did have the ability to change his own mind on reacting to new operational information and that would be the key – not to have others change his mind for him, according to their own opinions, but to allow Hitler to believe that he had changed his own mind.

The Soviets had prepared for this with a new piece of misinformation regarding heavy tank build ups in the Leningrad area, but Lehmann knew this would never be enough. What he needed was a second bit of intelligence that was independent and that gave credence to the first. He could then forward this to i.G Borgmann, who could then pass it on to Hitler himself. That way, they may just have a chance of getting inside the mind of Hitler, allowing him to re-arrange the old facts in accordance with the new.

But he was beginning to have doubts about Borgmann. Oberstleutnant i.G Borgmann was an army liaison officer attached to Hitler's HQ at Rastenburg. Lehmann and Borgmann had been in the SS together. Lehmann had always had him in his pocket, so to speak, but since his move to Rastenburg, Borgmann did not seem as receptive to RHSA communications as he had been before. Perhaps it was the sway and pull of the Wehrmacht, perhaps because he was so close to Hitler, maybe even because he did not need Lehmann to advance his career any further. Whatever the reason, the centre of gravity in their relationship had changed. Getting to Hitler had never been a problem before, Borgmann being the perfect conduit for any information Lehmann needed to pass down the line, but that last link was not as strong as it had once been.

Dressed for the part in immaculate double-breasted black wool jackets, matching trousers and boots, the five men strolled through the streets of Paderborn, catching the eye of every girl who passed.

Were they not warriors? Had they not lifted the veil of shame that hung over their countrymen since the Treaty of Versailles? Was Germany not now at ease with itself?

To von Schroif, the memory of his hard times in the Freikorps seemed distant – a torn and divided country – as did the times of economic hardship, but now look at it! The streets bustled under the warm May sky, shopkeepers busily selling their wares, children playing safely in the streets – this was what they were fighting for! They were fighting for peace! This glimpse – this was not just a snapshot of what Germany had become through its own striving, but what it would become – this was not just part of the present, this was a vision of the future!

The local cinema was screening the latest Wochenschau newsreel as the Tiger men called in and surreptitiously took their seats. Each feigned nonchalance, but each was secretly excited. After a well-cut sequence of tank combat, the narrator began his frantic commentary.

'The Eastern Front! Outside Rostov, a fierce tank battle results in the destruction of twenty Soviet tanks. These fearless fighters have become known as the Lions of Rostov. Their heroic deeds were recognised by the award of various decorations from the hand of the Führer himself.'

A wide shot of the five crewmen receiving their awards from Hitler filled the screen.

'Hey, it's us!' gasped an excited Otto Wohl.

'And here are the heroic crewmen who crewed the panzer in combat against the red menace. Led by Hauptsturmführer Hans von Schroif, the crew consists of just five men – a commander, a gunner, a loader, a driver, and a radio operator who is also the hull machine-gunner.'

A big close-up of a smiling von Schroif filled the screen.

Otto Wohl gave a whoop of delight. 'Hurrah, it's the boss!' He was quickly shushed by the others, who were eager to hear the commentary.

'The tank commander is responsible for

the vehicle and the crew. He is the brains of the outfit and has many duties. He indicates targets to the gunner, gives fire orders, and observes the fall of shots. He keeps a constant lookout for the enemy, observes the zone for which he is responsible, and watches for any orders from his commander's vehicle. In action, he gives his orders to the driver and radio operator by intercommunication telephone, and to the gunner and loader by touch signals or through a speaking tube. He receives orders by radio or flag, and reports to his commander by radio, signal pistol, or flag.'

What concerned von Schroif was the fact that, behind himself and the crew, the mantlet and 88 mm gun of the Tiger could be clearly seen. This was obviously a deliberate inclusion on the part of the propaganda ministry. Rumours were rife, and a glimpse of the new machine was no doubt intended to give substance to the rumours, and to help bolster morale. Given the choice, von Schroif would have preferred no information to leak out, but then he was not the expert and, if he was honest about it, he was rather proud of his new life in the spotlight.

There was a cut to a close-up of a smiling Michael Knispel. In his embarrassment, Knispel couldn't help let slip, 'God, it's me! My mother always said I'd be a movie star!' As Knispel looked on in amazement, the narrator kept up his rapid delivery.

'The gunner is second in command. He fires the turret gun, the turret machine gun, or the machine carbine, as ordered by the tank commander. He assists the tank commander in observation. In the action at Rostov, the actions were carried out by Michael Knispel, the Berliner born in 1910, who has achieved greatness in the boxing ring and has beaten Max Diekmann, who himself has beaten the great Max Schmelling!'

There was a spontaneous ripple of applause in the cinema and Knispel slouched down in his seat to avoid recognition. As the camera cut to a close up of Wohl, gurning into the camera, the young man fell uncharacteristically silent as he drank in every moment of his short burst of fame.

'Otto Wohl, the laughing loader, is a young man from Munich who typifies all that is best from that proud area of the Reich. The loader loads and maintains the turret armament under the orders of the gunner. He is also responsible for the care of ammunition and, when the cupola is closed, gives any flag signals required. He deputises for the radio operator in an emergency.'

'If Knispel farts and he has to bail out, you mean!' quipped an excited Otto Wohl, who was quickly silenced by a look from von Schroif.

161

Bobby Junge's beaming face now filled the screen.

'The driver is SS-Panzerschütze Bobby Junge from Heidelberg. Junge is renowned for his pre-war performances against Rudolf Caracciola and the tragic Bernd Rosemeyer at the Nurburgring, which indicated a trajectory of great success. Once the war is won, we hope that racing will once again be a part of the young man's life. He operates the vehicle under the orders of the tank commander, or in accordance with orders received by radio from the commander's vehicle. He also assists in observation, reporting over the inter-communication telephone the presence of the enemy, or of any obstacles in the path of the tank. He watches the fuel consumption and is responsible to the tank commander for the care and maintenance of the vehicle.'

Last but not least came a close-up of an embarrassed Karl Wendorff. Unlike the others, Wendorff didn't smile or mug for the camera. He squirmed in his seat as the narrator turned his attention to the radio operator's role.

'Finally we have the Funkmeister, SS-Panzeroberschütze Karl Wendorff, the quiet philosopher, who turns his abilities to the practical duties of a panzermann. The Funker operates the radio set under the orders of the tank commander. In action, when not actually transmitting, he always

162

keeps the radio set at 'receive.' He operates the intercommunication telephone and writes down any radio messages not sent or received by the tank commander. He fires the machine gun mounted in the front of the tank. He takes over the duties of the loader if the latter is wounded. These then are the lions of Rostov, five very different men, and now these great talents and personalities are combined, working together as one, for the glory of the Reich!'

The newsreel moved on to the subject of folk dancing in the Danzig region and von Schroif nodded to his crew. As a man they left the cinema and, as they moved through the afternoon crowds, the Tiger men knew the reason for the smiles and pointing fingers. For this week at least, they were movie stars. This unsettling fact was confirmed when a small group of workers stopped to applaud.

The only slight cloud on the horizon was the prospect of an evening spent listening to Wagner's Rheingold. Wendorff, of course, could barely contain his enthusiasm, but the others were less than thrilled at the prospect.

Sensing the mood, von Schroif knew it was time to ply his team with some pre-theatre anaesthetic. Settling down at a garden table in the Brauhaus, von Schroif noted that he and his crew were the centre of attention. At the next table, a four-man Sturmgeschütz team in their grey uniforms gave their undivided attention to the Tiger men.

'Hail the Rostov heroes!' They raised their glasses.

They permitted themselves a beer, which the host kindly donated. This gift was soon followed by flowers from two groups of girls who passed, giggling and smiling. This was almost peacetime, von Schroif reiterated to himself. This was contentment, this was to be treasured...

Suddenly they were interrupted by a very pretty girl whose face suggested that she was less than appreciative of the efforts of the Tiger men. She marched straight up to Wohl, arms folded, and with an obvious sense of purpose.

'So, here you are again!'

'Magda! What a surprise,' spluttered Wohl.

'Not as much of a surprise as when I found out you were romancing half of Paderborn! You two-timing little runt.'

'Look, that's not true.'

'Yes, it is, and you know it.'

Magdalena Klinsman had clearly been waiting for her moment and she was not about to let it go. 'I should have listened to my father. Damn Bavarians!'

'Look, Magda, don't be too harsh.'

'Harsh? You don't know the meaning of the word. Harsh is sending the same letter to two girls who work in the same factory. You're an untrustworthy pig. Never trust a Catholic, Dad says, and he couldn't be more right.'

'Too true, young lady!' interjected Michael Knispel, clearly relishing the fun. 'I don't trust them either ... especially this one.'

'No one asked you to speak, Mr. Ugly!' With that, she nimbly grabbed the beer mug from in front of Knispel and emptied it over the unsuspecting head of Otto Wohl before storming off into the early evening light.

A ragged cheer rose from the Sturm-geschütz crew.

Von Schroif did not like the look in the eye of Michael Knispel, who had lost half a litre of precious Weiss bier. 'Right boys,' said von Schroif, 'time to go home and get Wohl cleaned up.' Out of the corner of his eye he noticed Karl Wendorff's face drop. Von Schroif knew exactly why, but he was only fooling. 'But first ... let's sample a little Wagner!'

Karl Wendorff's beaming face was a joy to behold! And so all five men strode through the streets to the theatre for a performance of the first part of Wagner's great ring cycle.

The best seats had been reserved for the new national heroes and the five Tiger men were ushered in by a grateful staff and applauded to their seats in the third row. To add to the honour, Furtwängler himself, the greatest conductor in Germany, came on stage and made their presence known to the rest of the audience. 'Ladies and gentlemen, I present to you, the Lions of Rostov!'

Von Schroif and his crew rose uneasily to their feet and stood uncomfortably receiving the applause which came thundering down in gratitude from all three tiers of the packed opera house. Finally, much to their relief, because too much adulation does not go down well with dedicated soldiers, the conductor finally reappeared in the pit and turned and tapped his baton. The long drone of the orchestral prelude began to pick up pace and they were transported to another world, one with passion and drama so intense that it made the cares of this world seem almost insignificant.

Even for Otto Wohl, time seemed to pass quickly as the orchestra sawed away for a while on a strange but pleasant tune which whirled and danced like the river itself. Then he realised to his astonishment that the first bit of singing was to be performed by three young ladies of very pleasing appearance. So these were the famous Rhine maidens! Things were looking up! He could have done without the tall bloke pretending to be a dwarf, but the girl on the left... 'Wow! What a figure ... and she can sing as well!'

Otto Wohl realised in a moment that he

had been wrong about Magda, or whatever her name was. She was just a silly factory girl after all. The real love of his life had been revealed, and she was a Rheintöchter in a low-cut mermaid's dress that threatened to reveal her ample bosom at any moment.

To Wohl's surprise, the story began to take shape. He snatched the programme from Wendorff's surprised grasp and quickly scanned the cast list. Flosshilde... Stella Huehn... Mezzo soprano... 'Ah, Stella ... Stella! What a beautiful name! Just like its owner.' How had he missed this all his life? He resolved to ask the boss at the very next opportunity if they could name their Tiger Stella, after his new love. As his adoring gaze followed Stella's every move while she teased and taunted the lecherous Alberich, Wohl soon realised how strongly he identified with this unfeasibly tall dwarf in his frustrated attempts to attain the seemingly unattainable.

Wohl's fluttering heart sank back to his boots when the scene ended, to be replaced by some rubbish about giants and a bill for building a castle, with no Rhine maidens in sight.

'It's just a glorified building dispute...' thought Wohl. 'For God's sake, Wotan, tell the missus to pipe down and bring back the girls...'

With the Rhine maidens seemingly gone

for good, the production began to wane for Wohl, but then something magical happened. Onto the stage came the young Elvira Schorr, perfectly cast in the role of Fricka's sister, Freia, the goddess of youth, beauty and feminine love. Not only was she absolutely beautiful, she sang in a wonderful soprano voice that nobody who heard it could ever forget. Wohl now realised he had been rash to fall for Stella. The real love of his life had been waiting in the wings all along. Elvira... Ah, this was the real thing. 'Look how her chest rises and falls as she sings... What fine lungs, what an adorable face... Whoa, what a cleavage!'

As the evening raced by, von Schroif found himself enjoying the performance, as he knew he would. Even Knispel and Junge seemed content. Wendorff, of course, appeared transfixed, but what amazed him most was the rapt look of attention on the face of Otto Wohl. 'Well, miracles do happen,' thought von Schroif, 'Wohl, wrapped up in Wagner... Who would have thought it?'

Wohl was indeed wrapped up, and von Schroif would not have been the least bit surprised to learn his thoughts. He was so engrossed in the performance that, internally, he had in fact become a confused mixture of a dwarf and two giants. 'Beautiful, beautiful... No wonder everybody's after her... Elvira Schorr, my only true love... I wonder what she looks like naked?'

Wohl's vigil carried him through the production and before long they were into the final act, the orchestra careering towards the final coda, when suddenly the dream was shattered by the piercing wail of air raid sirens, a screeching wall of warning and discord, as the terrible reality of the twentieth century intruded on the world of fantasy.

Von Schroif looked around as, one by one, the audience started shouting words of encouragement to the orchestra. 'Carry on! Keep playing! To hell with the British!'

And so, Furtwängler, the revered conductor, knowing that he had the support of the crowd, rallied his players. The crowd could hear him calling for more from the orchestra: 'Forte! Molto forte!' The sound of the orchestra swelled and carried them across the final few bars to the great orchestral conclusion, which brought the audience cheering and standing to their feet. 'Bravo! Bravo!'

The Tiger men stood too, applauding, stirred by the defiance of the crowd, who stood as one with their countrymen from the front. Karl Wendorff cheered the most enthusiastically, passionate tears streaming down his face. However, in the distance they could now hear the low thunder of exploding bombs and the cast cut short their well-earned bows to leave the stage, the whole atmosphere changing as the audience realised that the performance was over. Their senses returned to this world. Get to the shelters, get to the shelters! The exodus was never a panic – the German people would never give the British terrorists that pleasure! – but it was brisk and, once out on the street, von Schroif marvelled at the orderly way the citizens of Paderborn re-acted to this outrage.

Luckily for Paderborn and its good people, the sound of the bombs receded, the city for now not being the target, but its effect on the Tiger men was profound. Who knows what war crimes the British and now the Amis were planning together? Who knows when and where they would attack next? Surely their time would come. But for now it was imperative to take care of the war in the east. The men returned to their quarters with renewed vigour and determination. Tomor-row they would be back on board a Tiger.

Professor Jacob von Stern walked briskly through the gates of Berlin University – how good it was to be back after all these years. The great names who had studied here – Hegel and Schopenhauer, Schelling, Marx and Engels, and Stern's own mentor, the poet Heinrich Heine! Memories of the pro-ductive and happy youth he had spent here flooded back – how glorious a period in a young man's life, before trouble and care insinuated themselves into all aspects of the more middle-aged term! But it was not just memories of the past that filled him with delight, it was anticipation too. How long had it been since he had last seen his oldest and dearest friend?

'Jacob! You are the picture of health! Come sit with me and regale me with your tales, stories, and, if I may add, what will be your incomparable insights!'

'Johan, you flatter me. It is you who shine with life and your insights which all men wish to hear!'

Professor Johan von Lieb did indeed look younger for his years. The academic life suited him, and Jacob felt a tinge of envy that financial considerations had prevented him from taking the same path all those years ago. No matter, it lifted his spirits just seeing his old friend.

'So, what times are these, afflicted by war and Herr Hitler? Who could possibly have predicted such a thing? We haven't discussed matters since the Röhm affair, I believe,' ventured von Lieb.

'Indeed, and no doubt we share the same opinion. This is a dark age, and all good men must hold true and hope that providence is not too hard on us.'

'All we can do is hope and pray and bear

silent witness. Resistance is not for the likes of us. I am not unsympathetic to that position, but those of us who have studied the classics learn to have too high a regard for the Fates!'

'Do you think the fever will pass?'

'I think that is our main hope. Even if Herr Hitler achieves his objective, and, let's face it, the obstacle proved insurmountable for another corporal, then the man, for all his devilish pacts, cannot live forever. Kinder forces will surely prevail and temper this 'fever', as you refer to it.'

'I pray you are right, dear Johan,' replied Jacob, 'but you know what Heine said, 'Burning the books is only a prelude. Next, they will be burning men.'

'My dear Jacob, demented though he is, Hitler is not that inhuman. Anyway, Heine, in that passage from Almansor you were referring to, concerned the Inquisition burning the Koran – surely we have moved beyond such depravities!'

'I do hope you are right, my old friend.'

'If I am wrong, it may be better for us to leave this vale of tears before our allotted time, my dear Jacob. Anyway, what is it that I can do for you?'

'It is a delicate matter pertaining to an old student of mine, whom I met after many years in the last week. He is a man of good character, who excelled in the field of radio communications. His name is Karl Wendorff. He now serves as a radio operator. He's one of the heroes of Rostov. You may have seen the Wochenschau? He told me of a strange incident of an intercepted message, of unknown origin, which he picked up outside Rostov. He noted the time and frequency and a few other details, and I was just wondering, with your contacts and experience, if you could help shed any light on this matter for him? Like you, I am no friend of these military adventures, in principle, but when you know one of the soldiers involved and hold him in high esteem...'

'I understand completely, Jacob,' replied Johan. 'These are innocents. They are sons, brothers and neighbours, and we may need as many good men as we can find in the future. Leave it with me. Our research work in conjunction with the University of Heidelberg is more orientated to applications of a commercial nature. For the military side, the people who know about these things are based in Abwehr 1-K, the crypto analysis section of department Z. If necessary, I can call in help from on high. Admiral Canaris is the man we would have to speak to. My wife is good friends with the wife of his number two, General Hans Oster. So, let's take a look shall we?'

The professor looked at the message and gave a chuckle.

'I don't think we'll need Canaris. Your old touch must be deserting you! On second thoughts, we may not need the Abwehr to decode this rather ham-fisted attempt at cryptology, but I am of the opinion that the content of this message may be of considerable interest to those at Tirpitzufer.'


# CHAPTER 6

## TIGERFIBEL

'Two hours to start her up. I know,' said Major Rondorf, 'that seems unnecessarily long, but it's like an athlete warming up, go too soon and you are in danger of causing damage to the cold muscle and pulling up. So, patience, and always run through the checks.'

'Fuel! Check!'

'Power! Check!'

'Water! Check!'

'Start up! Check!'

'6x Oil Check! Check!'

'Oil Pressure! Check!'

'Idling speed...'

Bobby Junge sat in his seat and ran through the position of his levers, slowly and methodically. Bottom plug – open. Fuel valves –

open. Main battery switch – on. Blower switch – land. Fuel vent – land. Throttle No 1 – down. Throttle No 2 – land. Throttle No 3 – open. Vent flap – closed. Fuel pump – on. Directional lever on '0'. Ignition key – in. Choke lever – forward. Clutch – depress. Starter button – push. Starter button – release. Choke lever – reverse. Throttle – touch lightly for first 5 minutes, warning lamp flickers ... do not race the engine! Clutch – engage slowly until transmission and steering gear start to heat up. Throttle – push in, increase engine speed to within 1,000 and 1,500 rpm. Slowly, slowly, think of the spark plugs ... fast idle, fast idle ... and then, with the cannon tied down to the six o'clock position, she slowly pulled off.

Hauptsturmführer von Schroif wanted to slowly take her up to top speed, so Bobby drove carefully over the open fields before opening her up and going up through the initial seven gears and finally letting her hit 3,000 rpm. She seemed to be handling it, but then he had trouble getting her into the final gear and then – Boom! – something blew and she came to a standstill. Bobby had learnt his first lesson! If you didn't take the correct steps before venturing out, she'd turn into a sixty-tonne metal mule – and there was nothing to do to get her to budge!

Bobby spent the rest of the day trying to find the problem. The main problem was obviously the Maybach engine, but the transmission and many other things felt wrong too, and that is where the investigation started. In the company of the Paderborn engineers, he checked the oil and cleaned the filter, just in case. He turned the wing nut to the right. He adjusted the limiter on the foot-operated lever. He checked the seating of the connecting lever to the relay box. He adjusted the lever on the accelerator shaft. Next he turned to the linkage on the selector lever. Then he applied lubricant to the linkages to keep them from binding. After that he checked the cables to the steering rods to ensure there was the required amount of play. He even cleaned the steering valve, despite being certain that this wasn't a problem related to the steering, but better to be safe and methodical.

He was now running out of ideas and had only one option left: checking if the mounting bolts for the sliding gear transmission needed tightening. Eventually, the engine had to be hoisted out and replaced. But now it was too late in the day to continue and so, in effect, they had lost an entire day.

Later that night, von Schroif voiced his concern. 'If that had happened in a combat operation, I fear, we – all of us – would be put at grave risk. What is your assessment, Junge?'

'Just as we were going at 2,500 rpm she

felt wonderful. This is an incredible piece of engineering. For her size, she is astonishingly responsive to the lightest of touches. In terms of manoeuvrability, turning especially, she is a joy. However, this all comes at a price: complexity. And here I fear we may come up against her greatest weakness. This complexity is necessary, given her size and weight, but it also makes her highly strung – all her demands, everything, absolutely everything, must be met. I'm not sure the Maybach is quite man enough for the job – it needs to be upgraded to something which generates more power ... 641 hp isn't enough, she needs 690 hp at least.'

'You make her sound like a spoiled child!' exclaimed Otto Wohl.

'In a way, she is,' replied Junge, 'however, if you do meet her demands, I have the feeling that this temperamental young lady – if in the right mood – will be able to pay us back ten times over.'

'Are you prepared to lavish that much time and attention on her, Junge?' asked von Schroif.

'I don't think we really have a choice,' replied Junge.

At that point Major Rondorf came bounding into the room and everyone sprang to attention. Rondorf waived them back to their ease. 'Gentlemen, I have just spoken to Kurt Arnholdt at Henschel.' Looking at von

Schroif, he added: 'He passes on his regards, Hauptsturmführer.'

'Good, I am looking forward to hearing the good doctor's opinion,' replied von Schroif.

'According to Arnholdt,' continued Rondorf, 'they are looking at an upgraded engine, but, for the time being, it may be that the best solution is to keep her under 2,500 rpm. This is far from ideal, and the designers are working on a solution for the next variation, but that was his suggestion.'

'Please pass on my regards to Doctor Arnholdt,' replied von Schroif, 'and let him know that, if the Sunday afternoon driving club say 2,500, then 2,500 it is!' This brought forth a gentle but hearty laugh from all present.

Korsak cast a knowledgeable eye over the experimental light tank he had requisitioned. Captain Androv stood by nervously. It had been some time since their horse riding adventure, and he was understandably anxious as Korsak outlined the features of the T-26B which had recently been delivered from Moscow. The machine had caused a great deal of comment, as it had obviously been adapted for use as a flamethrower.

'Please God, do not let him take us out in this,' thought Androv, all the while feigning readiness to leap into action in this death-trap. His unease increased as Korsak approached a tank driver who was inspecting the vehicle with professional curiosity. Androv knew that this was a three man machine, and now that they were three, it could only mean one thing.

'Have you driven the T-26, comrade?' asked Korsak of the curious driver.

'Yes, comrade, it was the tank we trained on. I have driven it hundreds of time, but this looks unusual.'

'Indeed, it is,' said Korsak. 'Many experiments have been conducted by our comrades in the tank development department of the Red Army to determine the advisability of converting the T-26B tank into a flame-thrower!'

'Well, that is certainly an unexpected development. Is it an effective weapon?' asked the driver, who was becoming increasingly interested.

Korsak continued with his explanation. 'That remains to be seen. As you are aware, this tank normally carries two 7.62 mm machine guns...'

'I have also served in these machines with one antitank gun and one machine gun, although the main gun is far from effective,' said the driver. 'On balance, I prefer the dual machine gun version.'

'I stand corrected, comrade,' replied Korsak, 'but here is an intriguing new variant. If the tank is converted to a flamethrower, only one machine gun can be carried. We need to find out which is most effective, the flame or the bullet.'

'Shit! Shit! Shit!' thought Androv. 'He's going to drag me off on one of his insane adventures. Please let me live. I don't need this man in my life. If I get the chance, I'll kill the bastard!'

'Will you help us in a test mission, comrade?' Korsak asked the driver.

'Willingly,' replied the driver.

'Good,' said Korsak. 'Now, pay attention. On this experimental model of the T-26B, the fuel tank for the flame-throwing apparatus is mounted on the tank, instead of being towed on a trailer. This does not strike me as a good design feature. Various tests on flamethrowers using crude oil, and some other similar fuels with a greater potential to cling to victims, show that ten gallons of fuel per second are consumed under high pressure through a three centimetre nozzle to obtain a range of 100 metres. At this rate, the blast could be expected to last from ten to eleven seconds. By lessening the pressure, the range is reduced to between 25 and 40 metres, and the stream of flame lasts longer. The question therefore arises whether it is worthwhile sacrificing the firepower of one machine gun for such a short-lived flame.'

Korsak gestured towards the tank. 'Shall we, comrades...?'

The three crowded in and the driver asked for orders. 'Where do you wish me to go, comrade?'

'Fucking Berlin, if I know this lunatic!' thought Androv, wisely keeping his own counsel.

To his great relief, the journey was a very short one. 500 metres past the workshops was a small barbed-wire holding compound for German prisoners; Fifty or so dispirited men lay on the grass and contemplated their ill luck. That luck was about to run out.

Korsak wasted no time and immediately sent a five second blast of flame into the compound. Almost thirty prisoners were immediately engulfed in flame, the screams and cries of agony and shock unearthly in their intensity. Korsak observed the effects of his handiwork as the burning men desperately tried to extinguish the clinging flame engulfing them in an unendurable anguish. The screams intensified and the smell of oily smoke and charred flesh filled the air.

A further intense blast of searing flame was directed towards the men who had avoided the first jet. Korsak lessened the intensity and amused himself by chasing the few un-touched prisoners with the jet of flame, like a father spraying his children with a water hose. The deadly game was soon over, as the flame gave way and flickered out.

Androv sat in his seat, shocked and catatonic with disbelief. He could not comprehend the horror he had just seen, and he was unprepared for Korsak's cynical suggestion: 'Come, Comrade Androv, we should not allow our prisoners to suffer. You have the machine gun...'

The screaming mass of writhing men presented an unmissable target, and Androv had little trouble in internally justifying his own part in the barbaric trial operation which was unfolding. The prisoners were suffering beyond human limits and their horrific plight needed to be brought to an end. Six long blasts from the machine gun silenced the cries of misery, but it was a scene which would never leave Androv, one that would haunt him for the rest of his life.

Day by day, the crew at Paderborn were getting, better and better. Bobby Junge was growing in confidence, and the longer he kept her at just under 2,500 rpm, the more confident he became that his spoiled young lady would not throw a tantrum! The next day they were to conduct some trials with armoured cars in the role of T-34s, duplicating their speed, movements and tactics. They were moving smoothly through some hilly terrain when a target appeared, coming up over a hill directly behind them, approximately 1,000 metres away.

'Target, 6 o'clock!'

Knispel immediately adjusted the position of his feet on the hinged platform and the turret began its slow traverse. The gun was at 12 o'clock and, to von Schroif's great disappointment, it took over thirty seconds for the turret to swing around. He knew that, in a battle situation, this would grant vital time for the Soviet driver to make up ground on him and become a potential threat. This was going to have to be accounted for, either by Bobby Junge swinging the tank around, or by an evasive manoeuvre. But this was why they were here, on the training ground. All of these potential problems had to be ironed out or, if not, alternative strategies which took note of these deficiencies would have to be developed.

There was one other thing that von Schroif had noticed during this training, and it exercised his mind greatly. He was blind in one eye. That is to say, because of the position of his cupola on the left-hand side of the turret, there was an area to his right which rendered him completely unsighted.

'How could this be? How could any commander operate with a blind spot?' He was going to have to speak to Kurt. For now, his mind focused on the immediate task at hand: gunnery practice. The first part of the exercise would use a Panzerstellung, an 88 mounted in a concrete turret.

The first practice involved a target with a range over 1,200 metres. Using the knife and fork technique, von Schroif and Knispel scored highly. Simply put, the fork technique was a way of eating up a target. They would drop one shell in front of the target, noting its position. Then they would drop another 400 metres behind, again noting its position. They could then divide the distance between the two into four sections of 100 metres, add 100 metres to the first shot, and the third shot would be deadly accurate. If they were unable to see the terrain behind the target, then they would use the knife technique. This was more difficult, but essentially involved dropping the second shot in front of the first, again in front of the target, and then using these two locations to estimate the distance of the final shot.

Added to this was the beauty of the Acht-acht, which, with its wonderful flat trajectory, meant that the gunner only had to lift the barrel a little to gain more distance. This was bread and butter stuff to Michael Knispel, his obvious prowess inevitably impressing his instructors so highly with his ability at under 1,200 metres that there was talk of retaining 'the Prussian cannoneer', as he was now known at Paderborn!

This, of course, was never communicated to Knispel personally, but was suggested to von Schroif. Unfortunately, results over the next few days were not all that they could be, but good enough to pass. Experienced, well-balanced crews were everything, and once one had secured the services of a top-class gunner like Michael Knispel, one did not let him go lightly. There were Ivans to fight, and Knispel was a born fighter.

Occasionally, after training, if the weather was acceptable, the crew would take their evening meal down by the river and talk and reminisce until the sun went down. At other times, tired and careworn, they would sit in silence, just watching the gentle flow, each man deep in his own thoughts, a situation every soldier knows.

On this particular night though, Otto Wohl was in fine form, regaling his comrades with tales of the Munich drinking halls, of scrapes and women, and too much drink. In the middle of one story about heading home late at night, he abruptly broke off and asked von Schroif about his own family situation, at which point the rest of the group started to listen in earnest. Not through any motive that was ill-mannered or intrusive, but simply out of great interest. In all the time they had known Hans von Schroif, they had never once heard him speak about these matters. The boss, truly, kept himself to himself.

'So, boss,' asked Otto, 'what was your father

like?' Only Otto could have asked a question like this. Coming from any other man, it would have seemed impudent.

'My father,' started Hans slowly, 'was born in Berchtesgaden, as I was, and I think he took his nature from that area. A very proud man, who loved his family. He owned an estate and took his living from the land. But I don't remember ever having to break into his house after a drinking expedition! I don't think I would have survived such an experience! But I think of him often, and I can see parts of him in me.'

'Is he...?' continued Otto.

'No,' answered Hans, second guessing the question. 'Those Red bastards took his estate from him and he never recovered. By the time we chased them out of Munich, it was too late. He thought he'd lost everything. He took his own life.'

The conversation ended there. It had gone too far.

Korsak was surrounded by his attentive subordinates. He stood by a makeshift blackboard, carefully outlining his strategy for the next action.

'The key to the entire action will be surprise. Everyone must understand that. The trap will only be sprung once the fascists have been drawn over the river and lulled into a false sense of security by our apparent

186

retreat. The camouflage of five hundred tanks across a wide area is crucial to the operation, and presents a number of problems with certain unique features created by the general summer background, the operational characteristics of the tanks, and in the conditions of employing them in combat.'

Korsak paused and surveyed his audience. Satisfied that they were paying proper attention, he carried on.

'This will influence the work to be done to camouflage them. In winter, the snow makes things easy. In summer, we must work even harder. A factor which must be considered of vital importance from the point of view of camouflage and concealment is the greater clearness of the sky; this helps reconnaissance activity by enemy aviation. In view of the fact that vehicles can be spotted by the shadow they cast, they should move on the side of the road nearest to the sun, so that their shadow falls on the road, which is darker than the grass next to the road.

'Movement along the roads, especially at great speeds and over dry and dusty earth, gives itself away by clouds of dust. For this reason, all movement of vehicles towards their attack positions must be at low speeds, especially over sandy ground. The tracks left by the tank treads in the dust stand out clearly as two parallel strips with tread impressions. These must be obliterated by teams tasked with sweeping the roads leading to the assembly areas. When tracks are left on the grass verge of the existing road it is necessary, instead of sweeping, to remove them with the aid of spades and rakes.'

Pausing briefly to ensure himself of the continued attention of his audience, Korsak went on to list the minute details of the operation.

'When the tanks pass through places where turns are unavoidable, little heaps of up-turned earth appear everywhere; these are characteristic marks and betray the movement of tanks. To prevent this, turns must be made gradually in a wide arc whenever practicable, or else the heaps of earth which are formed must be cleared away. The reflection from the lenses of the tank headlights will also give away their movement. In order to prevent this, it is necessary to cover the headlights with green fabric covers, or some other material.

'Finally, among the most important factors betraying the movement of tanks to ground observers is the clank of the tracks. Unlike the fascists, our tracks are of all-metal construction. The noise of these can be heard better at night as the temperature falls. Naturally, when operations are in the immediate vicinity of the enemy, you must make full use of all the ordinary precautions employed in summer for the prevention of noise.

'The peculiar characteristic of inhabited areas from the point of view of camouflage is the motley appearance of the landscape due to the presence of dwelling places, barns, gardens, roads, and paths. This wealth and variety of outline affords considerable opportunities for concealing the position of tanks from air and ground observation by the enemy.'

The listeners were impressed by Korsak's uncanny attention to detail and his grasp of the fact that a battle could be lost by what appeared to be insignificant consideration. They would have been less relaxed had they been aware that Korsak considered them to be an idle, feckless bunch of incompetents. Normally he would have shown no hesitation in having them all shot as an example to the others. However, time was against him and Korsak had decided to work with the material he had. He therefore adopted a mild approach.

'You have not made the best of the time available to you, comrades. I am disappointed by this. I see tanks in winter camouflage. By the end of today the tanks are to be painted to avoid observation. The open country is characterised by a profusion of variegated colour. Two-colour disruptive summer paint is to be used where the ground presents a variety of colour, where there are forests, underbrush, small settlements, exposed patches of earth, etc. Painting in two colours with large spots can be undertaken by painting only part of the tank surface, leaving about a third of the tank's surface in the original green; the new scheme must either be green and dark grey, or green and brown. It is necessary to avoid mechanical repetition of patterns and colours. Make sure this is done.'

With some of the detail out of the way, Korsak moved on to give his orders concerning the concealment of his force.

'Once the vehicles are in attack position, for camouflage you must use nets made of cord which have fastened to them irregular green and brown patches of fabric, about 1 metre across. But the construction of these camouflage masks involves special considerations dependent on the characteristics of the background. The principal camouflage materials employed are irregularly shaped pieces of fabric or painted green matting. In addition to the green patches, dark patches should be fastened to the material to give the appearance of bushes, tree tops, or other natural ground features. For dark patches one may use tree branches and other similar materials. As with covers, the use of brown patches alone, or of a combination of green and dark patches, will depend entirely on

the terrain and the coloration of the surroundings.'

Korsak noticed an enhanced level of interest as he began to detail an unusual feature
of the plan.

'Those of you who have been responsible
for their construction will know we shall also
be using dummy tanks during the forthcoming operation. Their purpose is, of course, to
draw the attention of the enemy air forces to
the dummy tanks and has the aim to deceive
the enemy concerning the disposition, types,
and character of our real tank activity. They
will lure the Stukas away from our tank
forces, which will be fully concealed.

'As a rule, all vehicles in attack positions
should be placed under the roofs of sheds
and barns, leaving the dummy tanks exposed to draw in aerial attacks in the open.
Where there is an insufficient number of
such structures, or where the size of the
vehicles makes it impossible to place them
in the existing shelters, it will be necessary
to build shelters resembling the existing
structures in the given locality. The roofs of
these shelters must be covered with a layer
of hay so that they will not look any different
from the roofs of the existing structures.

'These camouflage structures may be built
either as additions to existing structures or as
separate structures. The separate camouflage
structures should be situated along laid-out

paths, and the tracks of the caterpillars which lead to the place where the tanks are stationed should be swept or dragged so as to resemble an ordinary road.

'Woods, orchards, and brushwood can be used for camouflage, but leafy woods offer the best concealment in summer and completely hide the vehicles from air observation.

'Finally, if no covers of any kind are available, the vehicles should be covered with branches, straw, hay, and the like, and earth placed on top in irregular patches. When the tanks are stationed in open, flat country, then the camouflage of the tanks can be achieved by scattering here and there patches of pine needles, straw, and rubbish... The ground should also be laid bare, as tanks which are painted a dark colour will not be easily discovered against a dark background, either by visual air observation or by the study of aerial photographs.'

Korsak was not a man to leave any detail unattended, and as he continued with his briefing his audience was becoming more and more impressed by the meticulous manner in which he approached the preparations.

'In open country, the ground assumes a naturally mottled appearance; when the tank is stationed in a gully, it is to be covered with solid green covers of any kind of fabric or matting painted green and, brown, or by the regulation net, with green and black patches attached to it.

His audience expected this to be the end of the briefing, but they had not worked with Kommissar Dimitri Korsak. There was much more to come.

'Now, comrades, let us consider our tactics...'

The day at Paderborn was an important one. Instead of firing from fixed positions, the crew was now to practise firing from the tank itself. In order to locate the target, they roamed over the range. Bobby Junge was sure he had a grip of her now.

For von Schroif, the thought process was quite simple: 'Preparation! Observation! Penetration! And don't push her too hard, let her live within herself.'

Hans eventually found the target they were searching for – an old French Char B in a stationary position.

'Target spotted. 700 metres.'

'800,' replied Michael, giving his best estimate.

'Average 750,' replied Hans. 'Anti-tank 39.'

'Mo-Fu-Fa-La-Ba,' replied the crew in turn as hatches and lamps were checked before firing, after which Otto Wohl loaded and Bobby Junge stopped her in her tracks.

Then von Schroif gave a new turret position and Knispel rotated the turret, Otto set

the gear emergency lever up, Bobby acceler-
ated, and Karl set the selector lever for the
turret position. Then more measurements.

'750.'

Michael adjusted range, aiming for the
centre of the target.

'Fire!'

'Direct hit!' exclaimed von Schroif proudly,
but he had not really expected anything else.
'Satisfying, but strangely unsatisfying,' he
thought. 'We need to be a little more stretched.'

'Wendorff,' he barked through the intercom, 'request moving target!'

Wendorff duly did so and the instructors
indicated that they would roll an old Soviet
truck down the hill.

'Junge, take her back 500 metres.'

This was ambitious. Taking a shot at a moving target over 1,200 metres was not usually
attempted in the field. After reversing the
prescribed 500 metres, Bobby Junge then
positioned the tank in the direction of the
target.

Hans, through his binoculars, could see
the truck being readied and then, with an
almighty heave, being pushed down the hill
by a small team who scattered like rabbits,
all running back up the hill as fast as they
could.

Now this was going to be difficult, and not
just because of the distance, but because the

truck, as it hurtled down the hill, would be accelerating. Normally, the calculations for hitting a moving target involved estimating the speed of the target and deciding how far in front of the target to aim the shot. In firing at a moving target at over 200 metres, the gunner did not aim at where the target was, but where it was going to be!

Many would consider this request to be folly, the result of overconfidence or cockiness, but the opposite was in fact true. Hans knew that, if you pushed yourself further on the training ground, anything within those parameters that were encountered on the battlefield could be approached with more confidence. He also knew that, at these kinds of distances and circumstances, the science would be of absolutely no help. Gunnery in this situation was more of an art, and Michael Knispel was an artist. A landscape artist whose brush was his gun, his shells his paint.

Knispel estimated the speed of the truck at 10 km/h, giving a lead on the main reticule – by the book – of three notches. But the target was starting to speed up. Throw the book out the window! Just feel the notches.

'Ready?'

'Target acquired,' answered Knispel.

'Fire!'

The high-explosive round hurtled towards

its target with the expectant instruction team watching ... waiting ... from the safety of their foxholes. Then, boom! A direct hit with high-explosive and the target was blown to smithereens! A loud cheer, not just from the crew in the tank, but also from the watching instructors who were enjoying the novelty, and the fireworks!

# CHAPTER 7

## KERCH

On the plains of the Kerch peninsula the fireworks were very real; the green flares rising into the pre-dawn sky indicated that the combat teams had done their work. Voss prepared to push the attack. He thought very briefly that it would have been good to get von Schroif's input, they had worked as a very effective team since the invasion of Poland, but he reassured himself that the plan was a sound one, and he was sure that the mission could not have been compromised.

The battalion workshop had worked overtime, and the new batch of Panzer IVs with the long-barrelled Panzerkamfwagenkanone had arrived at the railhead and were being rushed to the front. New tanks were heartily welcome, but with them, Voss knew only too well, would come new crews, unused to the ways of the frontline. A repeat of the tactics which had brought him a much lauded victory at Hill 15 was out of the question. Ivan was a fast learner and would be vigilant, watching for a repeat. Voss was ordered to force the issue, and his objective from division was to seize the vital bridge and push on to the town of Chersoniev.

The officers gathered to hear the briefing seemed suddenly so much younger. Had it not been so depressing, Voss would have laughed to himself as he realised that was because they were younger. The days when mature and experienced officers like von Schroif could be relied upon to instinctively understand their duties and define their own parameters were over. As each day took its bloody toll, the dismal reality was that the experienced officer cadre was becoming thinner and thinner. Looking at the circle of young faces, Voss began to carefully outline the battle plan once more.

'The advance Vorausabteilung will operate much further forward than usual, providing combat reconnaissance in strength, and will be supported by a battery of Sturm-geschütz. The Vorausabteilung will seize the bridge in a surprise attack. This group will be followed by a heavily reinforced attack group, and this main Angriffsgruppe will incorporate a force of fifty tanks, advancing to the jump-off point by forced marches, with its infantry riding on tanks.

'The Luftwaffe assures me that they have destroyed large concentrations of enemy armour which they discovered in the open. We do not therefore anticipate strong armoured resistance. However, the main attack by the Angriffsgruppe will only go ahead in the event that the bridge is seized and a wide perimeter is held by the Vorausabteilung. It is vital that the bridge is secured. A strong detachment of anti-tank guns and infantry has therefore been detailed to advance as a bridge guard. In the event of a strong Russian counterattack, the consequences of being trapped on the other side of the river do not bear thinking about.'

Voss's plan was necessarily a simple one and, initially at least, all appeared to proceed smoothly. By the evening of the 5th of July, the most advanced elements of the Vorausabteilung had reached the vicinity of the bridge and had concealed themselves in readiness for the assault. The force chosen by Voss for this important assignment consisted principally of an army bicycle company and a platoon of Waffen SS assault engineers. An SS cavalry battalion awaited nearby, ready to add its mobility to the coming battle. This detachment was to assemble and, supported by the battery of assault guns, take possession of the bridge and keep the crossing open for the main attack group.

As soon as the bridge was secure, the main Angriffsgruppe would come rushing up from its jump-off point, five kilometres to the rear. The main Angriffsgruppe was to follow the advanced detachment and push on through, towards Chersoniev. A defensive force, the Verteidigungabteilung, was tasked with guarding the bridge. It consisted of one platoon of light infantry howitzers, one anti-tank platoon, and a company of infantry.

Plans for the support of the advance by strong artillery, emplaced as close to the front as possible, had been put into readiness for action. From its bridgehead positions, the battery of assault guns attached to the Vorausabteilung advanced detachment was to cover the dash to the bridge and assist in its seizure and the subsequent advance beyond.

It has often been said that the best laid plans do not survive the first five minutes of contact, but Voss had good reason to curse as things began to go wrong, even before contact. The reinforced bicycle company and the assault engineers had arrived at the jump-off point only to find that the battery of assault guns which had been ordered to the bridge had not yet arrived. The incomplete Vorausabteilung waited as precious hours of pre-dawn darkness vanished.

'Where the hell are they?' barked Voss at his radio operator.

'No report as yet, sir!' The operator knew it was a rhetorical question and continued with his quest to make sense out of what was becoming a confused situation. The time was not entirely wasted.

'Sir, the forward reconnaissance elements report that a weak enemy force with machine guns is holding the southern end of the bridge. However, at the far end, the Ivans are well dug in with concrete emplacements. The assault guns will certainly be needed.'

This report triggered a frantic series of calls to find the location of the Sturmgeschütz. Finally, a report came back.

'It appears the commander took the wrong route ... he estimates a four hour delay.'

'Damn these children!' bellowed Voss. 'Well, it's his funeral. The attack will have to commence in full daylight...'

Eventually, the Sturmgeschütz arrived, and amends were made as they effectively threw their weight into the attack. With their help, the Vorausabteilung succeeded in throwing the enemy back and seizing the bridge. The concrete emplacements at the far end of the bridge were no match for the high-explosive rounds blasted into the firing slots from murderously short range, although reports were coming in of a few isolated individual

Russian soldiers who continued to fight stubbornly from the woods beyond the bridge. It was clear that the main enemy force had withdrawn to the east, and they continued to harass the rapidly advancing Vorausabteilung from that direction by means of rifle and machine-gun fire.

Meanwhile, Voss now learned that the Angriffsgruppe, too, had been somewhat delayed by skirmishes with enemy snipers and isolated groups of partisans on this side of the river, and would be late in arriving. In order that the attack of the main body should not be held up because of this delay, Voss desperately ordered the main body to force march the remaining two kilometres, before the bridge could be reoccupied by stronger enemy units.

As he waited and seethed in frustration, the first prisoners arrived. Under interrogation from Voss himself, the disorientated and terrified prisoners stated that the Ivans were not intending to mount an immediate recapture of the bridge. Their statements were at first regarded as incorrect, especially in view of the general estimate of the situation. However, a short time later, an air observation report came in that enemy motorised forces were indeed retreating, and this appeared to confirm the prisoners' statements.

Voss now decided to go forward himself, and quickly ascertained that enemy artillery, which he reckoned to be one medium battery, was shelling the road south of the bridge as far as the regimental command post. Voss took heart from the fact that the sound of battle indicated that the enemy was not resisting stubbornly.

In order to force the attack forward, Voss rushed to the bridge to rendezvous with the fast-approaching main Angriffsgruppe. He wanted to ensure that they immediately surged on to engage the enemy. He received a new and disconcerting report that signal flares, indicating enemy tanks, were now going up from the wooded area on the other side of the bridge.

The situation appeared to have changed. Were the Ivans about to reverse their plan? A further unconfirmed report arrived – what appeared to be an enemy tank concentration had been spotted in the woods to the south, and was now being engaged by the artillery.

At the same time that all of this was going on, messages began arriving from the advanced detachment saying that fire from enemy artillery, tank guns, heavy mortars, and infantry howitzers, in addition to well-aimed rifle fire, was preventing any forward movement. Some elements had got as far as the woods beyond the river; there, however, they had been stopped by enemy, machine-gun fire. Consequently, though the assault guns were on the far bank, no infantry or engineers were firmly emplaced as yet. Voss therefore ordered the available artillery to switch targets and engage the enemy on the north bank.

As Voss waited and seethed, the situation became increasingly confused. The enemy artillery fire, increased; it was estimated at forty heavy, eighty medium, and ninety light pieces. Furthermore, it was reported that the enemy was installed in field fortifications in the woods beyond the far bank, and that numerous light tanks were engaging the attacking force. The most advanced German infantry was involved in stubborn close combat with the enemy in foxholes and small trenches.

No report that the Vorausabteilung had succeeded in moving forward was forthcoming.

'Where the hell are those reports?' bellowed Voss. 'What's happening over there?'

The only good news was a subsequent report which confirmed that the assault guns had got across the river, expended their ammunition, returned to resupply, and then crossed again with more ammunition. It could not change the general picture that a continuation of the attack did not appear to promise success under the methods employed so far. Moreover, it was ascertained that the main Angriffsgruppe had lost much time in its advance by deploying across open terrain and that it was still lagging behind; early assistance from this battalion was not to be expected for another hour.

As random runners appeared at the half-track command post, the situation became less and less clear. Voss therefore had no option but to issue oral and fragmentary orders to hold the main attack, as the heavy artillery was needed elsewhere and there was no longer the guarantee of the strongest possible artillery support.

Towards 11:30 am the situation took a new turn. Voss was heartened to learn that the aggressive élan of the attacking elements was able to accomplish what had not been considered possible in view of the estimated enemy situation. By exploiting the bold forward thrust of the returned assault guns, elements of the infantry and parts of the engineers had succeeded in forming an advanced bridgehead, thereby clearing the way for a sweeping manoeuvre by the cavalry, and paving the way for a general attack across the bridge by the main attack group. If reinforcements could come up soon, the whole attack was likely to be successful.

Finally, the Angriffsgruppe arrived at the bridge. Voss immediately collared the liaison officer with the attack group.

'The situation is fluid; there has been a change in the situation since the issuance of the order for a hold on the main attack. It now appears possible for the forward movement to gain sufficient momentum for a successful advance. I have countermanded my order. You must attack now and push on towards your objective.'

'Jawohl, Sturmbannführer!' barked the liaison officer, and the column roared off. Without further ado, the Angriffsgruppe swept over the bridge and into the attack. It was now imperative to prevent the attack from stalling; this was the moment to press forward with all available strength.

A considerable element of danger was recognised by Voss in the fact that, during the sweeping continuation of the assault, the attacking force might run into its own artillery fire. However, efforts to shift the fire to a box barrage succeeded in time and, falling directly in front of the panzers, it greatly facilitated the attack. The liaison officers with the attacking units were ordered and rushed forward with the new and final order to dispense with any preparation for a coordinated attack and to press on with the attack now in progress.

Frustrated by the lack of a complete picture, Voss took a decision to move his command post to the far bank. The Gefechtsstandfahrzeug roared over the bridge. Voss observed that there were one or two dead Russians lying in every foxhole. Now and then, shots were still being fired by some individual Russians who had obviously simulated death, but Voss was satisfied that the mopping-up operation was already underway.

In the far distance, it was obvious that only a few Russian light tanks were still resisting. They were disabled by the assault guns, and some of them were abandoned by their crews. The Ivans had apparently been forced to give up any intention of defending, both by the fierce attack and by the effective artillery fire. The enemy had been caught in the ferocity of the attack by the main Angriffsgruppe.

While a few enemy riflemen and heavy weapons, supported by tanks, were holding out until the last, everything else appeared to be in full flight. Enemy riflemen, approximately two companies in strength, were observed to the northwest in scattered retreat. This was apparently the enemy's infantry reserve. The encouraging signs were that the enemy artillery left some single guns behind in their emplacements. The rest withdrew to the northeast and, caught in the pursuit fire of the medium artillery, were soon abandoned by the enemy.

Voss, flushed with the thrill of success, pushed on beyond the bridge in an effort to keep up with the changing situation. As he breasted the hill, he ordered his command half-track to halt under the spreading branches of a tall oak tree. From the back of the Gefechtsstandfahrzeug, he anxiously scanned the advancing panzers. Initially, all appeared to be going well. The tanks advanced in the textbook manner, arranged in the standard breitkeil, or 'broad wedge', when suddenly a series of violent explosions rippled through the lead tanks.

The radio burst into life. 'Anti-tank gun screen!'

More and more panzers rolled to a halt. In next to no time, Voss could count twelve flaming wrecks. The attack lost momentum, and his concern rose as they began to reverse. As if from nowhere, there came the whoosh of an incoming round. Voss was knocked off his feet by the blast. As he stumbled up, his dazed brain came back to life, and his eyes focused on a terrifying sight.

Arranged between him and the bridge was a force of around 100 Soviet tanks. Before his eyes, the thin screen of German defenders and anti-tank guns screening the bridge was rolled up. He looked back in horror as another wave of Soviet armour emerged from the north. They were led by T-26 light tanks, each spouting thin bursts of flame.

He was trapped. Voss could see his infantry force fading away under the assault of the flame-throwing tanks. Burning grenadiers, reduced to human candles by the

Soviet terror weapon, dotted the battlefield. He was merely a spectator as his panzers were picked off, one by one, by a large force of T-34 tanks which appeared to come from nowhere.

For a brief moment, Voss and his adjutant mentally prepared to fight to the death, but the simple truth was that the situation was so obviously hopeless that the will to commit suicide evaporated. As a KV-1 with the stencilled outline of a White Devil hurtled towards them and pulled up beside the Gefechtsstandfahrzeug, Voss and his small command group left the vehicle and raised their hands in surrender.

The commander of the Russian tank climbed out and stepped down. As his feet hit the ground, he was joined by four T-34 tanks, each bearing a full complement of desyanti. The tank riders, too, dismounted, and formed a circle around the five German prisoners, binding their hands behind their backs.

'SS-Sturmbannführer Helmut Voss, if I am not very much mistaken...' began the Soviet tank commander in perfect accentless German.

'That is correct,' replied Voss, offering the absolute minimum of information, but apprehensive as to why it was necessary to tie their hands behind their backs. 'I demand that my men are properly treated.'

'Don't worry, they will be...' said the tank commander, removing his cap and wiping the sweat from his brow. His thick black eyebrows contrasted with the bushy shock of pure white hair.

'Stenner!' gasped Voss.

Voss said no more as the Soviet commander flashed a dagger across his throat, severing his vocal chords and his windpipe. On Korsak's signal, a member of the tank crew stepped forward with five rope nooses and began to loop them over the bough of the oak tree. With no ceremony, the cords were fastened around the necks of the German prisoners. One by one, the prisoners were strung up and left to die like dogs.

From the ranks of the curious Soviet spectators, an official photographer was on hand to record the gruesome sight. Korsak made sure that he took a good shot which featured the KV-1 with its White Devil motif prominently displayed in the foreground and the dangling bodies behind. Justice was being visited on the fascist beasts and Korsak was anxious to make sure Moscow knew that the Weisse Teufel had been at work.

The news of the ignominious death of SS-Sturmbannführer Voss struck home hard, but there was nothing that could be done at Paderborn. Until the new tank was combat ready, von Schroif and his crew had little option but to work hard and push the machine through its paces in readiness for what was projected to be a combat debut in 1943.

Throughout July, the testing programme continued. Other tanks emerged from the factory and other crews appeared to take charge and begin the complex task of learning how to maintain and operate the Tiger. As the nights slowly became longer, the senses sharper, the bonds tighter, von Schroif estimated that by April 1943 the Tiger would be ready to be tested in combat. It was frustrating to have to wait so long, but the machine was still a prototype.

In the meantime, it was certainly good to be back in Germany, away from the hell that was the Eastern Front, but Hans von Schroif never forgot for one moment that he was going to return there. Despite the moments of levity, this was no holiday, it was a mission. A mission to keen the eye, the hand, and the mind, to become one – yes, one! – with the awesome capabilities and technology of this fantastic new marvel, bestowed on them by the genius of German engineering. It was their job to become one with the machine...

Hans smiled when he thought of it this way ... it sounded like a marriage! A marriage in which the bride was so powerful that, like a queen bee, she could call on five suitors, each of which would pledge themselves. Married to a tank! In a way, there was some truth to this.

'Truth be told,' Hans thought to himself with a smile, 'she may be more faithful!'

However, he still had reservations: the blind spot, the turret speed, the preparations. At Paderborn, the preparations were not too difficult, but how would they be in the heat of battle? How would she perform in the mud, or in the freezing ice and snow of winter, or in the dusty furnace of summer? What would happen if the supply chain got disrupted and spares started to run out? What about the terrain and the distances?

'Yes, we've seen the tables for armour protection, but that was only theory. How would she respond in reality to being hit by Ivan's shells?'

This led Hans on to a new line of thinking. Perhaps it was time to leave the warm bosom of Paderborn, and request that the tank and crew go east for further trials, trials which more ruthlessly exposed both man and machine to the extreme conditions of war on the Eastern Front. This, he believed, would provide a real test as to whether or not the Tiger was truly ready.

Before he could mention this to Major Rondorf, it was Rondorf who approached him.

'Well, von Schroif, I am afraid you have to

leave this little idyll and head back to the front.'

'Strange, I was just going to talk to you about that. I agree, our time here should be over, but I was going to suggest further testing and training in conditions that more closely resemble the front.'

'I feel that your crew know their way around the Tiger now, but I am afraid further testing is out of the question,' said Rondorf.

'But she is still very much a prototype. I have written various reports...' replied von Schroif.

'Yes, the blind spot, turret speed, drive chain... Unfortunately, there is nothing I can do. These are manufacturing decisions. There will be factory modifications, but, for now, you must content yourself with what you have.'

'With great respect, I believe it to be premature to put this tank into action.'

'That may or may not be the case, Hauptsturmführer, but the order came from the Führer ... or from someone close to him.'

'Don't tell me... It's Borgmann again, isn't it? It's almost as if he wants to throw this opportunity away. If one of these falls into Soviet hands, everything is compromised.' At which point von Schroif suddenly clammed up. He realised that he had crossed the line. There was no point in continuing his line of reasoning. 'When?'

'Tomorrow,' replied Rondorf.

'How?'

'Pick up five new machines from the factory at Kassel tomorrow, then entrain for the front. The Führer wants to see the Tiger in action.'

'Then we must oblige,' said von Schroif, his mood changing. 'It will be good to see the unit again. It's great tank country, down in the southern sector.'

'Don't plan on it,' said Rondorf curtly.

Later that night, Hans von Schroif gathered his crew and told them the news.

'I don't think she's ready,' said Bobby Junge, 'she is still basically a prototype.'

'I know,' replied von Schroif, 'we all have reservations.' But then, feeling he should engender a less anxious state of morale amongst his comrades, he decided to shift emphasis. 'However, as far as the gun and the communications go, I don't think any further improvements need be made. They are ready to go.'

'So is the loader, sir,' added Otto Wohl, '...he's never been fitter!'

'Is it back to the Division...? Rostov?' asked Bobby Junge expectantly.

'I would imagine so... They've done well without us. Rostov is back in our hands. We're missing the party. They'll need us to help push on beyond. Rostov is great tank country, and we have to remember our mission. Rostov is where we suffered our first setback, so it is entirely fitting that we return and, with this great tank at our side, let Ivan know the reverse was only temporary. In fact, now that I think about it, this is where we could make our most valuable contribution! Now, let's get some sleep.'

'Sir, has anyone ever loaded a section of these things on a train before?' asked Michael Knispel as the men readied to leave.

'I don't know,' said von Schroif with a shrug.

'Me neither,' said Bobby Junge.

Junge, Knispel and Wohl stood up, then made their excuses and left. None of the men betrayed their true feelings over the matter. Soldiers very rarely did.

Staying behind, Wendorff sat without speaking, but had the look of a man beset by problems.

'Are you sure it's Rostov, sir?' asked Karl Wendorff, finally breaking his long silence.

'No,' replied von Schroif truthfully, '...perhaps it was wishful thinking. We can only hope. We have to trust those above us.'

'Assuming that it isn't ... given the importance of this new weapon, surely you could make representations?'

'The order has come from the top, and we will follow it.'

Wendorff knew there was no point discussing it further. He rose and saluted.

'Goodnight, sir.'

'Goodnight, Wendorff.'

Hans von Schroif sat looking out over the river, the fierce red heat of the sun fading into cooler night. In the distance he could see the cathedral and, without wishing it, couldn't help thinking of Saint Liborius, the patron saint of a good death. It wasn't a thought he wanted to have at that time, but once present in his mind he could not easily dismiss it ... a good death... What was a good death?

## CHAPTER 8

## ELVIRA

'Elvira,' answered Karl Wendorff, '...Elvira Schorr, according to the programme notes, trained at the Staatsoper in Munich.'

'Hah! A Bavarian. I knew it... Does it give an address?' asked Wohl hopefully.

'It doesn't reveal that kind of information, Wohl! I'm afraid you will have to do your own detective work.'

'Unless, of course, you have good contacts in the Gestapo,' suggested Knispel.

'Not my kind of people. Jumped-up cops, if you ask me,' replied Wohl. '...I just don't want to forget her face.'

'I didn't see you looking at her face,' said Junge.

Ignoring the barb, Otto Wohl glanced across to a mother with a young child sitting at the window on the other side of the railway carriage.

'Excuse me, Madam, may I borrow one of your son's pencils?'

'Of course, sir. Heinrich, please give the soldier one of your pencils.'

The child obliged and Otto smiled at him. He then looked around for something to write on.

'Use this,' suggested Bobby Junge, offering a page from his Tiger manual. 'It's practically unreadable. Perhaps you can brighten it up!'

Wohl picked a page and started sketching Elvira from memory. Of course, his only memory was her performance as a Rhine maiden on stage in Paderborn. If the performance of Das Rheingold had appealed to Karl Wendorff's ear, then the sight of Elvira on stage had appealed to Otto's eyes, which widened as he sketched Elvira's long blond hair and fulsome bosom! Of course, Otto Wohl, being Otto Wohl, the dress started to remove itself, and before too long poor Elvira was completely naked.

'One Reichsmark for a copy of the lovely Elvira standing with her back to you, two for her...'

'Wohl...' interjected von Schroif, motion-ing with his eyes.

Otto looked across and could see young Heinrich staring at the disrobed Rhine maiden with a look that was rather inappro-priate for one so young. Otto immediately shut the book and quickly stared out the carriage window as the train slowly ground to a halt for the thirtieth time that morning. Everyone knew the reason. There had been a heavy raid during the night, targeting the rail network north of Kassel.

'God, if I get my hands on one of those RAF villains, he'll pay,' said Knispel. 'What a damned waste of time!'

'We don't have to waste the time,' said Wendorff.

'I'm not volunteering to fill in bomb craters, if that's what you're suggesting. I can't run this war single-handed, you know.'

'No, this is brainwork.'

'Well, that rules out Knispel!' exclaimed Wohl.

'Careful, Wohl,' warned Knispel.

'Gentlemen, please,' interjected Wendorff, '...I think we may have finally found a posi-tive use for both of your talents. Why don't you, Wohl, put your skills as a cartoonist to use and make a Tiger primer for all the other kids coming to Paderborn who will follow in your shoes. Your own Wundertüte, but with a purpose... you could make Elvira the star of

217

the show. That would certainly hold the attention. Who knows? She could even lose a few garments along the way!'

'That's a brilliant idea!' exclaimed von Schroif enthusiastically. 'There will soon be thousands of young idiots like Wohl at Paderborn; we need something more memorable than reams of paper, full of charts and tables. Something accessible, with lots of memory aides. Some of your technical drawings could be useful too, Junge.'

'If it saves lives, I'd be only too happy to oblige, Hauptsturmführer.'

'Then let's get started,' said von Schroif.

Without any further prompting, the five Tiger men set to work to create an illustrated manual which would incorporate all the tricks of the trade in an accessible way. The rest of the journey flashed by as the Tigerfibel, a primer for Tiger students, was hastily created. It featured a combination of jokes and limericks from Knispel, with the text supplied by Wendorff and von Schroif. Wohl's risque cartoons and Junge's excellent technical drawings helped to illustrate the simple lessons on maintenance and combat, including the simplified lessons involving the clover leaf, meal times, the anti-Goetz, and a hundred other things which the coming waves of Tiger men might need to know.

Wohl couldn't resist weaving a new and bold hero into the creation, a purely fictional gun loader called 'Hulsensacke the indefatigable', who wins the hand of the beautiful Elvira.

Eventually the line was repaired, and the train began its painful progress. The crew had just completed the work and were settling back to a well-earned rest when von Schroif glanced up just in time to see the refection of a tall, formally dressed man standing over him.

'Gentlemen, may I join you?' came the request, his hand motioning to the one empty seat opposite Wohl.

'Of course,' answered von Schroif.

The man sat down, put his briefcase in his lap, and made himself comfortable. There was then a pause, followed by a question.

'Ah, the Lions of Rostov we have read so much about... Where are you going today?'

The manner was direct and too forward for a civilian. There was something about the plain and formal dress, the way he guarded his briefcase, and also a lack of sincerity in the voice which antagonised von Schroif and encouraged him to adopt a less than friendly manner.

'You know I cannot give you such information.'

'Of course. Do forgive me. Well, we can share some time. Kassel is also my destination. May I say what an honour it is to meet men such as you, men who are in the very

219

vanguard of this noble and historic mission?'

'Noble? A fine word, best reserved for those who know nothing of war,' replied von Schroif, rather disparagingly.

'But surely, however difficult the waging of war, there is still nobility in its overall purpose, the protection and furthering of the German people – and, of course, in carrying out the will of the party?'

'Party? You mean the gangsters who run this country?' snorted Otto Wohl, his antipathy spilling over into venom. His tone surprised even himself, let alone the well-dressed stranger who sat opposite.

This was dangerous talk. Who was this gentleman sitting opposite? And how did he know they were headed for Kassel? It took von Schroif to draw the situation's sting.

'SS-Panzerschütze Wohl is doing no more than any soldier in his circumstance would do ... he is not making a political assertion... Soldiers get tired, and soldiers through the ages let off steam, and it is usually their superiors who feel the brunt of it ... but I can assure you, sir, his actions tell a different story. This is one of the bravest warriors on the whole of the Eastern Front.'

'That may very well be the case, Hauptsturmführer...?'

'Von Schroif,' replied Hans, curtly but politely.

'Yes, that may very well be the case, Hauptsturmführer von Schroif, but, no matter how well a man has fought, if his purity of thought becomes degraded, this infection could spread not only to his greater self, but also to others. I have to tell you, I am quite shocked to hear words such as these from men of the Waffen SS. Men from within the Führer's personal bodyguard division! If I may, it does not reflect well on the commanding officer of such a unit.'

The stranger opened his briefcase and took out a notepad on which he began to make a record of the conversation.

'I am sorry,' replied von Schroif calmly, 'I don't believe you have introduced yourself yet.'

'I, too, am sorry, but there is no need for introductions...' said the stranger. 'Certainly not at this point,' he added, rather ominously. 'I am afraid this conversation is over. For now... Good day, Hauptsturmführer von Schroif, gentlemen, and ... er ... SS-Panzerschütze Wohl?' adding Otto's name in the way a man does when he pretends to be asking a question whilst already knowing the answer.

The smartly dressed stranger rose and left the carriage.

'Bastard,' muttered Knispel, out of earshot of any of the passengers who might be listening, and then flashing out his right fist in a pretend blow. 'I'd give him that! Who was he?'

'Heinrich Bremer. Kriminalrat, Geheime-staatspolizei... RHSA...' Wendorff informed them. 'Well, that's according to the letterhead on one of the letters in his briefcase.'

'Gestapo, eh?' added Junge. 'You should have asked him for Elvira's address, Otto!'

The crewmen laughed, except for von Schroif, who saw only the serious side.

'For God's sake, Wohl! I order you to make this the last time your stupid mouth opens when it should stay shut. If they come to take you, there's nothing even Knispel here can do to stop them.'

Wohl's smile faded quickly as he stared out the carriage window, the rain sleeting against the glass.

The dismal conditions were also informing the thoughts of Hauptsturmführer von Schroif. Soon they would be back in Russia, and incidents like the one that had just occurred sapped at one's resolve. It was completely unnecessary, given the sacrifices they had already made, let alone those that were still to be made, but it did beg an uneasy and unwanted question.

'How many enemies were they actually fighting?'

Dimitri Korsak was a dedicated enemy. He was happy to be back in the vicinity of his native Leningrad. The city itself was under siege, but he was only ten kilometres from Mga. A big offensive was in the offing, and it hadn't been too difficult to arrange a transfer.

Arriving in the Volkhov front, it had proved predictably troublesome to obtain a KV-1, and he found himself having to have a few words with Moscow with regard to future requirements, but, for now, one tank was enough. His new crew was less than inspiring, and he had found it necessary to shoot his first driver. After all, no one wanted to go into action with a driver smelling of vodka.

Sergei Ovanovich, the new replacement, was well aware of the fate of the previous incumbent and was understandably nervous as Korsak began to outline the advantages of his favourite tank, known to the troops as the KV-1.

'As you know, comrades, twelve months of war have seen substantial changes in the design of tanks available to the Red Army. The best of these, you see here. It is the Klementi Voroshilov. You will notice that it has many fine features.'

Korsak began pointing out the advantages of the tank as he spoke.

'It has a good, high road-clearance. It can ford streams 2 metres deep. Its length of 6 metres permits it to span trenches 12 to 14 feet wide. Our comrades in the design teams have worked hard on this machine, and improvements have been made in the track plate, as well as in the method of interlinking them. There are no projections on the outside edges of the track plates on which snow or mud can become firmly lodged. You will notice that the tread of the track has a grid pattern which insures a firm grip in snow and mud, and reduces sideslipping. Thus, snow and mud cleats are not required.

'A new method of joining the track plates has been devised. Observe that each section or plate of the track has nine links, which are interlocked by a full-floating pin. See how the pin itself is held in position by small disks, or lock washers. These in turn are held in place by a spring collar fitting in a recess between each of the nine links of the plate. A broken track pin is thus prevented from working out of the links and causing the track to separate and thereby immobilise the tank ... ingenious.

'The contoured turret is cast in one piece and weighs approximately 10 tonnes. The frontal armour of the turret is 90 mm thick and, as I can assure you from long experience, it is exceptionally rugged and capable of withstanding sustained enemy fire. It can be revolved 360 degrees, either by power or by hand. These heavy steel bars you see are laid on edge and welded at the base of the turret to deflect shells which might cause it to jam.'

Korsak now turned his attention to the armament.

'Observe the 76 mm long-barrelled gun, and one 7.62 mm machine gun mounted coaxially. Do not overlook this weapon, as many targets do not require high-explosive. Machine gun bullets will do the job just as well. Conserving ammunition prolongs missions and aids the motherland in her hour of need. You will also note the forward 7.62 mm machine gun. As you know, there are two spare 7.62 mm guns as replacements for the turret or hull guns. Remember that one may be mounted on top of the turret for anti-aircraft fire, or even used on a tripod for dismounted action.

'My concern as commander is the fact that we carry only ninety rounds of armour-piercing and incendiary shells for the cannon. My preferred ratio is 40% armour-piercing, which the loader must ensure are carried at all times. We should also ensure that we have at least 4,000 rounds of machine gun ammunition in drums.'

Korsak now moved towards the rear of the vehicle, the crew following smartly in his wake and hanging on his every word.

'The Klementi Voroshlov is propelled by a 600-horsepower 12-cylinder V-type diesel engine. Unlike the fascists, it is driven through a transmission and final drive to the sprockets at the rear of the tank. The motor is noisier than I would like, but this serves to frighten the fascists. The tank is equipped with both electric and compressed air starters.

'The Klementi Voroshilov carries 600 litres of fuel inboard and can carry an additional supply in saddle tanks. Do not forget to fill the tank at every available opportunity. The normal range of action without saddle tanks is 110 to 125 miles across country.

'Our recent experience of tank warfare has taught the designers many lessons which have influenced this tank design. The turret is located well forward to permit desyanti tank infantrymen to use it as a shield while riding atop the tank. Every provision has been made to prevent unwelcome riders from getting aboard. You will note the lack of external fittings, tools, and sharp projections. You must keep it this way. This uncluttered surface meets the double purpose of eliminating hand grips for enemy hitchhikers and reducing the chance that a firebomb or other missile could lodge on the tank. Also observe that the fender of the tank is very narrow, so that 'tank hunters' who seek to jump aboard run the risk of being caught in the track. As a further protective measure for the tank crew, the hatch in the top of the turret is so constructed that it cannot be opened from the outside. A special tool is required to open the hatch from the inside. Do not, at any time, take it out of the tank, and do not lose it.'

Eventually, Sergei Ovanovich plucked up the courage to speak. 'Excuse me, Comrade Korsak, but I was trained on the T-34, and it appears to me that the T-34 is the equal of the KV-1.'

The other crew members stood back in terror, expecting a blast of rage from Korsak, but none came.

'That is an intelligent question, Comrade Ovanovich. The T-34 has indeed a high level of manoeuvrability, and a relatively spacious interior arrangement. It makes the tank a favourite of tank crews seeking comfort over fighting capability. The fascists themselves have expressed the opinion that the T-34 is the most effective tank they have encountered. It can surmount the same cross-country obstacles as the KV-1, except that its length limits the width of the trenches it can jump to about three metres.

'The turret is the problem. I can share with you the information that a bigger turret is in design. You will recall, Comrade Ovanovich, that your previous tank was manned by a crew of four. Your commander also acted as loader. When every second is vital, and watchfulness must be maintained at all times, this is an inefficient and dangerous arrangement. Until that design flaw is overcome, the KV-1 is the deadliest predator on the battlefield, and today, comrades, I shall teach you why. Let us begin.'

The crew piled back into the tank and, under Korsak's eagle eye, were soon pressing along the road to the front, his new driver responding swiftly to every command.

'Now pull off the highway and aim straight across country,' ordered Korsak.

'But, Comrade Korsak, it's swamp. We'll never get through.'

'Has anyone tried? Mother Russia demands courage in her hour of need. If you want to learn to fight with me, you have to learn what is possible. I know the hunter's route to the Leningrad main road. Every tank man should make it his business to learn what's possible. Our wide tracks will take us where the fascist machines cannot hope to go.'

To the amazement of the crew, the terrain did indeed prove passable, but the journey was not without its difficulties. Eventually, the KV-1 managed to reach the main Leningrad road, known to the Germans as the Rollbahn Nord, the only supply route of the German force located in the northern wilderness.

Korsak intended to blood his new crew and block that lifeline. He had chosen his spot with extreme care, the KV-1 emerging from the forest at the bottom of a natural dip, the Rollbahn Nord rising straight and true in either direction for a distance of 1,000 metres, which afforded a clear view in either direction.

To their left, at a distance of 700 metres, was a small wooden bridge. A column of trucks was waiting to cross. Through his binoculars, Korsak could see that papers were being checked. To their right, in the distance, Korsak could discern a column of ambulances, halted to allow the supply column heading north to pass. Hugging the tree line, Korsak ordered the font of the tank to be swung south to face the bridge. He was careful to maintain an angle so that the front of the tank did not face directly down the road. The rear and side of the tank was protected by the thick trunks of massive mature trees.

They now waited in tense silence. Soon, the first unsuspecting trucks began to cross the bridge. At last, Korsak gave the order to his anxious crew. 'Fire!'

A high-explosive round hurtled into the first truck, which immediately exploded in a violent eruption.

'Ammunition truck. Our lucky day!' exclaimed Korsak.

The rest of the column was soon shot afire by the accurate fire of the KV-1. The few escapees from truck crews were ruthlessly machine-gunned. By swivelling the turret,

Korsak was able to take the ambulances under fire, and he had no qualms in sending a stream of high-explosive shells crashing into the column.

As Korsak had expected, the noise of combat and the resulting explosions soon drew an infantry detachment. Korsak calmly directed his crew to engage the infantry with the machine guns. Without heavy weapons, there was simply no possibility of the infantry eliminating the monster. The infantry detachment blazed away at the KV-1, aiming for the vision ports.

Korsak ordered his crew to stop firing, as if the tank had been knocked out. Eventually his ruse worked and, assuming that the tank had been disabled, a landser ran at the tank, carrying a flaming bottle. Korsak calmly allowed him to approach, then cut him down in a flurry of machine gun bullets. The body provided an interesting diversion as it burned brightly, lit by its own Molotov cocktail.

Soon there was a long jam of vehicles stretching in either direction. Korsak knew it was impossible for the Germans to bypass his KV-1 because of the swampy surrounding terrain. Neither supplies nor ammunition could be brought up, and the severely wounded could not be removed to the hospital.

Korsak's crew felt they had achieved a

success, and were understandably anxious to leave the scene. Their none-too-subtle hints mounted, but their attitude changed as a Panzer III began to cross the bridge. They obviously felt themselves equal to the next attempt to put the KV-1 out of action. The Panzer III, returning to the front, now attempted to engage the KV-1 with its 50 mm cannon. Knowing he held all the aces, Korsak calmly allowed the Panzer III to close to a range of 600 metres.

'Do you want me to open fire, Comrade Korsak?' asked the gunner.

'No, let him come nearer.'

The Panzer III rumbled over the bridge and halted at 500 metres before opening fire and sending a stream of accurate armour-piercing rounds crashing against the steel hide of the KV-1. The Russian tank remained undamaged, in spite of the fact that the crew inside the KV-1 felt the impact of nineteen direct hits. Between shots, Korsak calmly dismounted and took his gunner on a tour of the impacts. The gunner was amazed, but gratified, to see that all of these violent strikes had merely produced blue spots on the impermeable armour of the KV-1.

To the terror of the gunner, Korsak did not allow him to climb back into the tank, but instead drew him aside, into the trees, where they watched as an armour-piercing round flew from the German tank, hit the sloped armour of the KV-1, and ricocheted sky-wards. Despite the violence of the impact and the shock wave which flooded over them, the gunner seemed to grow in confidence under Korsak's calming influence.

'Now you see why you should have confidence, comrade,' said Korsak.

'I understand, Comrade Korsak, but should we not destroy the fascist?'

'The time will come ... but we must first let our comrades see that there is nothing to fear.'

Each of the crew in turn was required to dismount and observe the effect of the German gunner's efforts. Eventually, Korsak decided that his men had learned the lesson that the KV-1 was a veritable fortress compared to the puny fascist tanks. At last he gave the order to fire, and the armour-piercing round which flew from the KV-1 blew the Panzer III apart. Its armour, at such a murderously short range, seemed to offer little more protection than the thin metal of the trucks which lay smoking on the Rollbahn Nord.

Eventually, common sense prevailed in the disorientated German forces, and, amidst a screen of leaves and branches, what was obviously a camouflaged 88 mm gun was trundled up towards the stationary tank.

To the terror of his crew, Korsak calmly permitted it to be put into position at a distance of 1,000 metres. 'Load with high-explosive. Fire when ready,' was his only command.

Growing in confidence in the presence of the icy Korsak, the KV-1 gunner took the proper time to allow for careful aim, and, with a single high-explosive round, smashed the gun to pieces before its crew was even ready to fire.

For the rest of the long summer's day, all was quiet. By cover of night came the anticipated attempt by German engineers to blow up the KV-1 by the light of the full moon. The crew watched in horror as Korsak allowed two German combat engineers to approach right up to the tank.

'Patience, comrades. They will require a far bigger charge to cause us discomfort... Have courage and learn.'

In the midst of their terrified silence, the crew could discern soft voices talking in German as the engineers laid the prescribed demolition charge on the caterpillar tracks.

The engineers sprinted for cover in the opposite ditch, and the charge exploded according to plan. To the surprise of the crew, a series of shots rang out from the trees opposite and the two German engineers slumped lifelessly to the ground.

'Ah, that must be our visitors,' said Korsak, opening his hatch. 'Come, comrades, let's meet our guests.'

As the bemused crew dismounted from the KV-1, they could see that the charge laid by the German engineers was insufficient for the oversized tracks. Pieces were broken off the tracks, but the tank remained mobile and could expect to make the journey home.

It was now that the crew was able to discern a series of shadowy figures in civilian clothing emerging from the trees opposite.

'Comrade Korsak? Everything OK?' came an inquisitive voice.

'Never better. Comrade Stankov, I presume?'

'The very same. We brought you some dinner.'

Boiled eggs and hard sausage were handed round, and Korsak's crew watched in amazement as Korsak and Stankov smoked and talked casually, as if they were in a Leningrad cafe.

'So, you are a new group?' asked Korsak.

'Yes, Comrade Korsak. It's our first mission.'

'Then you have done well – two fascists killed, and a significant contribution to our mission. I'll make it my business to ensure that Moscow gets to hear about this,' replied Korsak.

'Thank you, Comrade Korsak. Do you have any further orders for us?'

'You must act on your own initiative,

Comrade Stankov... but that bridge looks like a target which would be worthy of your next effort...'

'Consider it done, Comrade Korsak.'

'Good! I wish you success. Our work here is over, for now.'

To the delight of his crew, Korsak ordered the driver to start up the engine and follow their tracks back to the Russian lines. Soon the KV-1 was gone, and Stankov and his team quietly slipped back into the trees.

# CHAPTER 9

## WERK 3

The Henschel und Sonne engineering works at Kassel had begun as a locomotive manufacturing business, but had long since diversified into supporting the German war effort, and had played a key role in providing heavy armaments in both wars.

As the train pulled into the railhead, the weather had still not lifted, and it was not possible to fully appreciate the size of this massive operation. There were three huge complexes: Werk 1, which was devoted to locomotive work, the giant foundry which comprised Werk 2, and, finally, Werk 3, the panzer plant, to which they were now headed. It dominated the entire area.

The crew looked on in awe at the activity around them as they strode through the plant, led by Doctor Kurt Arnholdt and a group of other representatives of the Henschel Company. Amongst the party was the familiar figure of Major Jurgen Rondorf. As they passed a wall covered in propaganda posters, Otto Wohl paused before a yellowing placard for the Winter Relief Fund and began to read.

'No one will be allowed to go hungry!' screamed the poster.

'So, we're not even allowed to do that now!' said Wohl mischievously.

A glance from Knispel conveyed the message to Wohl that he was on thin ice, and the loader wisely decided that it was best if he didn't criticise Knispel's beloved party, for now at least.

Eventually the party came to a hospitality area where bottles of beer and wine were being opened by pretty waitresses. Glasses were soon filled all round.

'Gentlemen! My good friend, Major Rondorf here, tells me that the term 'flying colours' is too inadequate a description to describe your achievements in passing all the tests at Paderborn! Congratulations, and proscht!' exclaimed Kurt Arnholdt.

'Proscht!' bellowed the Tiger men, draining their glasses, and, by their body language, indicating that they would happily engage in a further toast.

'Major Rondorf is too kind and generous a man to admit to the extent of our daily struggles. He is also too modest to admit to his invaluable efforts at cajoling and educating us Tiger novices!' said Hans von Schroif.

'Come now, Hauptsturmführer,' replied Rondorf, 'it is you who are being too modest. Good teachers could not exist without willing and able pupils. How was your journey?'

Hans von Schroif could have elaborated on the unfortunate incident on the train, but he chose not to. Instead, he opted to be positive.

'The journey was slow, but it may yet prove invaluable, Herr Major. Wendorff here has hit upon an ingenious plan to create a new manual, which the Tiger men hope will be interesting and accessible... Without going into too much detail, it involves an 'assistant' who, we could say, troops at the front may find rather ... how shall we say ... "fetching".'

Major Rondorf accepted the new illustrated Tiger manual and, with Arnholdt looking on, began to flick through the pages with interest.

'My dear von Schroif, anything that helps our men memorise the vital information in that manual is to be welcomed,' said Arnholdt.

'Let's just hope your "assistant" is not so well drawn as to be distracting!' noted Major Jurgen. 'But this is a good idea. I'll pass it on to Guderian's office with a recommendation that it be published.'

'Thank you, Herr Major. The idea is that it should be small enough to fit into a battle dress pocket.'

'Rather the Tigerfibel than Die Wundertüte, eh, Wohl?' said Major Rondorf.

As they laughed and joked, the small group moved on to the first part of the factory. Thousands of workers found employment here. The all-pervasive hum and buzz, and the unremitting crash of metal upon metal, indicated an industry and effort which could only give comfort to those who served at the front. Places like these were indeed the engines which helped the German army move forward and on!

'Now I shall pass you over to Herr Arnholdt, who has arranged a brief tour of the facilities here, which will hopefully add to your appreciation and knowledge of the vehicles which are about to pass into your care.'

As Kurt Arnholdt led the group off to the giant doors at Werk 3 to begin their tour, Hans received a gentle dig in the ribs from Bobby, who motioned to another group of men some way off, one of whom was the very Heinrich Bremer that they had encountered only an hour ago on the train.

Hans fell into line beside Major Rendorf and discreetly enquired about the group.

'Our friends from RHSA,' replied Rendorf.

'But why are the Gestapo here?' asked von Schroif.

'It's a delicate matter, but there have been rumours of plans to sabotage production,' interjected Arnholdt.

'Sabotage?' replied von Schroif incredulously. 'Take them out and have them shot! What kind of German worker...? That's treason!'

'As I said,' continued Jurgen, 'it is a delicate matter, and not all the workers here are of good German stock and foundation. There is a shortage of labour. Production must be maintained. So, workers are drawn from what might be termed less 'patriotic' pools.'

'You mean you have foreign workers here? In the name of God, you are not telling me that Soviet prisoners have been entrusted with the job of building tanks which they know are being sent out to kill their comrades? That's insane!'

'Soviet prisoners, hopefully, I would doubt. I think the vast majority are from Germany, or our allies, but I fear – and this goes no further – that there may be a large measure of malcontents: social democrats, communists, religious extremists ... and the situation is not helped by their working conditions.'

Hans von Schroif was outraged. He had heard rumours of forced labour, but there was a war on, which allowed for a slight relaxation of civilised norms. There would be time enough for considerations of an ethical nature. It was the practical aspect that perturbed him the most at that moment. The lives of his men depended on these machines. At each and every moment, he and his crew had the right to expect that everything possible was being done to make them as reliable as possible. They had to trust every gear wheel, every weld, and every join. It reminded him of the old saying: 'Would you accept a meal served up by a bitter cook?'

'I can sense your anger, Hauptsturmführer. The situation is not ideal. Circumstances dictate. Let us just be confident that these arrangements do not end in tragedy.'

Kurt Arnholdt then called them together to commence the tour. He seemed full of pride, so von Schroif decided that it was best to put his concerns to one side and let Arnholdt take centre stage.

'Gentlemen, this is where the hulls arrive. We do not have the correct facilities here for construction of the hulls, or the turrets for that matter, so they are prefabricated at Krupp's and Dortmund-Hoerder Huettenverein, the turrets by Wegmann and Company, and delivered here to be precision-tooled and transformed into fighting machines worthy of the Wehrmacht. The assembly line consists of nine discrete stages which we refer to as takt. At the moment, each takt involves around six hours per tank – a time which we can hopefully reduce in order to meet, and exceed, our production targets.'

Kurt Arnholdt was in his element as he led the group along the line, pointing out all the functions and roles of the workers, the piles of stacked components, and the special tools and presses needed to assemble one single tank. Granted, he was having to shout to be heard over the din, but here was a man who had found a role he obviously relished!

'Takt 1, gentlemen. After taking delivery of the prefabricated hulls by rail, we carry out the great endeavour of unloading. As you can see by this hull here, there is almost everything still to do. Notice that the only post-fabrication work before it arrives is the boring of a few holes; everything else is carried out in these works.

'Next, we move on to takt 2, where we prepare the hulls by boring holes for the suspension arms. This is done by this six-spindle borer. The next stage of takt 2 is carried out by a four-spindle borer, which finishes the holes for the final drives and idler arms.'

Hans von Schroif found the whole thing fascinating, and was pleasantly surprised to see Bobby Junge paying close attention and engaging Arnholdt in conversation with intelligent and informed questions. Michael Knispel too, seemed transported. He also noticed Heinrich Bremer and his associates peering closely at the group and talking together. Surely they were not under scrutiny?

'Takt 3,' continued Arnholdt, 'is mainly concerned with fixing the turret, as you can determine by the presence of that lathe. Which leads us, gentlemen, out of this shop and on to the next where, and I am sure this is the part of the process which will interest young Herr Junge, the Maybach engine makes its first appearance!'

As they left takt 3 and headed on to takt 4, Hans turned round to check if they were still being followed by their friends from the Gestapo. Sure enough, the little gang was still on their trail.

'Shouldn't they be out catching traitors and subversives?' thought von Schroif.

Just then he saw one of the workers dart out of shop 3 and head diagonally across in front of them. Then he heard Otto Wohl call out. 'Herr Jensen! Herr Jensen!'

The man looked startled and, for a moment, embarrassed, as if for some reason he did not want to recognise Otto.

'Herr Jensen! It's me, Otto ... Otto Wohl!'

Finally the man turned and smiled and walked towards Wohl, but in a hurried, almost nervous, limping manner.

Otto then turned excitedly to von Schroif and said, 'Boss, this is Peter Jensen, my old art teacher. Any worth I have in drawing came from the encouragement of this one man!'

Otto's initial excitement paled as the man came closer. Otto recalled that he had once been a burly athletic type – they had played in the school football team together – but now he looked emaciated and haggard, a gaunt spectral reflection of the hale figure he had once been.

'What are you doing here?' asked Otto.

The man looked furtively about, as if assessing whether he could be truthful in his answer. Seeing the others walking off toward shop 4, he must have judged the company of Otto Wohl to be less threatening. He spoke with a whispering, halting voice.

'When the war broke out, because I was a Danish national, I was stripped of my papers and found myself to be stateless, unable to keep my job at our old school, or to find a new job. I was sent here. Conditions here are not good, Otto. I do not know how much longer I have left, or how much I can tell... but you are looking well. Hopefully, when this is all over, we may meet again. It is a great and natural talent you have. I have to go now, but please give me your word you will not tell anyone you have seen me like this. Forgive me.' And with that he was gone, leaving Otto pale and shocked.

Hans von Schroif knew that Otto's childhood had been less than stable, he even referred to him on occasion as 'the little urchin', but this man, this Peter Jensen, had perhaps been the sole guiding light in Otto's troubled younger years. It must be a cruel blow, seeing someone he had held in such high esteem so humbled and so broken.

On entering shop 4, Hans von Schroif struggled to regain full concentration, so affected had he been by Otto Wohl's encounter. It was terrible to observe someone so full of spirits having those bright feelings dashed. However, von Schroif was the only witness, and the tour of the factory was about to continue.

'To our engine, gentlemen, the Maybach HL 210,' announced Arnholdt, raising his arm and pointing at the twelve-cylinder behemoth that was being swung into place over the empty engine compartment by a giant overhead crane.

Through his left ear von Schroif could hear Bobby Junge exhale in wonderment, but then something else, another sound, something altogether more ominous, crept into his range of hearing. A tearing sound, tearing metal, and then the shout of the crane driver.

Von Schroif looked up and saw the engine list suddenly and hang for a moment. Without even thinking, he shouted, 'Look out!'

The huge engine came crashing down onto the side of the hull and careered off towards them, bouncing and skidding along the ground.

Hans picked himself up off the shop floor. To his great relief, he saw Bobby Junge, Michael Knispel, Karl Wendorff and Kurt Arnholdt all do the same – but where was Otto Wohl?'

'Oh no,' thought Hans, 'please God, no,' as he turned and looked in the direction of the now-stationary engine and saw blood spurting from underneath it. Then he heard the unmistakeable sound of Otto's voice.

'Boss! Boss! Help! Help! It's the major!'

The men rushed round the back of the engine and were greeted with a sight too awful to properly relay – poor Otto, on his knees, with blood running through his hands, cradling the crushed remains of Major Jurgen Rondorf.

Although von Schroif's first impression was that there was no possible help that could be directed at the situation, his instinct forced him to seek aid – a crane perhaps to lift the engine from the crushed body – and so he turned his eyes upward and just then saw the figure of a man, high up in the building, running behind the crane. Even at that distance, there was no mistaking the outline. It was Peter Jensen, the former art teacher, but, before he could assimilate this knowledge, he heard a barking voice from behind him.

'Halt! You there, halt!' It was Heinrich Bremer. 'Halt, or I will shoot!'

Peter Jensen did not heed the warning and carried on running. Hans heard the crack of a pistol shot, then another, and Otto's former mentor staggered, slumped, and fell from the roof, the only noise a crumpled thud as his body fell fifty metres onto a stack of ring gears before landing on the factory floor.

'No, No! You bastard! You murdering bastard!' shouted Otto Wohl.

Von Schroif immediately motioned to Knispel to restrain him. The former boxer struggled to hold Otto Wohl as the loader directed his rage at the Gestapo man.

Hans was operating in survival mode now. They had lost Major Rondorf. The last thing they wanted now was to lose Otto Wohl. What had happened here? Had the art teacher sabotaged the crane? Is that what he meant when he said to Otto, 'Forgive me'?

Hans felt the anger rise in himself too, but he didn't yet have the facts. If that bastard art teacher had sabotaged the crane, Hans would have willingly torn him limb from limb himself. But had he? And why? However, he understood Otto's rage, and the last thing he needed was for Wohl to get in trouble with – or even, God forbid, be shot by – some trigger-happy, faceless Gestapo man.

'Arrest that man!' Bremer shouted to his colleagues, who ran towards Otto, reaching for their guns.

'Wohl!' shouted von Schroif with all the force and authority he could muster. 'Leave this to me!'

This was crucial. If Otto Wohl heeded his plea, von Schroif was sure he could defuse this already-worsening situation. If not, and Wohl continued to struggle, then his life was in danger. There must be no escalation.

Fortunately, in one of those moments in which a soldier's absolute faith and trust in his commander can mean the difference between life and death, Wohl heeded the call and slowly stopped struggling.

Hans von Schroif immediately put himself between Otto Wohl and the onrushing Gestapo men.

'Halt!' he shouted. 'I am SS-Hauptsturmführer Hans von Schroif, of the Leibstandarte SS Adolf Hitler, veteran of the Freikorps, and holder of the Knights Cross. In the name of the Führer, I order you to halt.'

Hans's upright posture and the tone of his order quickly succeeded in stopping the Gestapo men in their tracks. Like all true underlings, they now adopted the only course possible; they looked back to their leader for guidance.

'SS-Hauptsturmführer, this matter is no concern of yours. My authority comes from the highest levels of the Reich Main Security Office. My quarrel is not with you, it is with that man there, SS-Schütze Otto Wohl,' shouted Bremer.

'Good,' thought von Schroif to himself, 'he is backing off. Now is the time to raise the stakes.'

'No concern of mine? I think you are badly mistaken. We are here on the direct orders of the Führer, to carry out a mission vital to the future of the Reich, and this man is pivotal to that task. But please, don't take my word for it.' Von Schroif turned to his driver. 'Junge, I want you to go with Doctor Arnholdt to make immediate contact with three men. One, Obergruppenführer Sepp Dietrich. Two, Albert Speer, Minister for Armaments. And three, the Führer himself.'

Hans then gave Bobby a look which, although powerful, was indecipherable, until he added: 'We are doing this for Elvira. Bring her here.' At that, Bobby and a still-shaken Kurt Arnholdt headed off to the rear entrance of shop 4.

Refusing to let up, Hans then continued his tirade against Bremer. The thing now was to hammer a wedge between Bremer and his men.

'If, as I suspect, there has been a mistake here, then, however unfortunate that mistake, there will be consequences. For all of you.'

'Good,' thought Hans. A quick look at the faces of Bremer's men revealed flickering glimpses of doubt and the crumbling of resolve.

Bremer, however, was not going to give up that easily.

'SS-Hauptsturmführer von Schroif, you were present when this man referred to the Führer in terms that are completely unrepeatable and seditious. Were you not?'

'Damn!' thought Hans to himself. 'He has me on the back foot. If I admit to this, his colleagues will be re-energised.' But von Schroif knew that excusing Otto's 'gangster' comment would only lead to the same outcome. He needed to try a different tack to buy time.

'Herr...?'

'Bremer, Heinrich Bremer.'

'Can I see your papers please?'

Two grown men were now reduced to sorting out their differences by displaying stupid bits of paper, but it was a request Bremer could not refuse. He flashed his credentials and pressed home his advantage.

'Answer the question please, SS-Hauptsturmführer.'

Hans von Schroif changed tack again and adopted the voice of reason. 'Of course I'll answer the question, but may I study your papers first, please?'

Bremer could not refuse that request. However, von Schroif knew that his stalling could only work for so long. 'Where was Junge?'

Bremer reluctantly showed von Schroif his papers. Hans took as much time as he could verifying them, but he couldn't take forever.

'Now, SS-Hauptsturmführer, answer the question.'

Then, just at the right time, Karl Wendorff intervened.

'I am SS-Panzeroberschütze Karl Wendorff. If your memory serves you correctly, I was also present when the alleged comment was made. I have known Otto Wohl for over ten years, I have fought side by side with him in some of the most vicious combat situations imaginable, and he has never been anything other than a loyal and patriotic German soldier.'

'I am SS-Hauptscharführer Michael Knispel. I have nothing to add to my comrade's comments, other than that they are entirely correct, and I am willing to stand by them with my honour and my life,' added Michael, stepping menacingly close to Bremer.

'Fine words,' answered Bremer. 'No less than one would expect from loyal comrades. However, the question remains. SS-Hauptsturmführer, you are a man of honour and you cannot lie. One final time, did you hear what your loader called our Führer?'

Hans knew he that could not lie, and that time was running out. 'Where on earth was Junge?' From the corner of his eye, he noticed a group of workers gathering behind Bremer. These men looked hungry, and angry, and had bitter retribution in their eyes.

Michael looked at Bremer and said quietly: 'I think we have a situation.'

However, Bremer refused to look behind him. He raised his gun and pointed it directly at von Schroif. The crowd was growing and continued to move quietly upon Bremer, who continued to fix his gaze on Hans von Schroif.

'This is your last chance, von Schroif. Tell the truth, or else.'

Then one of Bremer's men noticed one of the workers lunging at Bremer from behind with a tank road wheel above his head.

'Sir! Behind you!'

Bremer turned immediately and shot the worker through the face, igniting a tinderbox. The rest of the workers charged him and his men with whatever tool or component they had at hand.

Hans knew they could be next and that, outnumbered, they stood little chance against this crazed, blood-scenting mob. Just at that moment, out of nowhere, came the huge roar of a tank engine. Hans turned and saw a Tiger roar through the gates of shop 4. Here was Junge at last!

'Quick, into the tank!'

All four of them dashed for the safety of the Tiger 1, clambering up over its frontal armour and into the turret. Arnholdt fired some rounds to frighten off the baying crowd. From the commander's hatch, Hans could make out the pitiful sight of Heinrich Bremer being pulverised by a massive Tiger suspension arm, his bloodied hands outstretched, begging for help.

The small security garrison was running into the factory and shots were already being fired. The situation would soon be under control.

'Leave them, Junge. Reverse gear, and let's get out of here!'

Dimitri Korsak half-dozed as the KV-1 made its way back to the Russian lines. The full moon lighted their way and it was simply a matter of following the tracks they had left on their outward journey.

The marshy forests outside Leningrad had a marked influence on German strategy. Such roads and railroads as existed in the wilderness were not first-class. Moreover, a demolition which would be merely a nuisance on dry terrain would be disastrous in a region where any detour from a roadbed meant becoming hopelessly bogged down in bogs and swamps. The marshes could not be effectively penetrated by the narrow tracks of the fascist tanks and they were now safe from pursuit.

The German axis of advance was determined by the disposition of highways and railroads. The fascists had no tank capable of following in their wake. So, for once, Korsak could relax and allow his tired brain to taste the sleep it craved. As he dozed off, he took confidence from the fact that brave men like Boris Stankov were in these woods and marshes in considerable force, and were beginning to seriously harass the German flanks and rear.

The situation in the woods and marshy flanks could not be ignored. At every crossroad or junction, a German task force had to be constituted to cope with a possible Russian attack which, if neglected, might threaten the flank or cut off communications.

Korsak drifted off in satisfaction at the knowledge that the fascists were becoming irked by the cost of the operations, knowing that a full-scale battle had to be fought for each miserable forest village, which was tactically, operationally, and strategically worthless in the first instance, and a useless pile of charred wood and rubble when captured.

Hans von Schroif listened intently as a still-shaken Kurt Arnholdt paced up and down his office.

'Spies, saboteurs, shootings, executions, and the murder of four agents of the Gestapo... This does not look good, Hans. Where were our factory guards? What will Berlin make of our security arrangements? Production has been held up... This does us no favours at all...'

'There are various factors, some of which you have no control over, Herr Arnholdt. Major Rondorf told me of the labour shortages and the calibre of men now being forced to work for you. This does you no favours. Neither do the working conditions, which are obviously going to be a breeding ground for resentment. I understand your concerns.

'However, that does not take away from the magnificent work you and your team have done on this tank. It is my firm belief that this is where the final judgement shall fall. If this tank lives up to expectations, then I believe all other considerations will slowly fade. Trust me, once good German crews get their hands on this wonderful Tiger, Ivan will not know what has hit him, and there will be dancing in the halls and corridors of the Reichschancellery!'

'I hope you are right, Hans! And there is no better crew to show the world, and particularly Ivan, what this machine can do! Speaking of crews, how is your loader, Herr Wohl? Has he been adversely affected by events?'

'SS-Schutze Wohl reacted as he does. It was a visceral reaction, there is not a political bone in his body. All he saw was a favoured old teacher, he was not aware of any political changes his old teacher may have undergone, but I would be loath to lose him. In fact, I would go so far as to suggest that eventuality might fatally undermine our combat effectiveness... and on this matter, if I may, I would appreciate any discretion you could afford. You know how sometimes a man's name can appear on a bit of paper, then another, then an investigation... It can take up valuable time.'

'Indeed. In fact, I shall make you a deal,' replied Kurt, slapping Hans heartily on the shoulder. 'My recollection is already a bit vague, but if you make over fifty kills in Rostov in this new tank, I will completely wipe this entire incident from my memory!' Both men laughed nervously.

Hans said his goodbyes and left Kurt's office. As he was walking out into the dim evening, he couldn't help but remember the Danish art teacher. At first impression, he did not seem a bad sort. In fact, Otto had attested to his previous character, and there was still no absolute proof that he had in fact sabotaged the crane. But, if he had, what would drive a man to embark on such a hateful and reckless course of action?

Walter Lehmann was furious.

'Damn Bremer! If he hadn't been so trigger-happy, he might just have been able to throw a spanner in the works. Maybe I should have sent someone a little less zealous, a little less than a true believer,' thought Walter Lehmann to himself.

But then people like Bremer provided excellent cover. Anyway, Bremer was dead now. Lehmann thought he'd better just leave it like that. No point in stirring things up. The less his fingerprints were found on any of these investigations the better. Fingerprints could be linked to patterns, and patterns to motives.

Walter Lehmann had been an active Soviet agent for over ten years now, and this was one of the secrets of his success. Remove yourself from the scene of the crime. He had sent Bremer to investigate Otto Wohl, but there had been no paperwork, until now.

256

This would be the report.

'Bremer was acting on a tip-off about a communist art teacher who may have been selling information to the Russians. Bremer confronted him. The spy ran. Bremer shot him, and was then turned on by an angry criminal mob. Died a hero. Case closed.'

Time to move on...

Lehmann returned to shuffling through the day's paperwork on his desk. Routine, routine, routine... But then one report caught his eye. A Soviet agent in custody in the cells. Red Orchestra. Walter Lehmann's mind started putting pieces together.

The walk from Prinz-Albert Strasse to the holding cells was pleasant, all the more so because Walter Lehmann took the time to sit in his favourite cafe, before buying a bottle of an expensive Asbach Uralt. Then, looking for all the world as if he was on a Sunday afternoon stroll, Walter Lehmann walked smartly into the corridor and asked one of the guards if he could possibly spend some time with Dieter Kleimer, in charge of the cell block. Making the visit look as accidental as he possibly could, of course...

'Kleimer! How are you, you old dog!' exclaimed Lehmann on meeting his old Gestapo colleague.

'Walter! The sun has just burst through the clouds! How the devil are you?' replied Kleimer.

'Just passing, on my way to Joseph and Anna's – one of the children's birthdays – had this fine bottle of brandy in my hands and thought you might want to share a glass!'

'Well, funny you should say that, because I have this box of excellent cigars liberated from a communist, and I was just wondering when on earth I was ever going to get a chance to acquaint myself with their glorious flavour,' replied Dieter Kleimer, pulling up a seat for his old friend and opening a cabinet which housed his favourite cigars.

The two men exchanged pleasantries, each asking about the other's wives and children and sharing stories of old acquaintances, before Dieter Kleimer asked about Lehmann's new position.

'We are doing good work, my old friend. Just yesterday we disrupted a Soviet spying operation at one of our largest engineering works. Unfortunately, we lost four men, but the value to the Reich is immeasurable.'

'Quite,' replied Kleimer admiringly.

'Most of these Soviet attempts at espionage are clumsy, as you would expect from such an inferior race, but there is one group who are proving a little more stubborn. This damn Red Orchestra. I don't know if you have heard of them.'

'Funny you should mention that, my dear Walter. We may have one in our cells just now. In fact, I sent over a report this morning.'

'Well, I have not seen it... Damn secretaries!' said Lehmann, feigning anger.

'You hire your secretaries according to looks and not ability, my old friend!'

'Yes, that is something in need of a proper revision ... but maybe not immediately!' laughed Lehmann. 'So, who is this suspect?'

'Maria Himpel. She works as a secretary for a Swiss textile company. Our informant tells us that she may have links to the Rote Kapelle.'

'Interesting,' replied Lehmann, his demeanour taking on a more serious hue. 'Has she revealed anything yet?'

'We are having trouble breaking her...' replied Kleimer.

'Give me five minutes,' said Lehmann, with more than a hint of menace, 'but first, let me see her records.'

Soon after perusing her records, Walter Lehmann found himself alone in a cell with Maria Himpel.

# CHAPTER 10

## SSYMS

The railhead at Kassel was a clanking bustle of tracks and marshalling yards. At this rate, they would have little chance to sleep before meeting up with the crews of the other four Tigers, loading, and heading back to Rostov. The new SSyms carriages were here on time, and the Tigers appeared ready to go.

'Change the tracks? Why the hell do we need to do that?' shouted Otto Wohl above the noisy din.

'They are too wide for transport by train,' replied Bobby Junge.

'Surely they should have thought of that before they built them! Do these designers never leave their stuffy little offices? Did they think we were to drive them to the front line?'

'Changing the tracks should only take twenty minutes ... there are other procedures ... but you've seen the size of this thing!'

'Hmmph ... Elvira needs to go on a diet, if you ask me...' grumped Otto Wohl. 'So, where are the transport tracks?'

'They were supposed to come direct from the factory...' said Junge.

The implication began to sink in.

'Look, can't we just load with these?' said Wohl.

'No, not if you don't want to be in a train crash!'

'Oh well,' said Wohl, taking out a cigarette. 'Time for a break then.'


'She was prepared to talk,' said Lehmann to Kleimer, as they walked the long dark corridor back to the front gate. 'Interesting intelligence. Apparently, there is a massive build-up of Red armour near Leningrad.'

'That was quite impressive in such a short time,' replied Kleimer. 'What did you say to her?'

'Trade secret, Herr Kleimer ... but you will call me next time you have a potential informant of the same type. Please send a full report – to me personally this time – when you have her statement.'

'Of course ... and what shall we do with her?'

'Well, bury her of course...'

Kleimer looked puzzled.

'Unfortunately, she didn't survive the interrogation ... but we did get the information we needed. These are the kind of small mercies her God might smile upon. Heil Hitler.'

Walter Lehmann then turned and walked out into the bright sunshine of a late afternoon Berlin summer day.

'The brandy did not come cheap,' he thought to himself, 'but i.G. Borgmann now has a second source of information about Leningrad to relate to Hitler. She talks, she dies. Fingerprints, fingerprints, it's all about fingerprints...'

Lehmann pulled his leather gloves over his chubby, lily-white fingers and strode off back to the office, perhaps stopping at another cafe on the way...

The infuriating business of changing tracks was a new experience for everyone. No one appeared to have thought things through. The tanks were fitted with cross-country tracks when they should have been fitted with transport tracks, but where were they?

Then, through the incessant noise, smoke, steam and arc lights, there was a knock at the door. Hans answered it to reveal the immaculately dressed figure of SS-Sturmbannführer Heinz Egger.

'Ah! Von Schroif. I presume you and your men are in a state of readiness for the ardours of embarkation in the morning.'

'Indeed, sir,' replied Hans. 'However, you have that look about you that suggests there is a change of plan. Don't tell me the train has been delayed.'

'No such luck, SS-Hauptsturmführer. But you are right about the change of plan.

Departure has been brought forward from 12.00 hours tomorrow to 05.00 hours today. You had better get your men ready. I'm afraid that is not all. We've had a change in orders. We are not going to Rostov anymore. We are going to Leningrad.'

'Leningrad? Why Leningrad? That isn't proper tank country,' thought Hans to himself. He'd spoken to other commanders – it was a tank trap, a marshy swamp. Nothing at all like Rostov or Kerch – now that was tank country. But it was more than that. This new tank... Well, it might be unfair to call it a prototype, but it was certainly untested in anything resembling a theatre of war. What about the weight? The turret? The transmission? Paderborn was one thing; Leningrad was going to be an entirely different matter.

Still, in moments like these, all a soldier had left was trust. Trust that his commanders knew what they were doing. Trust in his crew. Trust in this new Tiger.

Before departing for the front, the Tiger men were to meet the mechanic who would not only accompany them on the journey, but offer invaluable advice on the art of entraining.

'Gentlemen,' announced von Schroif, 'I am sure you will be delighted to once again meet SS-Hauptscharführer Rubbal.'

The men were delighted. Some strings

had obviously been pulled. Rubbal was the best engineer any of them knew, and it was an obvious mark of the importance of the entire Tiger project that he had been spared from his work at the front.

'I have convened this briefing to illuminate you on the vital subject of logistics, particularly the science of moving these new tanks from one sector of the front to another. You could drive the tank to its objective, of course, but that would wear and damage the equipment, wasting unnecessary time for repair and maintenance – all this before you actually engage the enemy. Needless to say, transport by train is also faster. Now, of course, it is also possible to facilitate movement by sea. We have already done trials proving we can more or less drive the new Tiger into a ship's hold or, if necessary, hoist it by crane, but this will not be the subject of today's talk. Today, we shall stick to one of Moltke the Elder's axioms – that military operations will suffer if the railhead is more than 100 km from the front. To explain your own role in all of this to you, I am delighted to have Hauptscharführer Rubbal.'

The ageing Hauptscharführer now prepared to speak. Out of the corner of his eye, he noticed Otto yawn.

'I am sorry if there is some duplication here. You, as experienced tankers, know many of these principles. So, I have prepared some notes for you on the new procedures of training and detraining that are specific to this new tank, the Tiger. Now, as SS-Panzer-schütze Wohl will understand, the key aspect of this is changing the tracks so as to avoid collision with trains passing in the opposite direction. There are also other consider-ations.

'SS-Hauptsturmführer von Schroif, it will be your responsibility to request from HQ whatever transport assets are required, transportation tracks and the like. It is foreseen – but who ever foresaw anything in war? – that the equipment for loading – ramps, tie-down chains, spars, camouflage, and straw – will be carried on the loader cars themselves.

'Now, camouflage – protection from aerial observation – I cannot put too high a value on this. Therefore, you will load the Tiger tonight, as if this operation were taking place at the front. As you probably know already, loading should always take place at night. So, again, this will be good practice. The objective will be to keep loading times to an absolute minimum.

'SS-Hauptsturmführer von Schroif, as was customary with the Panzer IV, you shall personally guide your driver onto the loading wagon and supervise the tie-down. This is to be rechecked at every halt. This being the end of August, there should be no need for covering the tanks with tarpaulin, but, for secrecy, this will be the order of the day. Again, as with the Mark IVs, keep your eye out for overhead wires, keep your head out of the turret, take down your antennae, and close any weapons or optics openings.

'Now, at the risk of re-emphasising what you already know – but is not repetition your friend and not your enemy? – entraining is easiest if attempted on a straight piece of line. Then you can line up all five Tigers and drive straight on. As you well know, loading from the side is not a desirable procedure. Load distribution is the responsibility of the Ladermeister. In your case, it will be one tank per wagon, with other goods carried on each intervening wagon.

'Tie-downs are effected by crossing and tightening the wire ropes. When all five Tigers are in place, the recovery vehicle can take its place. Now, I can tell that you gentlemen cannot wait to get out into the clear evening air and prepare for this relatively simple operation, so I shall finish with two pieces of vital information, one good and one bad.

'The good news is that you will be travelling with a complete support crew, including, I am happy to announce, a tailor. The bad news is that the Feldeisenbahnkommando, since the inception of the 'Otto' programme, is sending nearly 220 trains east every single day, thereby resulting in a chronic shortage of rolling stock. Therefore, we are limited in the amount of passenger cars available. You will have to travel by the scenic route – inside the lovely machine. You may need that tailor after all: Good luck, gentlemen, and I shall-see you in Mga.'

The crew pressed SS-Hauptscharführer Rubbal with further questions, each aware how little time they had left before loading.

'What exactly is the Otto programme?' asked Otto Wohl as they returned to their quarters. 'Is it something along the lines of out, back in time for Christmas and an evening out with the lovely Elvira?'

'Not quite,' replied Michael, 'it's a DR initiative to double the German rail network capacity in the east.'

'Damn,' replied Otto, 'looks like Elvira will have to kick her heels a while yet.'

'SS-Panzerschütze Wohl,' interjected Wendorff, 'you do realise that in some quarters that last comment could be described as defeatist?'

A wry smile appeared on the loader's face.

The arriving train passed slowly, its passenger cars first, followed by the flat SSyms wagons. These were interspersed with normal railcars to ensure that the weight of the machines was spread evenly along the length of the train, as bridges were not certain to take the weight of the Tigers. In order to avoid the possibility of a collapse, great care had to be taken when loading.

Hans von Schroif had done his homework. He was keen to compete against the other crews to see who could load their Tiger the fastest. This was healthy competition; the kind of sport that could save lives one day.

The Ladermeister called forth the first of the crews, in readiness for the platform truck being shunted up to the ramp. Once secured, the loading vehicle towed the narrow transport tracks off the wagon and positioned them in parallel on the ground. The first Tiger crew then removed one of their tank's wide tracks and drove the tank onto one of the thinner, transport tracks. Using the sprocket hub as a capstan, they then hauled the upper run of the track into position using a wire rope.

While this was being done, Hans watched, whilst timing, the second part of the operation – removing the Tigers other wide track and running the bogies over the remaining transport track.

'So far so good,' thought Hans, 'but we can definitely go faster than that.' He did wince slightly though when he cast his mind forward to a time when this methodical operation might have to be carried out in the howling, freezing waste of the Russian Steppe, in a blizzard – and under fire...

He was then woken from this nightmare

vision by a pink flash off to his right. 'Must be a firework. Was there some sort of local celebration tonight?' He dismissed trying to remember being told of such a thing and returned to concentrating on the loading of the first Tiger, paying renewed attention as the crew took off the four outside bogies and waited for the half-track to tow the original, wider tracks to the front of the ramp. In such a position, the newly-tracked Tiger could drive over its old tracks, then carry them underneath by means of two wire ropes which were connected to the two lifting eyes. She was then driven onto the wagon, trailing her old tracks. Finally, once in the correct position, the trailing ends of the original, broader tracks were lifted by wires and pulleys, up and over the rear armour, and it was time for the next tank.

'Quite ingenious and straightforward,' thought Hans to himself, 'but surely we can get the time down to under twenty minutes!'

He then looked at the Ladermeister and listened for the next set of instructions, but was immediately distracted by another pink glow off behind the Ladermeister – and then it struck him. These weren't fireworks, these were flares, flares from British pathfinders! And then, if he needed confirmation, he was given it – the rising and then falling wail of the air raid sirens.

'How far behind were the bombers? And

what was their target?' Hans had little doubt. 'The Henschel Engineering Works. We have to get these tanks loaded!'

Hans looked across at the Ladermeister, who seemed to be in a state of confusion. Then came a huge explosion as a British bomb went off, the percussive wave crashing against the train and crews and throwing everyone to the ground.

Dusting himself off, Hans jumped to his feet and made a quick calculation. 'If it was a wayward bomb, they still had time to load the tanks and pull out. But what would they be pulling out into? Would they be closer to, or further from, danger? If it wasn't a wayward bomb, but just the first of the load, then they were all dead anyway.'

So, the conclusion he came to was this: 'Load the tanks as quickly as possible, and then make an assessment as to the risks, based on any information at the time.'

However, given all that, he knew, as every commander does, that the decision to release the train was not his to make. All that he knew was that they had to get these Tigers to the front.

'Ladermeister,' he shouted at the still prone Ladermeister, shouting again until he realised that he was shouting at a headless corpse. The poor fellow had been decapitated, probably by flying shrapnel.

Hans quickly took command. 'SS-Panzerschütze,' he shouted at Otto Wohl, 'inform all crews that normal loading will take too long. Every tank must simultaneously load from the side. Crews are to immediately locate material with which to build ramps!'

Otto acknowledged that he had understood the order and ran to pass it on. Hans then turned to the remaining members of his crew.

'Stones, earth, wood, straw, anything! Let's get this ramp built!'

Then the first real wave of bombs started to land, tearing up the earth in a deafening cluster of explosions off towards the Henschel works. The crew gathered whatever came to hand and packed it down against the side of the wagon. Otto Wohl returned to help. Hans von Schroif looked down the line and could see all the crews feverishly collecting material for their own ramps.

Hans knew that this approach was fraught with danger, requiring great manoeuvring skill from each driver, the ever-present possibility that, if the procedure was not carried out properly, the weight of the tank could tip the entire wagon over and end in disaster. 'Should he order the wagons to be uncoupled? It would take a bit longer, but... Yes, he had to, the alternative was far too risky.'

Again he called Otto over and instructed him to tell all crews to decouple their wagons, make good on the ramps – would they all hold? – and then, starting with their own Tiger, have the drivers drive the tanks up and on, spin them round into position, tie them down, and then recouple. Otto Wohl could barely hear the shouted order as the intensity of the bombing increased, the ground shook further, and a violent and unnatural gale threw dust and debris all around.

As Otto went off, Hans decided that it would be useless in this maelstrom to issue any kind of spoken order to Bobby Junge, so he motioned with his hands for the driver to prepare the tank for embarkation. He then motioned to Karl to help him uncouple the wagon. On finishing, he motioned Bobby forward, the great iron titan straining and pulling as it rode over the first incline of the ramp, the front hull lifting.

'Just keep on lifting,' prayed Hans von Schroif. 'If the ramp collapsed now, God knows how long this would take...'

Looking down the line, Hans could see the next four Tigers, all with their engines running, all slowly approaching their own ramps. Then back to Bobby. Hans was on the wagon now, guiding, he could feel the wagon tilting under him, the weight on one side pulling it down. It was all up to the driver now, all driver skill. Open her up, up, open her up more, and then ... crash! The front of the tank came down on the wagon and Bobby engineered a turn on a pfennig to bring her round and into place!

Hans then coupled up the car and went to oversee the rest of the operation. So far, so good, the next tank on safely, then the third, then the fourth. Just the final Tiger to go, followed by the towing vehicle.

Hans was then distracted by a series of explosions at the engineering works, huge explosions which sent flame and twisted metal high into the night sky. Hans couldn't help thinking of the poor souls – was Kurt safe? – trapped inside the inferno. 'These damn British! What kind of people were they? The Tommy soldiers had a good reputation, but these airmen?'

Hans felt hatred swell up inside of him. He was running pictures through his mind of what he would do if he ever got his hands on one of the terrorists when he heard a familiar jolt next to him. The train was starting to move! His first reaction was to shout, but there was no one to hear him. The engine was too far away.

Then he shot his gaze back to the last Tiger, just rearing up, when a backward jolt on the uncoupled wagon nudged it back – certainly not far – but enough to disturb the recently-built ramp, which collapsed just as the front of the tank was about to drive onto the wagon.

'Look out!' von Schroif screamed at one of the tank's crew who was standing next to the ramp, but his voice was lost and too late.

The tank fell, its massive weight pressing down on the long wagon, which flipped up and turned in the air, landing on a screaming crew member. There was nothing that could be done. He shouted and waved frantically to the rest of the crews to get on the slowly moving train before it pulled away.

Hans looked out over the grim scene – explosions and fires, the wail of sirens, the screams of the wounded and dying, and the sickening sight of the flailing arms of a man caught under a rail wagon from the waist down, the last frantic automatic movements of a man who, if there was any mercy in this world, would hopefully be dead already.

Von Schroif had to look away, not because of any squeamishness on his part, God knows he had seen worse, but because of a deep malaise that sickened his soul. He had killed many men, been responsible for the deaths of many men, but they were all sworn foes, enemies... It was always different when it was one of your own.

He hadn't personally killed the poor bastard, but it was his responsibility. He had given the order to side-load the tanks and, as it turned out, that was premature. No more bombs had landed near the train. Yes, the driver had pulled out without warning, but that could have been rectified.

Hans knew where he was headed – a dark slough of despair where no light ever shone. There might be justifications and excuses that the mind could throw up to help alleviate this sickness, but honest despair overruled them all. He had killed that tanker just as surely as if he'd hurled down the wagon with his own bare hands ... and this knowledge cut him to his very soul...

'Should I take the credit?' asked Walter Lehmann of himself. 'What a stroke of luck! One Tiger left behind and, probably more importantly, no towing vehicle! Yes, why not? It would make his negotiating position with the Soviets even stronger. How many more Swiss francs did he need? Well, there were certain necessities a man could not do without, and there were contingencies and plans for the future which needed certain amounts of capital.'

Then he thought again. The objective was simple: to capture a Tiger. The plans he had the art teacher steal from the factory would help, but would not have the same value as one of the beasts falling into the hands of Soviet engineers. The more tanks that got to the front, the more chance of capturing one intact. So perhaps he had better word the transmission carefully. How about...

'Guests arrive Mga. 0800 hrs 29th. One

guest has food poisoning. Will miss meal.'

The journey to Mga, the railhead to the east of Leningrad, was not ideal, certainly not cooped up in a tank on a train in the middle of a blazing hot August, but essential camaraderie would see them through, as it always had. Otto Wohl would cut hair and tell jokes. Bobby Junge, as was the custom with drivers, would be allowed to sleep as much as possible. Michael Knispel would regale the rest of the crew with useful and informative titbits, like the differences between German and Soviet rail gauges. Karl, as usual, was quiet, listening in on any radio traffic. Who knows what went through his mind. Perhaps he was listening to opera?

'This is it.' Hans von Schroif thought to himself. 'This was not why men went to war, but how men survived war.' In that moment, von Schroif realised that, amidst all the privation, the pain and the suffering, it wasn't the cause or the ideal, and certainly not the glory, which made it bearable. It was the unit, the platoon, the crew. These other men in this tank, these friends. When all was said and done, they were the reason why he would see this through to the end.

It was nearing dusk. With Wohl, Junge and Knispel asleep, von Schroif was about to shut his eyes when Wendorff motioned that he wanted to talk, in private. Hans von

Schroif agreed. Screened by the gathering darkness, the two men ventured out of the turret and walked to the front of the tank. This, of course, went against all the rules for rail travel, but Hans von Schroif knew there was little chance of the two men being seen.

'SS-Hauptsturmführer, there was an incident back in Rostov, the day we faced the KV-1. I did not mention it at the time, as I felt I needed more information before divulging it to you,' said Karl as Hans listened intently.

'Continue, SS-Panzeroberschütze,' replied Hans.

'As we were travelling along the road, just before the mine and the Russian attack, I received a signal, not one which I could readily understand or decode. It seemed to me to be significant, so I memorised it and then wrote it down. However, even after considerable research, revisiting my old study papers and the like, its meaning or even origin eluded me. Then, when we were in Paderborn, I took the opportunity to make a request to my old professor, who was kind enough to enlighten me in my search.'

'And...?' asked von Schroif.

'PNKTI.EH.SFTVOCE, transmitted by key. I thought I was dealing with something sophisticated, perhaps in Italian or one of the Swiss dialects, even one of the Russian languages, but I overcomplicated things. It's actually a very simple code, and the message is in German. It's not one of ours. It's simply the alphabet reversed, with roman numerals for numbers. Once decoded, it gives an attack target. Kmpgr.vS.hugelXV. It means Kampfgruppe von Schroif, Hill 15. Our unit designation and the objective... If you recall, Hill 15 was the objective.'

Hans von Schroif looked out over the Polish countryside as they sped towards the Russian border, quite unable to take in the ramifications of what he had just heard.

'There is more, sir...'

'Go on.'

'After we did the brief inspection before leaving Berlin, I picked up a message in the exact same code language. The signal was fainter, but it's essence just as disturbing. It detailed the exact time of our arrival at Mga. I think someone may be expecting us.'

Commander Kirill Meretskov studied the man who stood before him. So this was the infamous Dimitri Korsak, the man also known as the Steppe Fox, or to the Nazis as 'Der Weisse Teufel'. Meretskov knew of his reputation, and could have used him in the Sinyavino Offensive, but Moscow had decreed otherwise. There was no intimation as to what Moscow required of this man, only that he, Kirill Meretskov, Commander of the Volkhov front and the victor of Tikhvin, was to do everything in his power to help this tank commander, this Dimitri Korsak.

This rankled him. Was he not trusted by Moscow? This had echoes of his arrest by the NKVD in 1941, but he quickly suppressed those memories. Stalin, after all, had spared him. But why the secrecy? This thing had Beria's fingerprints all over it.

Dimitri Korsak could sense Meretskov's unease, which in turn gave him confidence in the importance of the task he had been assigned.

'So my requests will be met in full?' asked Korsak, the suspicion showing through in his voice.

'Impudent bastard,' thought Meretskov, but he knew now never to interfere with his superiors. 'Anything you require will be made available to you.'

At which Korsak saluted and left. 'Now,' he thought, remembering Rostov, 'it is time for unfinished business...'

The station at Mga was a throng of troops, trains and equipment. The detraining had passed without incident, apart from the obvious excited interest of everyone who had cast eyes on the new Tigers. When they had pulled back the tarpaulins it had been like the unveiling of a great work of art! This was no art gallery though, because the noise of not-so-distant artillery exchanges indicated that either they were not far from the front, or they had just arrived in the middle of a major offensive. In fact, both were true.

On the previous day, the Volkhov Front offensive had started, and Ivan had punched a 3 km hole in the German line. Catching the Germans by surprise, the Russian 8th Army had enjoyed initial success. Army Group North had been preparing for its own offensive, the Nordlicht Offensive, aimed at breaking Leningrad's spirit once and for all. Army Group North, however, had rallied, and the newly-arrived 170th Infantry Division, many of whom were still at Mga, had helped shore up positions, along with the redeployment of the 5th Mountain and 28th Light Infantry.

For his part, Otto Wohl was itching to get into a fight, and kept asking every five minutes if they had their orders yet. Hans von Schroif was a bit more circumspect. He was to rendezvous with Major List from the army. He was pleased that someone else would take the lead, with responsibility for the Kampfgruppe, and leave him to command his tanks. The sheer scale of the troop movements around the railhead was daunting. 'How many trains were arriving and leaving?'

Hans noticed a tall figure striding toward him, a figure who bore all the hallmarks of a man who knew his mission.

'Good morning! Hauptsturmführer von

Schroif, I presume. Welcome to Army Group North,' said the tall officer, giving the regular army salute. 'I can't tell you how pleased I am, not only to meet you, but to get acquainted with those magnificent new machines of yours.'

Instinctively, von Schroif clicked his heels and gave the German greeting. 'Heil Hitler! SS-Hauptsturmführer von Schroif, reporting for duty, sir!'

'Yes, yes, that's all very good,' continued the officer. 'Sorry, I forgot to introduce myself... Major List.'

'Despite his obvious lack of enthusiasm for the National Socialist cause, List seems an agreeable fellow,' thought von Schroif. The kind of man one could have confidence in. He would not have been selected otherwise. The feeling of confidence deepened as the new orders were quickly outlined by List.

They seemed straightforward. Join Kampfgruppe List at Mga, then drive north to the assembly and supply point. From there, the four Tigers were to take part in an attack on the southern flank of the Soviet advance. With simultaneous attacks from the north and centre, it was hoped to nip the Soviet attack in the bud. The Führer expected hourly updates on their progress and was informally reported to be 'on thorns' to hear how the Tigers performed in their first combat.

'So, all we have to do is single-handedly conquer Leningrad, and then on Tuesday we can turn our attention to Moscow, Herr Hauptsturmführer.' Von Schroif made no immediate reply, and List continued. 'Then, finally, on Friday, we head south to Georgia and decapitate the monster in his lair.'

List spoke with a tone not so much of irony, but from the viewpoint of a battle-hardened veteran who had long given up notions of the strategically grandiose. In this, he shared an opinion with many who, since Barbarossa, over a year ago, had come to the opinion that, however brightly it had started, this war was going to go the course and be fought river by river, hill by hill, and inch by bloody inch.

'I'm sorry to correct you, Herr Major, but we do not use the term Herr in the Waffen SS.'

'I stand corrected, Herr Haupsturmführer, but let's leave the politics aside and fight the Russians first, eh?' Even von Schroif had to smile.

List continued. 'As instructed, we have carried out a thorough reconnaissance of the route to the front, including checking every bridge for its ability to bear a com-bined vehicle weight of sixty tonnes.'

'Sorry to have to correct you again, sir, but it's not combined weight ... it's individual weight.'

'A single vehicle?' came the surprised response from Major List.

'That's right, sir. I suggest it might be best if we check the route again. We don't want any bridges collapsing on us.'

'Of course not. I'll get the Kübelwagen ready. We can go together and get to know each other.'

As the Kübelwagen carrying von Schroif and List travelled across the wooded and undulating terrain of the rollbahn, the two men began to realise that, politics apart, the other was not such a bad egg after all. After what seemed, to von Schroif anyway, a wary, start, they gradually relaxed and began to enjoy each other's company.

As experienced East Front veterans, they kept an eye open for anything untoward. Fortunately, there were few bridges, and the dry weather meant there were no culverts or water courses to concern them.

'The next bridge is about five kilometres ahead. It was just past there that we had the business with the White Devil in the KV-1 ,' offered List.

'Are you sure, sir?' replied von Schroif.

'Sure as can be. I lost two of my best combat engineers...'

'It's just that I thought he was on the southern sector. I have had brushes with him in the past.'

'Well, if you have any old scores to settle,

now's your chance. I'll show you where the bastard destroyed an ambulance column ... 500 wounded ... burned alive ... what a way to go. Horrible.'

'There are scores to settle alright, but how did he get onto the main rollbahn?'

'Came across country, though God knows how... Ours just bog down in these confounded swamps.'

This far behind the lines, there was no sign of danger. The dappled light of the sun streamed through the tree-lined route, and life seemed almost pleasant.

The brief idyll came to a crashing halt as they rounded a bend and began a long decline leading to a short wooden bridge spanning a narrow river. As they approached the bridge, the fact that there were no guards instantly alerted both men. Vital river crossings were guarded by platoon strength, but even small spans, however easily replaceable, should have at least a squad. This bridge had no one on guard.

As they approached, List slowed the Kübelwagen down, and von Schroif spotted the sight the men dreaded. Four field-grey figures lay sprawled in grotesque attitudes on the roadside. The terrifying conclusion was obvious and, for two Eastern Front veterans, it did not need verbalising – partisans!

Fortunately for von Schroif and List, Boris Stankov and his men were comparative novices. Emboldened by their first success, the previous night, they had slavishly followed Korsak's suggestion and had wasted no time. They had little difficulty in overcoming the unsuspecting bridge guards, but there had been too little time to plan and organise. The simple fact was that no one in all eighteen members of Stankov's unit knew for certain how to wire a bridge for destruction.

The equipment had been air-dropped and retrieved alright, but now all the men were gathered under the bridge, attempting to help wire the last of the explosives, or to provide advice on how best to do it. A great deal of advice, not all of it useful, was being given. Suggestions and helpful hints mixed with Stankov's urgent commands conspired to conceal the arrival of the Kübelwagen. It also masked the soft sound of two men slipping off safety-catches on automatic weapons and stealthily advancing down the bank.

Despite the relative confusion, some bickering, and more than a hint of panic, Stankov was pleased to witness the last of the explosives being wired into position and the detonator primed. All that remained was for the plunger to be rammed home. So intent were he and his crew on achieving their first independent blow against the fascists that, in their amateur enthusiasm, every one of the group felt certain that someone else was keeping a look out.

Keeping low, the grey-clad figure of Major List was now settled in prime firing position, watching as the black-clad figure of von Schroif slipped into his position on the other side of the narrow road.

The two men nodded to each other in an unspoken signal to attack and sprang into a firing position, their machine pistols spitting fire into the compact group of partisans, who fell like skittles as the bullets ripped into them. Bodies fell left and right and any return fire was directed impotently skywards as the few partisans who could bring their weapons to bear were swiftly mown down in confusion and chaos.

One of those bodies falling to the ground, industrially shredded by machine pistol bullets, was that of Boris Stankov. As the life drained from him, he determined that he would use his last instant in the service of his country in her heroic struggle against the fascists. Boris Stankov's last act was to reach out with a blood-stained hand for the plunger.

The force of the resulting explosion threw von Schroif backwards into a muddy pool, which certainly saved his life, as a cascade of falling logs and planking crashed into the ground where he had been standing only seconds earlier. List had been fortunate enough to witness Stankov reaching for the plunger and had dived into a water-filled ditch. As the last debris fell all around him, he rose slowly to his feet and ran over to the half-submerged, prone figure of Hans von Schroif. His terror turned to humour as the mud-encased figure arose floundering from the shallow pool.

'How was the fishing? Catch anything?'

'Only this...' retorted von Schroif, tossing a piece of hairy, blood-encrusted partisan skull.

'Ah! Lunch... How would you like it? Rare or medium?'

'I'll skip lunch, if that's OK with you,' said von Schroif.

The two men gazed at the wreckage of the bridge. Stankov and his team had certainly done a thorough job.

'Well, there's a bit of a problem. It's nearly two metres deep. The place where the 'White Devil' appeared is about 700 metres that way,' said List, pointing to the other side of the river.

'As long as the banks are capable of supporting the weight, we'll be OK,' replied von Schroif.

'So your tanks are submarines too?'

'In a way, yes... We can travel submerged up to three metres.'

'Well, you learn something new every day!' said List.

'The Tiger is quite a machine, designed by an old friend of mine. The wide tracks give it very low ground pressure... so it can go places where a Mark IV can't ... and it can certainly go anywhere a KV-1 can...'

'Are you asking for permission to follow the tracks of a certain KV-1?'

'I am, sir.'

'Permission granted.'

Back at the railhead, the four Tigers, after a quick inspection, were refuelled and ready for the short journey north to the supply point. Initially, things went well. Bobby Junge reported the engine to be running smoothly, the track they drove on seemed firm and substantial, and the crew's morale was boosted by the cheers and good wishes they heard from every group of infantrymen they passed.

'What confidence these new Tigers give our soldiers!' thought Michael Knispel, commanding the tank in von Schroif's absence, and now eagerly anticipating the coming engagement. In fact, he began to feel a surging wave of great confidence and pride, which began to encourage dangerous notions that these new tanks may somehow be decisive, and that they had the power to transform and save!

'No, no, no,' thought Knispel to himself. 'Never allow your thoughts to travel along these beguiling roads… how dare he dream such dreams! These were the dreams of the vain – glorious – and the soon to be deceased…'

So he reprimanded himself and returned to the time-honoured tradition of studying the landscape, the details of which were quite delightful. The sun-dappled trees and shimmering streams, the entire landscape bathed in a warm, soothing late-August light.

'Great hunting country! When this is all over…' Knispel thought to himself, 'I must return.'

His reverie was soon broken when he rounded the next bend to be greeted by the gun-metal grey and standard-issue camouflage netting of the supply area, carved out of the forest as if with some great steel clearing shovel. Knispel snapped back into attention. This was where the training took over. He could hear Bobby Junge lower the rpm, which was correct when approaching any assembly point. He noticed the grenadiers out concealing previous track marks into the area, which was again correct procedure, and he followed the signs assigning his tank to the correct location. Correct, correct, correct.

Then Junge manoeuvred the tank, amidst all those admiring eyes, under the nearest tree. Correct. Knispel made sure the turret was traversed to the side, so Junge and Wendorff could conveniently climb out through their hatches. They then set about removing the track marks and concealed the tank with branches and netting. Knispel then quickly reconnoitred the immediate area, checking for anti-aircraft spotters. These men would give alarm if any enemy aircraft were spotted. Best to know who and where they were.

According to the rules, the entire crew carried their individual weapons. In the event of a surprise artillery barrage, they also carried their steel helmets. Off to the right, Knispel could make out the supply vehicles gathering. Everything they were to need should be aboard those vehicles. Knispel did not need to tell Bobby Junge to carry out any essential maintenance and to help replenish the tank, he had already started!

Knispel had one last quick look at the land and sky surrounding them and then went off to find the cookhouse and sniff out the possibility of a bottle of beer. 'All is well,' he thought, noticing crews busy and some resting, others occupying alert position at the edge of the woods in case of enemy attack. Before he could get on to his mission, the Kübelwagen bearing List and von Schroif swept up to him.

'Ah, Knispel, just the man... Our reconnaissance is, how shall we say, lacking its usual comprehensiveness. Not surprising, given the unexpected events we have just encountered, but it does seem, even from the confirmed reports, that an old friend of ours is lurking nearby.'

'The White Devil, sir?'

'Got it in one, SS-Hauptscharführer. Time to go hunting!'

# CHAPTER 11

## ROLLBAHN OST

*Elvira* had little difficulty in fording the narrow river. The snorkel device worked perfectly, and they were soon at the spot 700 metres to the north where KV-1 tracks led off into the forest.

'Anywhere they go, we can go too,' said Junge with confidence. 'You can see what type of an opponent we are dealing with though. This is more like a rally.'

'Good. We all know a single tank should not be doing this, but the prize makes it worthwhile. We head straight to the rollbahn, and we destroy as many enemy vehicles as possible. Understood?'

'Jawohl, Hauptsturmführer!'

The journey through the forest was difficult and challenging in the extreme, but the deep track marks left by the KV-1 meant their route was unmistakable, and eventually they emerged from the trees, the Soviet-held roll-bahn stretching in front of them from right to left. It rose gently upward toward the left, and disappeared behind high ground after about 1200 metres. To the right, it ran flat and true for a distance of 3,000 metres. They were just taking up a position facing east when von Schroif's observation was interrupted by an unwelcome message.

'Oil pressure is very low, sir. I think we may have an engine problem,' reported Bobby Junge. 'Permission to check, sir?'

'Go ahead, Junge. Everyone else, keep vigilant.'

While the others kept an all-round watch, Bobby Junge busied himself with the engine. He had only just begun to open the engine hatches when, very faintly, in the distance, came the sound of what sounded like voices singing. Slowly, the noise got louder, and gradually started to mix with the sound of tank tracks.

It was Otto Wohl who first identified the source – a long line of Soviet tanks, each carrying a contingent of desyanti tank riders. This far behind the front, the Russian infantrymen were in relaxed mood, and passed the journey by bellowing their way through a favourite folk melody.

Through his binoculars, von Schroif

identified the first tanks – T-34s. The engine would have to wait. As quick as lightning, every man was back in his place. Knispel began to swivel the turret to bring it to bear on the first tank.

The Soviets rolled on, singing merrily, and didn't take any notice of the lone tank by the roadside, assuming it was a broken-down prototype vehicle. They certainly weren't counting on any form of enemy contact.

Wohl had an armour-piercing round loaded, and Knispel had his first target lined up. The firing couldn't start fast enough for him. Given half a chance, he would have been happy to ask Junge to ram them, so that he could let his fists do the talking. Knispel expected the order to start firing at any moment, but von Schroif remained silent.

The tanks rolled closer and closer. 700 metres, 600 metres, 500 metres. The singing grew louder. Knispel was convinced they would be discovered, but there was still no sign of concern from the Russians. How steely was his commander – in nerve and resolve! At last, with the lead T-34 just 100 metres away, the order came.

'Open fire!'

The mighty Acht-acht of the Tiger barked into life for the first time in anger, and the lead T-34 was simply blown apart by the huge kinetic force of the impact. The round

must have found its mark in the ammunition, as an almost simultaneous explosion
hurled the maimed figures of the desyanti in
all directions.

The singing stopped abruptly, and it was
now that the benefit of holding their fire
came into its own. The rear of the column
was so close that there was no need to re-
volve the turret. As soon as Wohl had
rammed the shell home, Knispel was able to
aim and fire. Even at 600 metres, the Acht-
acht simply ripped the T-34 apart. As
Knispel worked his way down the column,
Wendorff was busy with the hull machine
gun, spraying the fugitives with fire. The
surviving Russian infantry scattered to the
opposite rollbahn.

None of the T-34s escaped Elvira's wrath,
and Knispel felt a surge of power. Now he
was on equal terms, and there was no stopping him.

Bobby Junge had spent the entire combat
waiting for the order to start the engine. He
fretted about the battery which powered the
firing button of the Acht-acht and traversed
the turret. He thought hard about the likely
source of the oil pressure drop, and the
danger of fire if the oil was collecting in the
sump. He wanted this action to be over
quickly, and his prayers were soon answered.
The main gun stopped firing. There were no
more targets left. Eighteen T-34s lay smoul-

dering on the rollbahn, and the few survivors from among the desyanti were keeping their heads well down.

'Can you take us home, SS-Panzerschütze Junge?'

'It might be a slow journey, and we may have to stop a few times to top up with oil ... but I think we can do it.'

'Well, Elvira has had her baptism of fire ... so her well-wishers must be entitled to a beer,' added von Schroif.

'I'll drink to that, sir,' laughed Wohl.

'OK then, let's roll!' said von Schroif.


'So, now you are even.' said Major List. 'That's the kind of report to warm the cockles of the heart.'

'Well, not quite even, because there was no sign of the Weisse Teufel. It will only be when he dies that we are even. However, I do not think that moment is too far off. I get the feeling he'll be waiting for us when we make the main attack.'

'Which I am ordered is to be a mission to take an unoccupied and exposed village,' replied the Major, at which the two men exchanged meaningful glances.

An exposed target like this village was not the easy picking it was at the start of the campaign. The Soviets had learned, and so had the German soldier, the hard way. In 1941 there had been some easy targets, sometimes too easy, but as the war had progressed, so had Soviet tactics. Red Army fanatics sometimes stayed behind deliberately, so that their positions could be overrun and they could then launch attacks into the German rear and other devilish snares. It was this possibility which both commanders wordlessly exchanged with that knowing glance. The village had been deliberately left exposed as a trap.

'I will take all possibilities into account and approach with great caution,' offered von Schroif.

'I think that would be the wisest course of action,' replied List.

'We know the Tiger packs a punch, but we haven't seen one take a punch yet. Now, with regard to conditions... Don't be fooled. This may look like the kind of dry and firm ground that is ideal for heavy vehicles, but believe me, the whole area is a morass of peat bogs, the largest of which you are going to have to traverse to reach your target. Don't be taken in by the clement weather either, these things retain their moisture and sponginess all year round. I presume you were able to put the new tank through its paces in conditions at Paderborn which simulated terrain like this?'

Von Schroif hesitated, not wishing to denigrate the training course or its instructors. Exhaustive though it was, the course at

Paderborn had not covered every eventuality.

'I can tell by your hesitation that you are not going to answer in the affirmative, Hauptsturmführer. Still, the role of any commander is to adapt to new conditions and circumstances, is it not?' asked Major List, trying to finalise the conversation on as positive note as possible.

From his vantage point high above the hamlet, Dimitri Korsak could see through his binoculars the column snaking slowly through the woods. He was sure his identification was correct, but he rechecked the drawings in front of him just in case – and then a feeling of jubilation came upon him! Yes, the four lead tanks were definitely the Tigers. They were supported by six Panzerkampfwagen IIIs, a couple of companies of infantry, and some other trucks... probably support personnel.

He smelled fruition. However, this last phase had to be meticulous. He knew never to underestimate his foe. No point in sending in the T-34s now. Save them for later, use the artillery now. Let them reach the soft ground, pin them down.

'How stupid,' he thought. If he, Dimitri Korsak, could spot weaknesses in the design drawings of these new tanks, how could the engineers who built them not spot them too? Imagine thinking that Mother Russia, with all her features and stature, could be contained and tamed within the scribblings of some fascist engineers?

It reminded him of 1939 and the German liaison officer in Moscow gifting the Soviets a Panzer Mk III. Boasting about its prowess! 'What did we do? We sent it to the GABTU proving ground and laughed at it! The arrogance of these people!'

Hans von Schroif was nervous. He didn't quite know why. This should be the crowning point of his career. The prestige of leading out the pride of German armour should have left him feeling invincible, but strangely he felt a little vulnerable. That wasn't because of the terrain, which would suit any attacker who held the high ground off and up to his right. Nor was it because he was exposed – Hans von Schroif kept the hatch open, only occasionally buttoning up when a battle was at its fiercest. No, it was neither of these – it was intuition, and, however wonderful a quality, it lacked the certainty of other forms of knowledge. It never announced what was going to happen and when. It was far too vague for that. All one knew was that something was going to happen, and all one could do was be prepared.

Suddenly he started to feel the ground get softer and, rather alarmingly, when Bobby

Junge manoeuvred to avoid a tree in front of them, he could feel certain unresponsiveness in the tank's handling. He motioned to the tanks behind him to take the ground into account. It was then that he knew. They wouldn't be attacked now. They would only be attacked when the last of the tanks was on the softer ground.

He then had a flash of being in his opponent's mind and he was immediately reminded of the last time this had happened. The eyes, the white hair, the hands making the shape of a gun... 'Snap out of it, Hans! Concentrate!'

He was right to do so. Suddenly, he sensed there was indeed the suspicion of muzzle-flashes on the extreme edge of his peripheral vision, and those were what his eyes were straining for. This was one of the reasons he rarely buttoned up inside the tank, eyes before ears! The light of a muzzle-flash would reach him well before the sound of any firing, but where had it come from?

Hans put himself in the mind of the Russian commander. He has two options; proceed with an attack either from the village, or the high ground off to the east. The high ground was the obvious option, but the most astute commanders rarely used the most obvious option. In that case, he would open up from the hamlet, draw us in, and then let us have it from the high ground. Therefore...

But before he had time to work out a counter-strategy, Hans saw the bright, brief and unmistakable burst of a muzzle-flash. From the village, the house on the right! Michael had seen it too, as he had been measuring the fire control, pressing left and right, waiting for the order to fire. Then a massive thud! The tank shook. Then another ... and then another ... and again and again... Hans jumped back into the tank. Bang! Bang! Concussive blow after concussive blow! Otto swore he could almost hear shells spinning and burring their way into the tank.

'Achtung! One o'clock! 1,400 metres. HE!' shouted Hans.

Knispel could barely hear von Schroif's voice above the din and deafening crashes. He immediately slammed his foot on the turret traverse. The turret swung to the right. With his left hand he set the range on the sight, the whole tank now reverberating, a cacophony of crashing metal.

Again and again, Knispel, like every other crew member, felt stupefied and dazed, like someone had taken out his skull and started using it as a drum, but through his assaulted senses he still managed to crank the elevation hand wheel with his right hand ... the target came into view...

'Ready... Release safety... Fire!'

And up it went, the explosion sending the two bodies of a PATR crew into the air, one landing and remaining immobile, the other grotesquely attempting to stand on one leg, falling, and trying to crawl, but there was no time to consider such sideshows.

'Achtung! 11 o'clock, 1,300 metres. HE!' shouted Hans again, and Knispel, through the smoke, smell of cordite, and the shriek of steel, went through the methodical but precise procedure of swinging round the turret and finding his next target, and then the next ... and the next ... taking out every anti-tank gun and PATR position in that damned hamlet, one by one...

Hans could tell by the amount of fire that was pounding the village that the other three Tigers had adopted exactly the same strategy.

'Stop. Measure. Use your brains, pick your target, fire, and then repeat and repeat again...'

It may have been slower than the blizzard of shelling coming from the hamlet, but the fire from the Tigers was effective! Within five minutes, any offensive capabilities of the Ivans had been reduced to twisted, smoking wreckage.

Then it suddenly occurred to him – what had happened to any Soviet forces that may have been on the hill to the east? But before he had time to process this last thought, another muzzle-flash – this time in the trees behind the hamlet. 'Damn! Out of range!

We are going to have to go in!'

Hans von Schroif had Karl Wendorff radio the infantry and support wagons to have them stay where they were. He then ordered the four Tigers to split into two groups of two, each pair to traverse opposite paths round the hamlet. Bobby slowly started moving her forward, picking up speed, everything going smoothly – what a joy of a machine! – but no sooner had the thought crossed his mind than he could feel the engine straining and the tracks start to slip.

'Hauptsturmführer, we have a problem, sir. Behind us.'

Hans swivelled round in his cupola and saw, to his horror, the trailing tank spew smoke and stutter to a halt.

'Overheating!' explained Knispel.

'Halt!' shouted Hans to Bobby Junge, who immediately obeyed.

'There's no point in continuing,' thought von Schroif miserably to himself. He couldn't leave the tank stranded... There were always many courses of action and many outcomes, but one particular outcome was unthinkable – allowing a new Tiger to fall into the hands of the Soviets. It was either going to have to be defended until reinforcements arrived and it was towed back to the workshop area, or repaired...

'Panzeroberschütze Wendorff, get me Hauptscharführer Rubbal.'

'No need, Hauptsturmführer,' came the calm and reassuring reply, '...he is on his way!'

Hans looked up and over the trail they had just travelled down and saw a Kübelwagen hurtling towards them! 'Brave man!' thought Hans. It wasn't just the front line that had its share of heroes!

Hans von Schroif turned and surveyed the hamlet again for any change in the situation, but the guns had fallen silent and the whole sector seemed quiet. 'What was happening?' He should at least be hearing his other two Tigers...

'Have the other two Tigers report to me, Wendorff.'

Hans could hear the tone of the conversation without hearing the exact words, and it alarmed him. Karl Wendorff conveyed the bad news. 'Immobile. Both of them. Transmission problems.'

'Damn!' thought von Schroif, cursing this new circumstance. 'Could things get any worse?'

And then they did... The entire hill off to his east seemed to light up with a series of sequential flashes. The tell-tale trails of smoke streaking across the sky told their own story; Katyushas! Hans von Schroif threw himself back into the tank, buttoned up, and waited for the storm that was about to be unleashed.

The thunder struck again. The crew was violently thrown about as rocket after rocket screamed through the air, crashing into the tank and the ground around it. On and on it went. Each and every single one of them thinking, believing, for there was no evidence to the contrary, that their next breath would be their last. All they could do was pray that it would end soon. Every single one of them had the same nightmarish vision, the same supreme fear, that the next rocket was going to be the one that broke through and roasted them alive...

Hans was burdened not only by this nightmarish vision, but by another. A burden shared by all good commanders – a total humiliation. He had failed, letting down his country, his unit, his crew and himself. The next explosion would surely eviscerate him and his crew, and take any reputation he had with him ... but the next rocket did not break through, nor the one after that, nor even the one after that.

Finally, it did, after all, come to an end. It left an endless ringing in the ears and a stunned silence, followed by a radio message from the following Tiger that Hauptscharführer Rubbal was on his way and, a few seconds later, by a knock on the hatch.

'Hauptsturmführer! Don't shoot! Hauptsturmführer von Schroif ... it's me ... Hauptscharführer Rubbal.'

Without having fully returned to his senses, Hans gingerly pushed open the hatch. He was greeted by the smiling face of SS-Hauptscharführer Rubbal.

'Rubbal, how on earth did you manage to survive that in a Kübelwagen?'

'I did … but the Kübelwagen didn't. The crew behind me was kind enough to offer me shelter. Is everything alright, Hauptsturmführer…? You look shaken.'

Hans von Schroif was not a man taken to crude shows of affection, but he jumped up out of the hatch and hugged the gnarly figure of Hauptscharführer Rubbal. As he embraced the stunned engineer, wild thoughts ran through his brain. 'Defeat, death, humiliation! How dare he allow the notion to enter his mind. This tank's astonishing resilience, its highly-engineered ability to withstand the worst the Soviets could throw at it, this … this … changed everything…'

'I'm afraid the engine's overheated,' stated the Hauptscharführer, pointing to the immobilised tank behind them. 'Unfortunately, there is not much that I can do here. We need to get it back to the workshop area, so that I can attempt some real work on it.'

'Along with the other two,' smiled Hans von Schroif.

'You mean…?'

'Yes, SS-Hauptscharführer, you are presently perched on the only active Tiger on the Eastern Front! However, if it is your assessment that repairs cannot be effected here, then it is best that you return to the workshop area and wait for us there. You are too valuable to be endangered out here.'

'I need to. I've got to get together the resources to tow three stricken tanks, Hauptsturmführer. I don't know how I'll do it yet, sir, but don't worry, I soon will!'

Hauptscharführer Rubbal was a wonderfully reassuring man to have on the team. Many times Hans von Schroif had found himself in so-called impossible situations, and each time Hauptscharführer Rubbal had managed to extricate not just the tank, but the crew too. Many times there was not even a germ of an idea as to how he would achieve it, just certain knowledge that it could be done.

It was now an act of faith in Rubbal. Each of the Tigers was equipped with a purpose-designed demolition charge, fitted by the commander's hatch, and von Schroif was determined not to use it. He believed in Rubbal, he believed in the Möbelpackwagen, he believed in his crew, and he believed in himself.

Dimitri Korsak was another man possessed of strong reserves of self-belief. However, his first impression of what these new Tigers had just survived, almost an entire arsenal of anti-tank weaponry, was galling. These were not the usual flimsy fascist toys, built along the usual German lines, paying attention to the comfort of their crew. These were powerful and formidable foes. How on earth was he going to deal with them? He had no option; he was going to have to send in the T-34s he had requisitioned from Meretskov.

Even though the system of mental fortifications he had constructed around his own abilities and self-belief were ironclad, a tiny stray and unwelcome thought slipped past its well-guarded perimeter and into his brain. What if the T-34s, with their 400 metre range disparity, could not get close enough? Even if they did get close enough and, worse still, were unable to silence the monsters, then their failure would be his failure. He knew exactly what the consequences of that would be.

There were too many unknowns here, and Meretskov had not allocated him all the T-34s he had asked for, but he could not go back to Beria and complain about the lack of support and the uncooperative behaviour of Meretskov. He had been given a task – capture at least one of the Tigers for evaluation – and the task was given to him on the presumption that he would carry it out. Of all the options open to him, failure was not one of them.

Hans von Schroif surveyed the heights, looking for the slightest movement, but saw none. How would this game of chess play out? What options were open to the Soviet commander? He couldn't move his artillery any closer. There had been no indication of Soviet air superiority, so any threat from the air could be shunted back down the list of probabilities. So that left retreat, tanks – did he have any armoured support? – or something else. There was always something else...

However, Hans could, he felt, also allow himself the luxury of thinking that the Soviets had run out of alternatives. Had things not changed demonstrably? For the first time since the first days of Barbarossa, he could honestly say that he felt at an advantage, as a result of this fine new tank. The 88 mm gun and the extra armour gave him a new confidence.

Then he corrected himself. How many dead men believed themselves to have an advantage just before the final blow came? And so he returned to thinking about what that 'something else' the Soviet Commander may have up his sleeve might be.

'SS-Panzeroberschütze Wendorff, order the Mark IIIs to escort the SS-Hauptscharführer back to the assembly area. Have the infantry go with them, but order them to double back and take up a position below that last ridge.'

Hans then turned his attention back to the hamlet, unable to filter out the cries and screams of the wounded, who still lay unattended. 'No German soldier would ever be treated like this,' he thought to himself. Despite these considerations, the operational aspect of this hamlet and the area behind it played on his mind. There was at least one emplacement in the trees behind it, but, with three tanks inactive, did it justify the risk of moving off through this marshy ground?

In the end, he rationalised it down to this... Transmission and engine failure – these were the factors that a good crew and especially a good driver held some sway over – these were not accidents of fate or design – these were the responsibilities of the crew. So, this was the question – did he have enough faith in his crew to justify any further offensive action?

'SS-Panzerschütze, we are going for a short drive. Take her up to 4,000 rpm. 12 o'clock!'

'Jawohl!' chirped Bobby, never happier than when they were on the move. Moving out, they were just picking up speed when Hans noticed a machine gun crew popping up from what appeared to be a slit trench. And then another. And another. One had to admire the guts – or was it the stupidity? –

of these Soviets. Did they have any idea of what they were facing? He wasn't interested in these positions though, his focus was on the artillery emplacement behind them. Hans pulled down the hatch and prepared himself. He could see Otto readying the co-axial machine gun.

'SS-Panzerschütze, save the ammunition. The tracks will take care of them.'

The tank then sped up, heading straight for the trench. The machine guns opened up, but harmless would be too strong a word to describe their effect as they popped off the Tiger's steel shell like so many bits of cracked wheat. One of the machine gun crews then upped and ran from the trench, only for a fusillade of shots to ring out from behind them, cutting them down as a sign of brutal Soviet discipline.

Bobby could make out the look of fear on the remaining Soviet soldiers' faces as he barrelled the tank towards them. 'Why,' he thought to himself, 'did the Ivans believe that a shallow dirt trench would offer any kind of protection?' He had done this many times, come to a halt over the trench, spun the tank, and just ground the poor bastards back into Mother Earth, and turned them into beer! He smiled at the gruesome symmetry of it. Anyway, Elvira needed to be blooded...

Just as he approached the trench, he hit the

brakes and spun her around. Even through the hull, he heard the pitiful screams of the first machine gun crew as they were turned to bloody mush beneath him.

'No! No! No!' cried Hans.

Bobby looked up at him in confusion.

'Twelve o'clock,' shouted von Schroif, referring to the original order.

Now made well aware that his manoeuvre had left them side-on and track-exposed to a potentially deadly piece of Soviet artillery, Junge knew exactly what to do. 'Knispel!' he shouted, and spun the tank around, taking into account which angle the barrel was at, and the previous position of the Soviet artillery.

From years of fighting and training together, Knispel knew exactly what Junge was about to do. This was going to require the utmost precision... Through his sights he could see the tank spin around through 90 degrees, saw the artillery piece come into view, and then let loose... A split second later, the high-explosive round caused a massive explosion, followed by a ball of fire which consumed man and machine. Quickly refocusing, he could see no immediate movement, save for the sickening sight of a Soviet gunner staggering into the distance, his entire body aflame. Knispel looked away, not through disgust, but simple expediency. Years of experience had taught him this one brutal lesson ... this is war and war is hell.

'I am sorry, SS-Hauptsturmführer,' Junge said to von Schroif.

'The fault is mine, SS-Panzerschütze Junge. My order should have been clearer. You did well.'

Von Schroif chided himself. Any ambiguity in commands came from him, and was his responsibility. He could not, with any clear conscience, blame his crew if the target, as in this case, had not been made explicit. Anyway, even if Junge had been at fault, he had taken it upon himself to remedy the situation. No more could be asked.

Hans von Schroif then opened the hatch to re-evaluate the situation. Ivan held the high ground, but his artillery had proved ineffectual at that distance. But did he have any tanks? Would he wait until dark before sending any infantry in?

Von Schroif then considered his own situation. Three tanks down. Isolated. Should he evacuate the crews and return with reinforcements and recovery vehicles? That would be like handing the Tigers over to the Soviets without a fight. Should they stay and consolidate? For all the mechanical problems these new tanks were exhibiting, they had proved themselves in terms of their defensive and armour capabilities. There was only one real option. They would stay and see off whatever Ivan could throw at them!

Rubbal and the Famos would soon find him!

So how was he going to organise this consolidation? His plan was simple. Tow the Tiger behind him over to the two other Tigers, spin the other two around until they were facing the hill to their right flank, and then hull-down and wait for Ivan! The idea appealed to von Schroif, particularly for its simplicity, but there was one problem. Regulations prohibited the towing of one Tiger by another, due to potential over-heating of the towing Tiger's engine, which could lead to breakdown or fire.

To von Schroif there was a higher principle though – Mission Command, or Aufstrag-staktik. This tactical freedom, enshrined in the German Army since the previous century, allowed the commander on the ground – within his overall objective – the freedom to improvise to a degree unrecognisable in nearly any other army. This, reasoned von Schroif, gave him the freedom to break this particular regulation and proceed with his objective.

Suddenly liberated from his previous dilemma, he felt a personal pleasure any commander or leader would recognise, having come up with a solution to a seem-ingly intractable problem. It was warm and affirmative and allowed the freedom to con-centrate fully on the newly-decided strategy. One remaining piece of the new strategy needed attention though – were there any remaining artillery pieces in or close to the hamlet? And was it capable of being reinforced?

'Wendorff, order the grenadier captain to send in troops to flush out the hamlet of any remaining enemy resistance. We also require some scouts up on the hill on our right flank.'

Von Schroif then ordered the other tank commanders to prepare for towing. Emerging into the cool evening air, he could see, off, to his right, the two crews also emerge. Then he heard a crack and saw one of his tankers slump forward.

'Snipers! Wendorff, relay!'

As Wendorff passed on von Schroif's message, von Schroif himself reflected on the first time he had come across this tactic. Soviet snipers in orchard trees on the long dusty road to Leningrad, staying behind at supreme personal sacrifice in order to pick off commanders like himself, who preferred not to be buttoned up inside their tanks.

'Knispel! Find that damned rifle of yours!'

'Wendorff! Tell the grenadiers they have a third mission! Snipers in the trees at the foot of the hill.'

As soon as he had barked out these new orders, von Schroif reconsidered the situation. Plan A – towing the immediate Tiger into a hull-down defensive position near the other two Tigers and then turning them so that their flanks were 90 degrees to the hill was now impossible, with their crews pinned down. Plan B – wait for the grenadiers to clear the snipers, tree by tree, but did he have time for this? Plan C – lay down covering fire and send Knispel in on a hunting expedition. But could he risk losing his gunner at this juncture? Plan D, plan D... Come up with a plan D! But plan D was too horrible to contemplate... Plan D would not be his plan, it would be the Soviet plan – blow up the Tigers and get out of there...

Then, as if on cue, up on the hill, the sound and fury of dust, engines and smoke...

'Enemy! 4,000 metres on our right flank! Junge, get as close to our other two Tigers as possible!'

The tank spun around. 'God forbid it isn't our turn to have engine trouble,' thought von Schroif to himself. He quickly calculated one advantage of which they could avail themselves – the terrain. The Soviet tanks would be unable to advance en masse through the trees; they would have to split up into small groups. He then made a mental note to search for any tracks or trails leading out of the sloping forest that could lead to bottlenecks where they might concentrate their fire.

His first task was to take care of the snipers though. He had, as a matter of urgent necessity, to get his crews back into their tanks and get them firing!

'Wohl, reload with high-explosive.'

'Wendorff, radio ahead to the tanks and tell those that are outside to remain under cover until after the third incendiary.'

'Knispel, aim for the rocky outcrop one hundred metres from the base of the hill. Three shells, fifty metres apart, starting at one o'clock.'

The plan was audacious, but von Schroif could see no other option. He had to get those crews in their tanks before they were overrun!

'Fire!'

The first shell streaked out of the throat of the barrel, traversing its distance in almost a straight line, before smashing against the rocks at the base of the hill and sending a spray of rock and lethal shrapnel shredding through the tops of the trees directly in front of it. Knispel had no time to check if it had been effective in its task. Wohl had already loaded the next shell.

'Fire!' came the order, just as Knispel had shifted the required aim 50 metres to the right.

Another deadly spray of shrapnel ripped through the tops of the next group of trees.

'Fire!'

The third shell crashed into the rock at almost exactly its allotted slot.

Von Schroif peered through the dust and flame, trying to hold himself steady as the Tiger sped across the soft Russian terrain, and was filled with joy at the sight of four lifeless bodies cradled in the leafless branches, and to see the stranded crew-members jump back into the relative safety of their vehicles. 'Now Ivan has a fight on his hands!' he exclaimed, as he watched both Tigers swing their barrels to point at the onrushing enemy.

To his amazement, he saw one T-34 burst into flames, and then, soon after, another's turret blown up into the air. How could this be? None of the three tanks had commenced firing yet. Then he realised that these two T-34s had been picked off by the fourth Tiger, the one he had left behind – at a range of almost 3,000 metres!

His spirits buoyed, and it was not long before the other three Tigers joined in. Hull-down, man and machine worked in what seemed like a furious but simultaneously serene harmony, loosing off shell after shell, and scoring hit after hit! Before the Soviet tanks could even get in range, they were blown apart or put out of business. One after another, with methodical precision, the on-rushing enemy armour was turned from deadly harbingers of doom to lifeless smoking hulks!

Von Schroif knew that this was, in part,

due to Soviet tactics. 'When would they ever learn?'

A frantic charge to get close may have worked against some of the older panzers, but not these new Tigers, not these new 'Princes of the Steppe'. Within twenty minutes it was all over. The full Soviet attack had been blunted. Through the smoke and flame, the only audible sound was the laughing and joking of the grenadiers as they made their way confidently through what, until recently, had been a battlefield.

A strong guard was placed on each disabled Tiger. The rest of the party withdrew to refit and tax their tired brains for a solution to this new dilemma. No one wanted to destroy them, but, whatever happened, the stranded Tigers could not fall into Russian hands. It was now a race against time.

Hans von Schroif stared out over the assembly area, noticing smoke rising from the field kitchens, the distant sound of music, the snorers, the dreamers, and the active workers – those that could not allow themselves to stop, for fear of coming face to face with what they had just seen, heard or done... If the heat of battle was one way of determining a man's character, then the assembly area presented another. In battle, a man was revealed by his actions. In the supply area, by his inaction.

Yes, there were essential acts of maintenance and training, but the overall job of the supply area was to take broken and exhausted men and prepare them for the next step in this dance of death. Replenishment and revitalisation were the order of the day, and every man dealt with it differently. Some slept, some talked, some sang ... some ate because they were hungry, others because they joked that this meal would be their last ... and some could not eat at all. Those that managed to sleep, von Schroif considered the luckiest of all. Especially during these all-too-short Russian summer nights, when Ivan seemed to enjoy getting up early and turning to his guns.

Letter writing was something that he, along with others, grew to hate. How could you possibly describe what you had just gone through and witnessed? Letters home were a deception at best, a lie, a work of art. At worst, when writing to next of kin about the loss of a comrade... How could you honestly describe the manner of death? Could you mention incineration, the spilled guts, or decapitation? How could you write that a son or loved one died any other death than that of a hero? To Hans von Schroif, war itself was preferable...

He then looked out over the ditch his crew had dug for themselves. This was normal practice when not sleeping in the tank itself, to carve out a little trench and then drive the tank over it for protection. The only member of the crew who refused to sleep outside the tank was Otto Wohl – Elvira was now the latest in a long line of metallic mistresses!

Von Schroif had noticed that Wohl had not yet carried out his prescribed task – replacing any expended shells – which was unusual for one so scrupulous. It was a laborious and arduous task. Had Wohl reached the limit of his physical reserves? Von Schroif thought he had better investigate.

Thankfully, on entering the tank, he was heartened to find his proud loader hunkered down in the loading bay, busy scribbling away with pen and paper.

'Letter home, SS-Panzerschütze?'

'It is a missive of sorts, SS-Hauptsturmführer, but not so much to my former family as to my new family.'

Von Schroif could have questioned him further, but he smiled and gently reminded him of his duties.

'Apologies, Hauptsturmführer,' said Wohl, before adding rather cryptically, 'This endeavour on which I am embarked is not a form of idleness, nor a recreation, but hopefully, in itself, essential to our efforts here on the front.'

Then, seeing the slightly perplexed look on his commander's face, he added, 'You will, of course, be the first to see the fruits of this labour, which I have called 'Project Elvira'. Now, where are those shells?'

Von Schroif then went over to tap Michael Knispel on the shoulder to wake him for sentry duty. Whilst doing so, he couldn't help but notice Karl Wendorff looking particularly pensive, sitting wide awake against a nearby tree.

'May I join you, SS-Panzeroberschütze?' asked von Schroif.

Wendorff nodded, his dark demeanour adding to von Schroif's concern. Von Schroif sat beside his radio operator, choosing to remain silent, in order to give Wendorff the chance to talk first.

'We are going to return for those tanks,' said Wendorff, which unsettled von Schroif, as the manner in which it was delivered suggested more an answer than a question.

'I have not been briefed yet, but I imagine those may be our orders.'

'Hauptsturmführer, do you believe that a man can foresee his own death?'

'Yes, I have foreseen myself die many times over!' joked von Schroif, feeling that the implied darkness in Wendorff's mood needed some lightening.

'I dreamed of St Liborius last night. You remember, in Paderborn, the patron saint of a good death.'

Von Schroif was unable to reply. The seriousness in Wendorff's tone precluded an answer that was unsympathetic or glib. Von Schroif was used to lifting his men's spirits, but the depth and weight of this despondency was something that was starting to alarm him.

'Would you call me a good friend, Hauptsturmführer?' continued Wendorff.

'You are not going to suggest that you dreamed you died in my arms, SS-Panzeroberschütze?'

'I know what dreams are, sir, but this was a vision with far more ... substance.'

'SS-Panzeroberschütze, I really think you should get some sleep.'

'Sleep is coming soon enough, Hauptsturmführer.'

'Wendorff, please stop this.'

Just then, an adjutant of Major List walked up to them. 'SS-Hauptsturmführer, Major List would like to meet with you immediately.'

Von Schroif stood up. Before leaving, he whispered to Wendorff, 'Not a word of this to anyone.'

The ashen-faced radio operator did not even look him in the eye. His only acknowledgement was a slight shrug of his already heavily-stooped shoulders.

Another who saw his own impending demise was Walter Lehmann. In his case though, his vision was far more concrete than a dream.

He would have liked to say it came as a relief, but RSHA Kriminalassistent Walter Lehmann, former SS man and now Soviet spy, was a man who had made his decisions as career choices. Decisions made in order to further and furnish his already-pampered life, not have it taken away from him before he had time to fully enjoy the fruits of his many deceptions. His heart had sunk when he saw the men from the Abwehr at the door. Strange, he had just been looking admiringly out over Prinz-Albert Strasse from his balcony. Berlin had never looked so beautiful. Funny how one knock on the door could change everything.

Staring out the window at Tirpitzufer, Admiral Canaris weighed up his possible responses to the news that Walter Lehmann was about to be arrested. 'If only that damned professor's wife had got in touch with him and not Oster.' His second-in-command had travelled down the only road open to him. There was no doubt Lehmann would talk. The Old Intriguer had always known that it was a risk to use Lehmann as an ignorant dupe in his grand game. Fat, stupid and unreliable, the piggy-eyed idiot thought his cover intact. Fool! How easy it had been to insert Borgmann as Viper and feed him little titbits to Stenner – or as he was now lovingly referred to by his new comrades, Commander Dimitri Korsak.

Canaris had vivid memories of their time back in the Freikorps. Ha! Lehmann and Stenner, these scum were worse than Hitler! He did not blame himself however; Admiral Canaris' luminous, spidery mind was too used to strategizing and plotting to fret over one broken filament in a brilliantly-spun web. The tactic had been weighed in the scales. Getting close to Beria was one part of the prize, a worthwhile endeavour in itself. But, for now, it was all about covering tracks, which meant getting Borgmann out into the clear, and getting rid of Korsak.

Canaris reasoned that the best way for Borgmann to prove his credentials was by ensuring that he was the one who eliminated Korsak. That way, he could claim that Lehmann was a pawn in the game to ensnare Die Weisse Teufel, and also strengthen his position at OKW. A worthy aim, for he was sure Borgmann would be needed again in the future... And there was one other consolation. Whatever Lehmann did transmit under torture would come back to Canaris, and he, being at the centre of the web, was in charge of how it would be retransmitted. He could spin it any way he wanted.

Time to move on... It was a pity his friends in London would not get their hands on one of these new Tigers anytime soon... However, there were other weapons and other secrets, and the British were nothing if not patient...

'Gentlemen, I am sure that the objective of our next mission will come as no surprise,' announced Major List. 'I have it on the highest authority that no effort should be spared to ensure that those three stricken Tigers do not fall into enemy hands. If they cannot be recovered, they are to be destroyed.

'To forestall this unthinkable outcome, I shall take command of the mission, supported by SS-Hauptsturmführer von Schroif. We shall be ably assisted by a team of combat engineers from Division, and a number of the new support and recovery vehicles.

'The principal objective is to clear and hold the area around the three tanks, in order that essential maintenance can be provided, and that all four Tigers can return to the assembly area under their own steam. If this is not achievable, then we are to tow them back for any repairs that can be carried out in the workshop. Over to you, Hauptscharführer Rubbal.'

'Thank you, major. Our first determination is that the problems may be related to the gear boxes, a problem accentuated by the soft terrain. In engineering terms, this should be a straightforward task. Dismantle the flexible couplings in the half-shaft drives, and tow it out of the immediate battle area. If, however, closer inspection reveals that any of the tracks have ridden up over the sprocket teeth, this will require more time and horsepower. In order to expedite this process, may I respectfully ask SS-Hauptsturmführer von Schroif's permission to involve his excellent driver, SS-Panzerschütze Bobby Junge?'

'Permission granted,' replied von Schroif, 'as long as our tank is stationary and not in need of a driver,' which all attending found highly amusing.

'Now,' continued Major List, 'I have read SS-Hauptsturmführer von Schroif's reports and the latest reconnaissance material, and we are expecting a counterattack in the next 24 hours. I suggest we split our force into two – one part, under SS-Hauptsturm-führer von Schroif, returning to the hamlet near where the Tigers are situated, and the other part, commanded by me, to pivot behind the hill and attack any Soviet resupply of their previous position.'

This made von Schroif uneasy. 'With all due respect, sir, the assumption that the Soviets will return by their former route leaves us open to an attack from the north side of the hamlet.'

'I understand completely, SS-Hauptsturmführer. However, in the absence of any new intelligence, I have to make the assumption that the Soviets' most likely strategy in most eventualities is a repeat of the strategy before.'

This was a fair point. However, von Schroif had one more question. 'Are we afforded any air cover, sir?'

'Thankfully, the forecast for today suggests that the skies will be too overcast for flying. Thank you, gentlemen.'

Having just finished preparing for a conference with the OKW, Oberstleutnant i.G. Borgmann had to decrypt the recently arrived message from Admiral Canaris twice before he could be certain of its import.

'Lehmann to be arrested. Position untenable. Fox no longer our friend. Retain cover till Fox eliminated. Repeat Fox no longer our friend.'

So it was over. Well, nearly. The Steppe Fox had never really been our friend. Borgmann felt relief. Getting close to Lehmann in order to gain his confidence had been distasteful to say the least, but he had done well. Lehmann had believed that they worked for the same masters.

In all honesty, the plan to trade these new Tigers had not sat well with him. Surely you do not give your prize military assets away when not just men's lives, but a whole front, a whole war, may depend on them? But, if Canaris thought the trade worthwhile, then who was he to judge? He had often wondered what hand Canaris was playing here, but that was beyond his rank. All he had to do was trust that Canaris had the best interests of the Reich at heart.

Frustration, but frustration underscored by an unrelenting patience. That was how an observer would have assessed Dimitri Korsak's state of mind. Such distant observations were not the object of Korsak's focus. His mind was concentrated, and nothing concentrated Korsak's mind like hate. He recalled the long death march from Liborius, the agonising thirst, the unendurable hunger, and the shock of seeing his comrades shot like dogs.

He owed his life to his capacity to hang on to his hatred, and, following his escape, he realized that hate was easier to deal with if it had an object. In this case, it did. Hans von Schroif was the name it held on to...

It was his command which had machine-gunned Korsak's colleagues. Korsak was sure he would have died too, had von Schroif got wind of the fact that he was there. True, the dirty work had been done by the SS-Sturmscharführer whom he thought had the name of Braun, but von Schroif was the puppet master. He had ordered the massacre, and there was the name to boil his blood and stir his hatred. 'Once a vacillating little swine, always a vacillating swine,' thought Korsak to himself.

His days in the Freikorps came flooding back to him, adding to his hatred, that weasel Hitler and his apologist cronies like von Schroif and his ilk. It was now nearly twenty years ago, but the memories were still raw, the accounts still unsettled. Gregor Strasser was dead because of men like von Schroif. Strasser had been the movement's one true leader. Killed and usurped by Hitler. Of course, he had not been Dimitri Korsak then, he had been Wilhelm Stenner, but that was just a different name and a different set of papers. It was the hatred that mattered, and the hatred remained the same.

When von Schroif returned to his tank and crew he was relieved to see Wendorff sitting amongst them.

Otto Wohl seemed to be the centre of attention, holding court with his now seemingly indispensable notepad and pen.

'SS-Hauptsturmführer! Come and sit with us,' enjoined Wohl, 'I am conducting a seminar!'

'A seminar, SS-Schütze?' replied von Schroif, 'Since when did you enter the hallowed halls of academia?'

'Do I look like a professor, sir? No, this is a meeting of practical engineering minds. Wendorff here was saying that one of the principles of study, whether at the University of Heidelberg or the University of Life, is to list what one could term the 'good' and 'bad' points of any consideration. I am sure you employ the same principles in your application of battlefield tactics?'

'Indeed, SS-Panzerschütze Wohl', replied von Schroif, 'Good, bad, plus, minus... Personally, I prefer the terms 'strengths' and 'weaknesses'.'

'Exactly! Now, it is funny that you should use those terms, because that is precisely the point of this exercise. It's part of the still top secret project Elvira, but I promise you, if the benefits are being deliberately held from you now, they will be more than evident on the completion of the project.'

'Time you made a good woman of Elvira then,' interjected Michael Knispel.

'SS-Hauptscharführer,' replied Wohl, 'no man should get betrothed to a woman whose charms he does not fully know.'

'No man would get betrothed to a woman whose charms he did fully know,' joked Knispel, at which the group, even Wendorff, chuckled.

'Enough of this,' replied Wohl. 'Elvira and I remain close, but, as yet, not fully committed. Let us leave it at that. Anyway, allow me to warm to my major theme. The purpose of this exercise, SS-Hauptsturmführer, is to attempt to list Elvira's good and bad points – her strengths and weaknesses, as you so eloquently put it.'

'One major good point is that she hasn't started spending your money yet,' mocked Bobby Junge, joining in the fun.

'Enough!' cried Wohl. 'To business! Sir, this is what we have come up with so far. From a lowly loader's point of view, personally, I am more than happy with the amount of space provided for my duties. This allows me to conduct my profession with greater ease and efficiency. I am also delighted with the new flexible strips for attaching stowage.

'Knispel here is beside himself with joy over the binocular sights, and with – as I think we all are – the overall stability when firing the new electric trigger switch in the firing gear, and the handholds on the roof. When it comes to the Acht-acht, I think the gratitude and levels of satisfaction are un-animous. Likewise the armour.

'Junge, who often worries about the state of his ass when any tank he is driving is on the move, also admits to casting a jealous eye over your seat...'

'Careful, Wohl...' joked Junge.

'Of course, he means the two-position commander's seat and, of course, the über-comfortable backrest... Other strengths mentioned by the group were the ability to stow more ammunition, and how much easier it was to reach it... I think that was all so far... Wendorff's been quieter than usual, so I think we can take that as a sign of quiet contentment and that everything on the radio front meets with his satisfaction. Now, sir, is there anything you would like to add?'

'I like your list so far, SS-Panzerschütze Wohl, and the thinking behind it... Now what would I add ... let us see ... the new optics... I do not appreciate the way they are mounted in the cupola... The hatches could do with a big improvement... Much more responsive... Has anyone mentioned the mine and smoke generator dischargers?'

'No,' replied Wohl, 'but I agree that they should definitely be on the list ... anything else?'

'Not that I can think of at the moment, SS Schütze,' replied von Schroif, 'but please bear in mind that these are very early days, and to reach full comprehensiveness, perhaps your list should be enlarged and amended when we have all spent some more time with Elvira.'

'An excellent point, SS-Hauptsturm-führer, and one which I have already taken into account.'

'It might also be an idea,' added Wendorff, 'to compile a list of strengths and weaknesses for different terrains, different sectors, and different weather conditions.'

'An excellent idea, Panzeroberschütze. Write that down, Wohl,' ordered von Schroif, who was heartened by the fact that Wohl was now at least engaging in some real soldiering.

However, if Wohl was now fully engaged, it was obvious that Wendorff was still a long way from being his usual self.

'Now for the weaknesses,' whispered Wohl, jokingly looking around for Soviet spies. 'So, what do we have here? Knispel is afraid that he sticks his hand up your ass when he has to leave through your cupola? Knispel, why this obsession with the boss's ass?

'As far as I am concerned,' continued Wohl, 'I am not particularly enamoured by the amount of fumes that are sent back when the gun fires, or my lack of comms. There have also been questions raised about the armouring on bins, a certain difficulty in re-arming the co-ax, the size of the gun deflector bag, and the fact that there is no neutral position on the traverse control... anything else?'

'Well, far be it from me to complain about my own personal comfort, but I do find my position rather cramped,' opined Knispel in a rather plaintive manner, so much so that he left himself completely open to a scornful attack from his loader.

'Right, that's it boys. Get Henschel on the phone. Scrap Elvira now... This Tiger is more of a pussy than a big cat... Send the designers back to the drawing board... Elvira is too small for Knispel's liking and is causing him a little discomfort! What we need is a lion ... a real big cat!'

Amidst such mirth, the discussion and festivities came to an end, with von Schroif having the last word at Knispel's expense.

'Worry not, SS-Schütze Wohl. When your list is complete, I shall personally arrange a meeting between you and Kurt Arnholdt at Henschel, to ensure the new lion has specifications that meet Knispel's exceptionally high standards!'

Walter Lehmann's expression remained outwardly calm, but his mind was running through options like a rat trapped in a cage. Why were the Abwehr here? Was it routine? Was he to be questioned here, or taken away? If so, where? There was absolutely no doubt in his mind that, if the situation was as serious as he feared, his only hope of escape was to flee before he was taken away. But how could he achieve this? Was he to jump out of the balcony? Run for the door?

His Luger was in the desk drawer behind him, and he could see that the officers were armed, so how could he manoeuvre himself behind the desk, open the drawer, and kill the two men before they killed him? On top of that, if he did manage to kill them, where would he go? Russia, that was his only real option... Beria owed him. He decided to relax, give nothing away, and prepare himself for any opportunity or advantage that might come his way, however slight or seemingly unimportant.

'RHSA Kriminalassistant Lehmann. We would like you to come with us.'

That was it. Stark and unambiguous. If they succeeded in taking him for questioning, then he was as good as dead. Then the dreaded word 'torture' flashed through Lehmann's mind. He knew he was no hero. If he talked, they would torture him to get more information before killing him. If he didn't talk, they would torture him, and then they would kill him. Just then the phone rang.

'Of course, gentlemen. I will be with you immediately. I just have a quick telephone call to take from the Führer's office.'

That would disrupt their thinking and planning. Nothing like dropping the Führer's name into an ironclad procedure. Lehmann then walked slowly behind the desk, picked up the phone, and in an obedient, but authoritative, voice said, 'For the personal attention of the Führer?...Yes, immediately...' to the puzzlement of the internal caller at the end of the line.

'Jawohl, it's for the Führer... I will ensure the relevant documents are sent both to Doctor Goebbels and Reichsminister Speer... I have them here...' At which he slowly opened the drawer and pulled out a piece of paper, being careful to leave the drawer open, allowing quick access to the Luger.

'Jawohl, I am holding the document now...

Yes, I understand... I shall send the other document too... Is it the directive...?'

At which he slowly put his hand back into the drawer, quickly pulled out his Luger, and shot both men in the chest. He then ran round the desk and finished both of them off and ran to the balcony.

When his staff rushed in on hearing the shots they were greeted by the sight of RHSA Kriminalassistant Walter Lehmann standing at the balcony, shooting repeatedly into the crowd of pedestrians below and shouting, 'Down there! Down there! American spy!'

His staff ran to the edge of the balcony, saw a man lying in a pool of blood, and Lehmann pointing and shouting, 'That one! That one! He is the accomplice! Arrest that man!' Then, turning to his staff, he shouted: 'Get after him! Try and take him alive! The one with the grey hat ... look there ... get after him!'

His staff dutifully obeyed and turned and ran from the room. At which point, Walter Lehmann calmly returned to his desk, collected any papers he might need, picked up some spare ammunition, donned his coat, put the gun in his pocket, and quietly headed for the back door and left the building.

On returning to Elvira, Hans von Schroif briefed his men on the impending operation. As all set about their tasks, he called Wendorff aside.

'I have not forgotten, SS-Panzerober-schütze, what you confided in me earlier. You are as aware as I am how the mind can play tricks, particularly in times of stress, battle and deprivation – even when a soldier is awake. I presume that in the intervening hours you have now categorised your previous experience accordingly.'

'I wish that were the case, SS-Hauptsturm-führer,' replied Wendorff, 'however, what I saw ... no, experienced is probably a better word ... what I experienced was of such a clear and vivid nature that I could not pos-sibly categorise it as you would wish.'

'Please describe it to me then, SS-Panzer-oberschütze.'

'It was as real as I see you talking to me just now... However, it was not you I was observ-ing, but myself. I was standing outside of myself, looking in. SS-Hauptsturmführer, you know I have no great religious or spir-itual inclination, so when I describe what I saw, and what I felt, it is purely in terms of rational, honest, accurate description.'

'Go on, SS-Panzeroberschütze,' indicated von Schroif with a wave of his hand.

'Not only did I see the occasion of my own death with supreme, almost heightened, clarity, but the experience also suffused my senses. I could hear and smell with the

337

utmost distinction. SS-Hauptsturmführer, I saw you open the hatch and carry me from my position in the machine and lay me beside a tree, but not only did I see this event, I could also feel it, this ... end...'

'Well, feelings almost always follow perceptions – as I think we both agree, SS-Panzeroberschütze. If you saw something vividly, then in all likelihood that would inform your reaction to it. Vision comes first in my book, and all else follows it. Now, there are no secrets between us. We have always been honest with each other, and I am going to be honest now... I believe you are making an assumption, the assumption being that the clearer the dream, the more accurate it must be.

'We have both heard of comrades, indeed known comrades, who have foreseen their own deaths. I cannot argue with that, and many have died. This is true, but, SS-Panzeroberschütze Wendorff, I'm sure you will agree, not all. This is also true. You cannot deny that. Therefore, while we can say there may be a certain power in your vision, we cannot say with certainty that it will re-enact itself in real life as it did in your dream.

But one thing is certain, SS-Panzeroberschütze, beyond all doubt – we are about to go into battle, and I need you with me. I need that mind of yours to be at its sharpest and most responsive, not clouded or distracted in any way. I cannot make this clearer, if this vision does manifest itself, then you will die. If you die, you die. But if you do not die and, because of your present state of mind, this preoccupation, this disposition, causes the death of any of our crew, then I will find it very hard to understand, let alone to forgive you. It is on this basis that I want you to proceed. I promise to be even more vigilant, just in case what you have foreseen has some validity. But I cannot allow you to join us in this operation if your present state of mind remains dominant. Do you understand, SS-Panzeroberschütze?'

'Yes, sir,' replied Wendorff.

'Good,' answered von Schroif. 'Now, let us go and get our Tigers back!'

With that, both men took up their respective positions inside the tank, and, just like the von Schroif of old, the Tiger commander pulled his hand down as if pulling on that imaginary bell chain and gave the command, 'Panzer Rollen!'

Looking from the window of the Storch, Walter Lehmann cast a cold eye over the endless forest of beech trees which marked his new homeland. Living here would be a necessary evil; he thought to himself, but hopefully not an extended one. If the Soviet Union did win the war – and how on earth wouldn't they? – then he would have played no small part in that victory. Surely then his reward would be worth the small price of a short stay in this underdeveloped, peasant hellhole. But then he didn't really have a choice, so he quickly quelled any misgivings he currently had.

He had, after all, escaped the bony clutches of certain death, yet again. This was no small matter, and a state of affairs he was almost used to. Walter Lehmann chose to put this down to luck – the telephone call at the office in the presence of the Abwehr – this offered up even more evidence of the Great Lady's favours. Yes, he had to use his brains and mettle when the opportunity had presented itself, but over the years he had grown accustomed to this mode of operation – wait, wait, wait, it will come, don't force it, it will come, it always does. Just be ready, do not panic, do not overreact, wait, watch, listen, and keep a steady hand on the tiller.

It had served him well and, as he looked out over the vast Russian forest, he had no reason to think this state of affairs would not continue. After all, it was not as if he was flying in blind. No, he was arriving on a cresting wave of epoch-making providence. History was on his side. As was Dimitri Korsak, which made him smile, for here was even more evidence of the confluence of good fortune, both personal and historical. Who would have thought it? Not only had fate placed him on the right side of history, but alongside his old friend Dimitri Korsak, or Wilhelm Stenner, as Lehmann could not help remembering him. Somehow that weasel von Schroif had been cast into the same nexus, the same surging river!

Lehmann could not help himself but remember those heady days, back in the early twenties, when they were all in the Freikorps together. Granted, Stenner had retained his youthful revolutionary zeal, while his own path had been somewhat more tempered by comfort and the finer things in life, but nevertheless the betrayal still rankled. Hitler and his gang had veered to the right. How they had betrayed the principles of National Socialism, falling into bed and under the spell of any rich industrialist who courted them, aided and abetted by opportunistic cockroaches like von Schroif! And now they were to meet again. How beneficent was this Lady Luck, and how all-encompassing her embrace!

Then, turning his mind to the immediate rather than the forthcoming, Lehmann reminded himself that it would soon be time to make contact with his old friend Stenner. He would do that, then he would be able to relax, but it was not over yet. Though he trusted in the overall direction his life was

taking, Walter Lehmann was not so in-
cautious as not to peer from the speeding
Storch to scan the skies for any interceptions
that may have been made airborne by his
hasty and sudden departure. The skies were
clear though, and Walter Lehmann settled his
large, lucky frame back into his seat and
looked forward contentedly to the next phase
of his so-far charmed existence.

The fact that no fighters were on Walter
Lehmann's tail, or had appeared over his
horizon, had nothing whatsoever to do with
providence, fate, or the good lady some men
call luck. Nor was it an accident. On the
contrary, it was a very well formed design,
quite simply the result of a decision made in
the mind of a single man – Admiral Wilhelm
Canaris. If, as seen from his own point of
view, Walter Lehmann considered himself
blessed and favoured, from another point of
view, that of Canaris, he was simply fat,
bungling and stupid. Muffled and cocooned
in a cotton wool ball of self-delusion and
outrageous complacency.

How could Walter Lehmann think that he
could show up at Templehof, commandeer
an airplane, and fly off without thinking that
his every move was being tracked, logged
and second-guessed? Canaris knew this
turn of events had saved him some trouble.
No need to worry about what Lehmann

may say in the chamber. The tracks of this operation would be so well covered if all went to plan that they wouldn't even lead to Lehmann's corpse. Yes, Lehmann's very existence was in the hands of a higher power, just not the one he had so much faith in...

Oberstleutnant i.G. Borgmann had been kept informed as to Walter Lehmann's movements by Admiral Canaris, since his arrival at Templehof. Lehmann had tried his best to blend in with the crowds of soldiers coming and going. His papers allowed him to travel as SS-Obersturmführer Luther, and he was wearing the black panzer uniform which confirmed his identity. Borgmann could have had him arrested easily, but his orders were explicit – allow Lehmann and Korsak, aka Wilhelm Stenner, to rendezvous and eliminate both. He had also been given the tools, the codes and frequencies with which to listen in on their communications.

With Lehmann and Stenner gone, all traces between him, Canaris, and the Tiger project would be erased. How right he had been to trust in Canaris! The only slight worry Borgmann had was von Schroif. The way the Tiger commander had looked at him on the Führer's birthday had suggested a man with a suspicion. A man with suspicion alone is no great threat, but combine a man with suspicion and an ongoing operation whose ends are not yet fully in harness, and certain difficulties could arise. Much better a man with no suspicion. Better still a man with trust, complete trust. Then it came to him. The perfect plan.

Leaving the assembly area, the battle group moved slowly, following von Schroif's previous route until Major List and his units left and split the group in two. Von Schroif, his senses now at their fullest state of alertness, studied the landscape for the smallest movement. Everything seemed as it was. Even the dead lay undisturbed, save for the flies or rats. To von Schroif, this meant nothing. He had absolutely no doubt that the immediate surroundings harboured an, as yet, unseen threat, and that their every move was being scrutinised and evaluated. He sensed they would strike, but when would they strike, and from where?

In the middle distance he could see the three abandoned Tigers, exactly as they had been left. This did not surprise him. The aim of the Soviets, surely, was to capture these machines intact, for study and evaluation. The best way for them to do this was to secure the ground around them. He was also sure that this plan would have to fit in with the overall objectives of this part of the front, but even though he believed the Soviets intended to capture the Tigers intact as part of a wider operation and therefore would not have elected to destroy them, this did not mean for one minute that he did not think the Soviets might have sent out teams to tamper with them. With this in mind, he had warned all crews to check for booby traps – those damn F1 grenades! – and also for degradation of their ammunition stocks.

Drawing closer to the Tigers, he elected to approach the two which were closest to the hill where the last Soviet attack had emanated from. Then he noticed something. One of the T-34s, charred and abandoned, its hull still in the same position ... its turret had moved.

Von Schroif, if he had been nearly any other commander, may have spent a brief moment congratulating himself on his acuity of vision and his ability to memorise battlefields before, during and after conflicts, but that was not his way, and he was already weighing up in his own mind how best to react to this new information.

How big was the threat? It was too far away to present a significant threat for now, and any other burnt-out hulks were even further away, but if they proceeded further and the tank crews and repair teams were out in the open, then the magnitude of the threat would rise dramatically. What to do? Should he take them all out and reveal his presence, or send in some grenadiers to investigate? In little or no time he came to a decision.

He was certain that the Soviets were already aware of his presence, so there was no advantage to give away. Consequently, there was no need to endanger the lives of any German personnel. Von Schroif then relayed the target's position, Knispel lined it up, and the quiet morning air reverberated with the massive explosion which ripped through the stationary T-34. Von Schroif immediately felt a vindication of sorts, and a brief sense of satisfaction, when he saw one man emerge from the inferno, pulling on a comrade who emerged head, then shoulder, then chest, then nothing but bloody mangled pulp. He did not linger on this horror though.

In the course of an almost-mechanical few minutes he had moved in turn to each of the remaining suspicious targets and dispatched all of them to any metallic heaven or hell that may exist. Once he was satisfied that the area had been cleared, he moved the column up and took a forward position between the two stricken Tigers and the hill to the east of them. Behind them he could see the support teams, helped by the Tiger crews, carrying tools. Elements of the rest of the force formed a perimeter around them.

Von Schroif then returned his gaze to the hill, trying to peer between the trees and the undergrowth, searching again for movement, change, disturbance, but saw nothing, not even the flight of birds or the movement of small animals. Then, from nowhere, the unmistakable sound of artillery, what sounded like a massive barrage on the other side of the hill.

Then Wendorff, who had been listening intently to his radio, passed on some alarming news. 'SS-Hauptsturmführer. Major List is under attack ... outnumbered, huge force ... artillery ... T-34s ... and ... he's breaking up ... monsters...'

'Monsters?' replied von Schroif.

'I've lost him, sir ... hold on ... monsters, monsters ... KV-1's, sir.'

Von Schroif knew it was now imperative to get the Tigers, if not up and running, towed back to the supply area as quickly as possible. If neither of these two objectives were achievable, then the next best tactic would be to get the crews back in and buttoned down and prepared for what von Schroif considered an impending attack. He then felt a tug on his leg and looked down to see Wendorff motioning him back down into the tank.

'SS-Hauptsturmführer,' whispered the radio operator, 'I don't know if this is pertinent or not, but a few minutes ago I picked up the same kind of transmission as I did at Rostov, the one that gave away our position and strength. I did not mention it at the time, as I was unable to decode it, but then this came through from Oberstleutnant Borgmann at HQ.' At which point Wendorff handed von Schroif a piece of paper containing a new order.

'Proceed to coordinates. Detain. Wait for further orders. Highest priority.'

Von Schroif rolled his eyes in anger and frustration. 'Borgmann? That oaf again! Did he have any idea of the situation they were currently in? What in God's name is this all about! What was Borgmann's game? Could he be trusted? Was there more to this than bungling idiocy?'

As von Schroif fulminated, Wendorff added to his Commander's woes. 'SS-Hauptsturmführer, Major List is calling for reinforcements. Message reads: position untenable. Requesting air support.'

Von Schroif needed air. What was going on? What was he to do? On emerging from his cupola, he immediately turned his eyes skyward. A patch of blue! The clouds were clearing! How unreliable those forecasters were! He then motioned to Hauptscharführer Rubbal to proceed with the utmost haste and get the static machines moving again. The Hauptscharführer responded with outstretched arms, indicating that that was exactly what he was doing...

Von Schroif had an uneasy feeling concerning this present circumstance, men working out in the open, the skies clearing, the force split in two, with one of its halves under murderous assault, the sound of its plight, though distant, still shaking the ground beneath them. He then turned his attention to the possibility of air strikes. Oberstleutnant Siebold, the Luftwaffe liaison in his SPW, was best positioned. He could sight, then report as an alarm over the radio – this would save them time and allow them to prepare for any attack.

'SS-Panzeroberschütze, radio Oberstleutnant Siebold and request him to not take his eyes off the skies.'

Von Schroif then turned his mind to Borgmann and the coordinates stated in his new orders. He decided to open his map and check the position he had been given. A mile from the hamlet, to the north. Damn him! This Borgmann, he was going to have to wait. In von Schroif's mind, there could be no greater priority than ensuring that these Tigers did not fall into Soviet hands.

'Oberstleutnant Borgmann again, sir,' shouted Wendorff from below, interrupting von Schroif's train of thought. 'Asking if we have reached target.'

'Tell him we will proceed when the situation has stabilised.'

There was a moments silence after Wendorff relayed von Schroif's message. Then

Wendorff responded. 'Not an option, SS-Hauptsturmführer. An explicit order. On the highest authority.'

'SS-Panzerschütze,' said von Schroif, resignedly addressing his driver, 'SS-Panzeroberschütze will give you the coordinates. Take us through the tree line at the foot of the hill.'

Bobby Junge revved up the Tiger and headed for the trees at the base of the hill. Just as they entered the trees, Wendorff relayed another message. 'Oberstleutnant Siebold. Luftwaffe has arrived! Rejoice!'

This was the best bit of news von Schroif had heard all day and it lifted his spirits momentarily. He looked back with warm pride as the Hauptscharführer called over the towing trucks, directing them carefully to the Tigers, as if they were his own children. 'At least the Tigers will be safe,' thought von Schroif to himself. 'Our airmen will make sure of that.' But then he heard the whine of diving aircraft and saw half a dozen planes banking steeply, then commencing a dive towards them.

He picked up his binoculars to get a closer look and was barely able to contain his rage. 'Those planes are not ours!'

'Take cover! Enemy aircraft alarm! Take cover!'

'Damn those forecasters! We have no flugabwehr!'

The Il-2's dived out of the sky.

'All crews under their vehicles!' shouted von Schroif to Wendorff.

Von Schroif knew that he and his crew were relatively safe. The Il-2's were nicknamed 'The Black Death', but von Schroif, and any experienced tanker who had encountered them, apportioned the term to Soviet propaganda. 'Reinforced bathtub' would have been a better name. However, it was not the ungainliness and bombing inaccuracy von Schroif was worried about – most of the vehicles in his group would survive, unless unlucky enough to receive a direct hit – it was the Il-2's cannon, and the poor crewmen, support teams, and grenadiers out in the open who were the object of his concern.

Refusing to jump back down into his tank, von Schroif watched in horror as the first wave of Soviet planes strafed the scattering elements of his group, many cut down and shredded as they ran for cover. Then came the bombs, the shrapnel, and the flames.

'Get Siebold to call for air support!'

Ducking and wincing, von Schroif saw one Kübelwagen take a direct hit, its flaming chassis flying through the air and grotesquely pinning two hapless grenadiers to the ground. Picking up his binoculars, he desperately tried to locate Siebold's SPW, but, just as he did, an Il-2 screamed over the tops of the trees, its cannon ripping up the ground in front of the vehicle like it was unzipping the very fabric of the earth itself before tearing apart the SPW and its crew. Men and bits of men flew about the innards of the vehicle before one lucky shell hit the fuel tank...

In return, the ground forces were opening up with everything they had, but von Schroif knew this to be absolutely futile. Without proper air defence support, this was no more than wasted ammunition, mere fireworks. Two more runs and the attack was over, each succeeding run less effective than the last, as the German forces fled from the open and found whatever temporary sanctuary they could.

As the smoke cleared and the sanis went about their bloody business of saving, consoling and tending, von Schroif's mind was already thinking ahead to the next phase. All was quiet. Whatever had been happening on the other side of the hill was over. Von Schroif did not dare to imagine. Poor List. And now it would be their turn. The KV-1s and the T-34s would be streaming over the hill at any minute. It wasn't the T-34s that bothered him, it was the KV-1s. There was a new balance of power in favour of the Tiger over the KV-1, but he had only four, and three of them unable to move in any direction at all.

Instinctively, von Schroif guessed that the Soviets would be legion... It all came down to numbers... The cold, dead hand of the numbers game... It was at moments like these that a commander, a soldier, a man, had to look skywards and plunge both hands deep down inside of himself to try and summon up any fight, spirit, or resolve that may remain.

Then it came, that awful thought... This is it, this breath may be my last... But that way lay certain death. When a man gives up on himself, then all, truly, was lost. So, holding on tight to the sides of his hatch, as if the tank herself were feeding him strength, he dragged himself back into the moment with the thought: 'It is not my last, it is not my last – it is ... to the last! To the last!'

Snapping out of it, he felt relief. How could he have abandoned himself so easily? How could he do that to himself, his unit, his crew? His crew ... that is what kept him going...

Just then, Wendorff, his rock, looked up at him and, in the calmest voice imaginable, said: 'SS-Hauptsturmführer. Do you calculate that the Soviets will attack from over the hill like yesterday, or will they skirt around it, retracing Major List's tracks and attack from the rear?'

Von Schroif took an instant to assimilate the import of what his radio operator had said... Genius! For, at that moment, his mind had been operating on one single track, that of a massed force of KV-1s and T-34s charging down the hill. That option, from the Russian point of view, however, presented certain obstacles: incline, lack of surprise, and the physical obstacles of yesterday's burnt-out hulks blocking their way down the few tracks available... So, an attack from the rear now seemed the likeliest Soviet option, which meant ... which meant ... and von Schroif's heart leapt at the word ... bottleneck!

'SS-Panzeroberschütze, remind me to take you, and the entire crew, to Bayreuth when this is all over. Instruct all units to take up position 150 metres above the tree line on the hill, looking down on where the track leads into the valley. Tell the three other Tigers to train their guns on the exact point where Major List's group turned off to go behind the hill. Inform all groups that the hill now has a new name. Hill Gotterdamerung!'

'Jawohl, SS-Hauptsturmführer,' answered Karl Wendorff with a smile.

Now it was only a matter of time and guile. Could Kampfgruppe von Schroif wheel and reach their new position before the Soviets? No doubt ever crossed von Schroif's newly-crystallised mind. This was a German battle group, after all!

With his group in position, ready to rain fire down on the advancing Soviets, von

354

Schroif then had to decide where to position the Eastern Front's one and only fully-functioning Tiger tank. With a bit of luck, they could take advantage of the Acht-acht's superior range and position themselves up and behind the main group, thus providing oversight and protection against any attack from the rear, but would the engine hold during the steep climb?

'Damn it,' thought von Schroif, 'trust in the crew, trust in the tank...'

'SS-Panzerschütze Junge, take us up to that ridge behind the main group.'

Then the wait, always the wait. The combined firepower of Kampfgruppe von Schroif, concentrating and concentrated, some sensing victory, others fear, others revenge...

When the first Soviet tanks appeared, von Schroif, like every commander, was engaged in his own personal battle. When to hold, when to fire. The longer one held, the greater the firestorm unleashed, but also, the longer one held, the greater the possibility the trap would be sprung against the hunter... Hold... Hold... Von Schroif could feel the sweat start to trickle from his brow. Inside the tank, the heat, the tension, the silence, the sweat... Hold... Hold... Hold... 'Fire!'

Every gun and every barrel spat flaming death down the hillside, onto a trapped and unsuspecting foe.

'Reload Fire!' Again and again, three savage salvoes fired before the Soviets were able to respond.

Inside the tank, sinew and brain formed an inseparable bond within men and between men, and between man and machine. Wohl, in his shorts, the heart of this machine, feeding shell after shell of this pulsing, beating organism of death.

Desyanti and T-34s were blown together and apart. Flaming metal death swept the column in high-explosive wave after high-explosive wave. Many of the KV-1s were still functioning though, still alive, and almost all had their guns bearing up on the hill above them.

'Reload. Fire!' ordered von Schroif, but he heard nothing in response. No noise. No retort. Fearing the worst, he turned and looked back down into the tank at Otto Wohl and couldn't believe what he was seeing. The little bastard was sitting down, flicking through the pages of that damn book of his. But before von Schroif could open his mouth, his loader quickly ripped a page out of the book and handed it to him. It was a diagram showing the weak spots of the KV-1 and the relative effectiveness of different kinds of explosives at different ranges.

'SS-Panzeroberschütze, Wendorff. Pass this vital information to all Tiger commanders.

Wohl, thank you, but please resume your duties!'

And so it was that the tide was turned. Rearmed with this vital information, each Tiger commander was reminded exactly which round to use and where to fire it. Armour-piercing at 1,500 metres front-on, 2,000 metres side-on. High-explosive for track and running gear and engine ventilation systems. Soon the KV-1, which had reigned supreme from June 1941, was cast down amongst the mortals, and a new tank, the Tiger, rose to take its place on the pantheon of battlefield gods.

'Send in the grenadiers,' was von Schroif's next order, one which signalled the final phase of the battle, and one which brought relief to all those hardy souls on Mount Gotterdammerung. All except one – Commander Dimitri Korsak.

Back in the tank, Otto was the first to break the silence. 'Well, boss, I didn't want to upset you during the heat of battle, but I'm afraid that last shell was ... well, our last shell. How is that for portion control?'

'Good timing, indeed!' replied von Schroif, 'Now, let us get these Tigers towed back to base!'

But then Karl interrupted. 'SS-Hauptsturmführer. Borgmann again, asking for an update.'

'Damn this Borgmann!' thought von

Schroif to himself, but orders were orders.

'SS-Panzeroberschütze. Inform Borg-mann that we are approaching target. SS-Panzerschütze Junge, take us to the target as quickly as possible!'

Junge then increased the revs and Elvira tore through the woods, smashing through the undergrowth like a giant beast un-leashed, the tank careering sometimes at such a steep angle that von Schroif, if he had not trusted his driver completely, may have adjudged it would surely tip over.

'Five hundred metres from designated co-ordinates,' Junge informed his commander. 'Must be that panje hut in the clearing.'

'SS-Panzerschütze Junge,' ordered von Schroif, 'slow her own and take us to within 200 metres. SS-Panzeroberschütze Wen-dorff, you are coming with me.'

Then there was an almighty crash. All five of the crew were thrown about the inside of the tank like limp dolls. Then an eardrum-bursting roar. Coming to, von Schroif instinctively knew that they had been hit from the rear.

'Knispel, behind us!'

Michael Knispel, dazed and bleeding, got back into his position, but, try as he might, could get no response from the turret turn-ing mechanism. Then von Schroif remem-bered that it was futile anyway – they had no armour-piercing shells left. They were a sitting duck.

Peering outside, he could see a KV-1 approach, and, in the commander's hatch, the unmistakable face of... and then he remembered... It was familiar, he had known this 'White Devil', this 'White Fox' ... their paths had indeed crossed before ... in Germany ... over 20 years ago, in the Freikorps and KAMA ... Stenner, Wilhelm Stenner ... that was his name...

This flash of memory was no good to him now. No gun, no ammunition, and, by the sound of it, even no engine.

His crew looked at him for support and salvation, but he had nothing to offer. Nothing. They were indeed a powerless, motionless, sitting duck. There was only one hope. If it was the tank that Stenner was after, then in all likelihood he would not want it destroyed. Their only hope was to sit tight, safe for now in the iron belly of the beast. Then, suddenly, Otto Wohl collapsed. Bobby Junge was first to guess the probable cause, Karl Wendorff the first to rush to Wohl's aid.

'Engine shutoff, sir. Carbon monoxide, we have to get him outside.'

Hans von Schroif made one of the hardest decisions he had ever made as quickly as if it had been one of his easiest.

'Everyone outside ... at the double.'

He had no choice. He would not leave

Wohl or any other crew member to certain death. They would take their chances. To the last.

Laying Wohl on the ground, von Schroif then stood up and faced the KV-1, trying to squeeze one ounce of mercy out of Stenner's cold heart, if not for himself, then for his crew, but it was a pointless exercise. Slowly, the machine gun turned towards him. In a gesture of solidarity, Wendorff, then Junge, then Knispel, stood shoulder to shoulder with him. None were running. None were leaving their commander, or Otto Wohl.

Death did not come at that moment though, only another almighty roar. The back of the KV-1 reared up, its turret sagged, and von Schroif could make out flames sweeping the inside of the tank. Stenner bailed out, but no crew followed him. There was an attempt to break open the turret, but it soon petered out. Nothing could have survived. Then von Schroif heard the roar of a Panzer III, bearing the welcome sight of Major List.

'Von Schroif! Had to take evasive action. Thought we'd pop round and see if we could offer any assistance! Even I couldn't miss from thirty metres!'

'You have been most helpful, my dear major. Most helpful. We will rendezvous back in the valley soon.'

Knispel and Junge then helped to revive

Otto Wohl, and set to repairing the engine and correcting the turret mechanism.

'SS-Panzeroberschütze Wendorff, let us now head over to that panje and finally put this Borgmann nonsense to bed.'

Von Schroif and Wendorff made their way carefully through the few remaining trees until they reached the edge of the clearing. Von Schroif then motioned to Wendorff to approach the building from the rear and both men ran, crouched and as silently as possible, to either side of the wooden building.

Finding himself outside the building, von Schroif paused and listened carefully. A voice ... German. He listened a little longer to determine if there were any other voices, but heard none and, from the tone, made the assumption the there was only one man inside the building, and that he was operating a radio.

'There is no other way to do this,' thought von Schroif to himself, so he took a step back, kicked in the door, and pointed his machine pistol at the first person he saw. That person was Walter Lehmann, dressed in the black uniform of an SS-Panzermann, sitting alone at a radio transmitter. Here he was, after all these years. It was him. A bit older, a good deal fatter, but still with those unmistakeable red piggy eyes.

Lehmann looked startled, but, with

chameleon-like ease, his mouth broke into a broad grin. 'SS-Hauptsturmführer von Schroif! I am so glad to see you. You are probably wondering why I am here. It's a secret operation...'

'Shut up, Lehmann!' retorted von Schroif.

'This is not what it seems, SS-Hauptsturmführer ... dirty tricks, you know ... undercover... It's what men like you and I do for our beloved Reich...'

'Neither myself, nor any of the good men in my command, would know the meaning of the phrase 'dirty tricks'. That is, and always has been, your department, Lehmann. Now, I am not in full possession of all the facts – God knows what you have been up to – but I have been ordered to detain you.'

'SS-Hauptsturmführer, I am only trying to fill in the blanks between those facts you say you are not in full possession of. Let me...'

At which point von Schroif felt a whole campaign's worth of bitterness, anger and frustration rise up within him. He grabbed Lehmann by the hair, pulled his head back, and rammed his pistol into his mouth, viciously rattling the barrel against his teeth and almost thrusting it down his throat.

'Shut up! Shut up! Where is the other one! Where is the other one! There are two of you! Where is the other one?'

'Here I am,' came the reply as a hideously

burned Wilhelm Stenner kicked the back door open. He was holding a gun against the head of Karl Wendorff. 'Now put the gun down, or I will kill your clever little radio operator.'

Von Schroif knew he had little choice.

'In fact,' continued Stenner, 'just leave it in Lehmann's throat. Step away, and let our old friend spit it out.'

Von Schroif could feel Lehmann shaking and choking. He did as Stenner had said, letting go of the pistol and taking a step back. Immediately, Walter Lehmann threw his head violently forward and half-coughed, half-spat the gun from his mouth.

'Pick it up, Lehmann,' ordered Stenner, who then threw Wendorff across the room in von Schroif's direction.

'How many years is it now... since we last met... The day before Gregor Strasser was killed ... murdered... Seems such a long time ago ... and we were on the same side in those days... You know, I used to look up to you ... especially in the Freikorps... I always knew you would make a fine soldier, but you were never that committed. So, in a way, it was inevitable that you would find yourself on the wrong side of history with that lunatic Hitler... You did fight gallantly today, I will give you that ... but now it's over ... all the little traitors have had their day.'

'You are the one who is the traitor, Stenner. You and Lehmann here,' countered von Schroif.

'I have never compromised on my beliefs, von Schroif. Whereas you did, didn't you? You veered off course and fell in like a little snapping dog on the orders of your master Hitler. You jumped into bed with the financiers and the middle classes. You never cared for the German workers... Well, perhaps you did once, or said you did ... but then you betrayed those principles.'

'There are many forms of betrayal, Stenner, and the greatest is the one that you and Lehmann have committed. You have betrayed those closest to you, not in terms of ideology, but in life. Your family, your friends, your countrymen, those German workers you claim to love. Many of them are now soldiers, and many now lie dead in the fields behind us, because of you.'

'You still don't get it, do you, von Schroif? These are your last moments on this earth, and still the blindness persists. The Russians are not your enemy, nor are they the enemy of the German worker. The capitalists, always, they are our enemy. Anyway ... enough. You will never understand. It is time for us to part. History has made its choice.'

Stenner raised his gun and pointed it straight between von Schroif's eyes. Von Schroif stared back, searching for the slightest bit of hesitation, or humanity, or mercy in the other man's eyes, but found none. Just a cold, determined, steely blue. Just then there was a slight jerk of Stenner's head, a crumpling of the gaze, a spray of blood, and then the sound of a single shot. The unmistakable sound of a shot from a Sauer hunting rifle.

Reacting like lightning, von Schroif immediately turned and grabbed at Lehmann's pistol hand with one hand and punched him as hard as he could with his other. Lehmann went flying in one direction, the pistol in the other. Hans von Schroif slowly and coolly went and picked it up and pointed it at Lehmann, who was now on his knees before him. A Lehmann who looked as deflated as any man could look, a man who looked for the first time as if all his luck had just run out.

'What are you going to do with me?' he asked, almost plaintively.

'I have my orders.'

'You know they will torture me. Please, kill me now, von Schroif. It's all I ask.'

Von Schroif was struck by the tone of this request, one human being to another. Maybe the day's killing had reached its high point. Maybe he allowed himself to remember when he, Lehmann and Stenner were all on the same side. Young men with immature hopes and dreams.

'It's over,' continued Lehmann. 'I could

beg, but I don't want to. I could even lie, but I am sick of lying. If you do this for me, I will do one thing I should have done many years ago. I will be honest. I have two pieces of information to impart, and then I would like to leave this world. That is all I ask.'

Von Schroif remained silent, unsure of what to do next.

'Who issued the order? Was it Borgmann?'

Von Schroif remained expressionless.

'So it was Borgmann,' continued Lehmann. 'Borgmann is not to be trusted. Borgmann used to work with me. Be careful. He is a man of many faces. The second bit of information I would like to pass on, my final words if you like, are of a more general nature. This regime ... I have worked closely with many of its key figures. I have seen the way it works ... from the inside. I do not have the same contempt for the German worker and soldier that Stenner did, but be very, very wary of this regime. They will bring lasting shame upon all of us. I have seen and heard things done in the name of the German people which will bring shame on Germany for a hundred years. We are heading into an abyss. Your Führer is leading you down a path to ignominy and defeat.'

'Never! The Führer will win in the end.' Incensed by Lehmann's final speech, Hans von Schroif lifted his gun and, quickly and emotionlessly, put a bullet through Walter

Lehmann's head.

'What shall we do with the bodies?' asked Wendorff.

'Who cares? Leave them for the rats,' said Knispel, entering the room with his Sauer poised for action.

'Leave Stenner for his comrades to bury … but bring Lehmann.'

Normally they would have simply tossed the body on the back of the tank, but von Schroif insisted that Lehmann was carried inside the tank. After some difficulty, they finally managed to get the lifeless body of Walter Lehmann into the tank, and von Schroif gave the order to depart. They rolled back to the supply point in confused silence with the dead body of Walter Lehmann jammed in among the spent shell cartridges. Just short of the supply point, von Schroif unexpectedly ordered them to stop beside a large, spreading oak tree. Together they manhandled the black-clad body of Walter Lehmann out of the radio operator's hatch and laid him by the tree.

Wendorff sat motionless in stunned silence. 'This is the vision I saw. A body brought from our tank … from my hatch … but it's not me. Not me!'

Knispel and Wohl exchanged glances and rolled their eyes, but von Schroif simply looked, a faint smile coming to his lips. And then he spoke. 'Now there is a good death for you.'

With that, the body of Walter Lehmann was laid to rest under the spreading boughs of the oak tree. There was no ceremony. It was just one more cadaver among the thousands dotting the Russian landscape that day. The crew simply leapt back into the Tiger and roared back to the welcome embrace of the supply area.

The rasputitsa came hard and early that year, and in no time they were once again up to their knees in thick, cloying mud. After the Tigers had been successfully recovered and repaired, they saw mercifully little action in the next few days. In his quieter moments, SS-Hauptsturmführer Hans von Schroif wondered how the new tanks would fare in this unforgiving new season. The second Russian winter, which was now looking ominous, was just around the corner, but someone else would find out if the Tigers would survive the extremes of the Russian winter. They would soon be on the move for sunnier climes. The orders had just arrived. They were to be sent to join the fighting in Africa. The crew was thrilled at the prospect of some desert sun on their backs, away from the gathering misery. Amidst the hurried preparations, one task stood out, one that von Schroif had been looking forward to.

'SS-Panzerschütze Otto Wohl, may I have a word with you?' asked von Schroif.

'Of course, SS-Hauptsturmführer,' replied Wohl.

'I have received some correspondence from Dr Kurt Arnholdt at the Henschel works. He has asked me to thank you for your reports concerning the new Tigers. Not only that, but, without going into too much detail, he has intimated that some of your recommendations may be incorporated in future revisions of the Tiger.'

At which Otto Wohl beamed with pride.

'And one more thing. He asked me to pass this on to you.' Von Schroif handed his loader a book-sized package. 'You may open it now, if you wish.'

Otto Wohl hurriedly tore off the wrapping paper to reveal a superbly illustrated little booklet, the *Tigerfibel*.

# APPENDICES

## About Ritter von Krauss

Ritter von Krauss is the pen name of a former German army officer who was the author of a large number of manuscripts for novels based on his experiences as a tank man in the first and second world wars. Although von Krauss is not his real name, the literal translation, Knight of the Cross, has been widely interpreted as an indicator that the author is a Knight's Cross holder, a decoration gained as a result of his service in either the Wehrmacht Heer or the Waffen SS.

There are at least forty surviving von Krauss novels in manuscript form, all of which are thought to have been written between 1954 and 1968, during the time when the author is believed to have lived and worked in Argentina. They range from fully-fledged novellas to story outlines a few thousand words long.

During the 1990s, as part of the negotiations for the sale of the rights to the novels, the manuscripts and the supporting documentation formed part of an extensive legal due diligence exercise and were studied and verified by a number of experts. This allowed the sale to proceed, but with the strict stipulation that the author should not be identified and that no publication could take place during the lifetime of any of the author's children. As a consequence of this condition, the manuscripts went unpublished in the 20th century. The main barrier to publication during the author's life time was a legal challenge by the author's estranged children based on the legitimate fear that the family might be identified and associated with von Krauss, who is reputed to have been active behind the scenes in the movement which became the Hilfsgemeinschaft auf Gegenseitigkeit der Angehörigen der ehemaligen Waffen-SS, the campaign to restore pension and other legal rights to Waffen SS veterans. His family strongly disapproved of his work in this sphere and, as a consequence, the publishing contracts to this day contain strong non-disclosure clauses preventing the publishers from identifying the author or commenting on his identity.

Following the death of the last of von Krauss' children, the way for publication was finally cleared and Tiger Command!, the first published Ritter von Krauss novel, finally appeared in e-book form in November 2011. The film Steel Tempest, which is based on von Krauss' experiences in the Ardennes offensive, also reappeared in 2011, with the author properly credited for the first time.

Originally, von Krauss served in the Great War where he was rumoured to have briefly been part of the unit which drove the A7V, the first of the German tanks, into battle. During the early years of the war von Krauss is believed to have served as a motorcycle despatch rider and to have been an associate of Kurt Ludecke, who was later to emerge as a member of Hitler's inner circle. It has been widely speculated that he was on good terms with Sepp Dietrich.

He is known to have been descended from an aristocratic family and von Krauss suffered the humiliation of being reduced to poverty in the 1920s when hyperinflation wiped out the fortunes of both von Krauss personally, and the entire family. Following the Great War, von Krauss is thought to have served in the Freikorps and to have spent time in Russia, working on tank development at KAMA.

It is thought that his failure to find a place in the 100,000 man army of the Weimar Republic was the spur which led to his joining the Nazi party. It is also understood that von Krauss spent time in the SA where he knew Ernst Röhm as a result of an introduction by Ludecke. This is borne out by the fact that both Ludecke and Röhm appear in fictionalised form in the von Krauss manuscript Freikorps!

There are many references which are interpreted as being autobiographical and it is conjectured that, as a result of his experiences in the hungry twenties, von Krauss may have become a committed National Socialist and, in any event, undoubtedly harboured life-long Nationalist aspirations. He was obviously a strong supporter of the Grossdeutschland vision which led to the creation of The Third Reich. He may have therefore been an obvious and easy convert to National Socialism, however, von Krauss was clearly not an anti-Semite and his novels display no trace of this aspect of National Socialist policy. In common with Ludecke and many others, von Krauss appears to have assumed that the anti-Semitic aspects of the party manifesto were a side show to the main event, which was the unification of the German speaking peoples into a Socialist state.

During the 1920's von Krauss is thought to have come to a breach with Ludecke when a number of business ventures designed to revive the von Krauss family fortunes also came to grief, leaving von Krauss penniless. It is thought that this was the event which drove von Krauss to seek employment by joining the fledgling SS, although he was initially highly disparaging of this outfit, describing himself as nothing more than 'a glorified advertising sales man.'

In 1933, it has been speculated that von Krauss joined Hitler's regiment of body guards, the SS Leibstandarte. From the subject matter of many of his novels, it is also thought that von Krauss served throughout the war initially as an armoured car commander and later as a Tiger tank commander, either in the Waffen SS or the Heer (possibly both). The Gross Deutschland division has also been suggested.

In 1945 von Krauss is understood to have escaped capture by the Russians and also slipped out of a British POW camp. As a result, he was never officially deNazified, and, lacking the appropriate papers, he was unable to work in Germany, and so began a game of cat and mouse with the German authorities which saw him serve briefly in the ranks of the French Foreign Legion, from which he was invalided out, suffering from malaria, an illness from which he never fully recovered.

## Notes on the Translation and Sources

It is never an easy task to render the

thoughts of a writer from his native language into a secondary language and one has to be careful to guard against creating a new work. I have therefore resisted the temptation to provide a complete translation of every word of the original manuscript as I feel it was important to preserve the essence of the German roots of the novel. I have preserved a larger than usual number of German words which are hopefully sufficient to make it clear at all times that we are in a foreign army. This is especially true of the ranks of the political soldiers of the Waffen SS. I'd like to think the balance is about right, but please accept my apologies if you have to reach for the German dictionary more than you would like. I've taken out a number of phrases such as 'cleaned his clock', meaning to kill a tank, as there is no real English equivalent. Unfortunately, a large number of the jokes told by Otto Wohl have been lost in the re-writing process, as they did not survive the act of translation with any semblance of humour still intact. Other German references have lost some of their charm. If you don't know, for example, that the German word for farmer is Bauer and Müller translates as miller, then you won't get the reference made by the Blocklieter.

Other German phrases have survived. 'To bite into grass' is recognisable as our own

'Pushing up the daisies.' As it is a German setting, I have used the German phrase in preference to the English.

Tiger tank drills were especially difficult to render into English. The mnemonic rhyme Mo-Fu-Fa-La-Ba called by the crew is the first word of the checks which were run through to ensure that the hatches were closed, the lamps removed and the track clear before firing; the German words were Motor, Funker, Father, Lampen, Bahn. The Tigerfibel is a genuine war time publication and the German original can be found on the web. Really curious readers can also acquire the new translation which sets the original German alongside a complete English translation.

I'm pleased to report that Die Wundertüte is a real war time publication. I understand that extracts from this charming little publication will soon be available for viewing on the forthcoming Ritter von Krauss site.

Panzertruppenschule Kama, or KAMA for short, was a top-secret research and training facility, located near Kazan in the USSR. It was jointly operated by the Soviets and Germans between 1926 and 1933. Oberstleutnant Malbrandt was the Reichswehr officer who selected the location for the training and testing of military technology. The site was chosen to be as far away as possible from the prying eyes of League of Nations inspectors. It was a school for the study and development of armoured warfare. KAMA was the short form codename created by the fusion of words Kazan and Malbrandt. KAMA came out of the brief period of Russo-German cooperation that was agreed upon as a part of the Treaty of Rapallo of 1922, and the Berlin Friendship Treaty of 1924.

Between 1926 and 1929, at least 146 German officers are known to have completed training at the Panzertruppenschule Kama. A great many more NCOs and perspective officers received clandestine assistance. The most famous 'graduate' of KAMA was Ewald von Kleist, future Generalfeldmarschall Reichswehr.

Generaloberst Lutz and NKVD Kommissar Josef Unshlicht were jointly responsible for conducting the training. Security for the facility was provided by troops of the NKVD. Several armoured fighting vehicles were developed at Kama, developed under the alias of agricultural tractors. The German companies Rheinmetall-Borsig, Krupp and Daimler Benz were responsible for most of the development. The preliminary work at Kama resulted in the designs for the Panzer I, II, III and IV. The training and development which took place at Kama made the Panzerwaffe a reality.

For more information about Tiger Tanks and Ritter von Krauss, visit www.tiger-command.com

The publishers hope that this book has given you enjoyable reading. Large Print Books are especially designed to be as easy to see and hold as possible. If you wish a complete list of our books please ask at your local library or write directly to:

**Magna Large Print Books**
Magna House, Long Preston,
Skipton, North Yorkshire.
BD23 4ND